L

Lynne Bryan is the auth
Cheese Handout (Fab
(Sceptre, 1999). She live
Cowan and their daughter Rose. *Like Rabbits* is her second
novel.

Also by Lynne Bryan

Envy at the Cheese Handout
Gorgeous

Lynne Bryan

Like Rabbits

SCEPTRE

First published in Great Britain in 2002 by Hodder and Stoughton
A division of Hodder Headline

A Sceptre Paperback

1 3 5 7 9 10 8 6 4 2

A CIP catalogue record for this title
is available from the British Library.

ISBN 0 340 73971 1

Printed and bound in Great Britain by
Clays Ltd, St Ives plc

Hodder and Stoughton
A division of Hodder Headline
338 Euston Road
London NW1 3BH

To Rose, her grandparents
and great grandparents

—LINCOLN, HUP! GOOD GIRL, LINCOLN. AND
AGAIN! LINCOLN, HUP! GOOD GIRL! GOOD GIRL,
LINCOLN.

That's Grandad. He's better than my Bugs Bunny alarm.
His batteries never run out. He normally wakes me.

—Christ.

That's Mummy. Grandad normally wakes her too.

—LINCOLN, HUP!

Mummy looks me in the eyes.

—Hello, Mummy, I say.

Her hair is all over her lacy pillow, some in her mouth.
She pulls it out of her mouth.

—LINCOLN, HUP!

—Every bloody morning, she says.

—Hello, Mummy.

—Move your knees, Lily, she says.

My knees are curled up and are touching her belly.
She pushes at my knees. Her hands are cold. They always
are in bed.

—AND AGAIN! LINCOLN, HUP!

—I've had this, she says. —Off the pillow, Lily.

I do as I'm told.

Mummy sits up and puts the pillow behind her back
like a cushion.

—IT'S EVERY BLOODY MORNING! she shouts.

—Ow! I say.

—HUP! HUP!

Mummy puts her head in her hands. —Christ.

—You hurt my ears, I say.

—LINCOLN, HUP!

—I can't stand this, she says. Her hair flops. She has black hair with grey bits. She doesn't like the grey bits. —I can't stand much more of this.

—You hurt my ears, I say, and I poke her and feel wet on my fingers.

It's not wee because Mummy doesn't wee herself. I do that. It's blood. I know. Mummy bleeds a lot. Sometimes she even bleeds through her knickers and trousers and leaves red splodges on the sofa. Blood means you can have babies. I want a baby sister.

—That's enough, Lily.

Mummy slaps my fingers away, then dabs hers at the blood on her nightie.

—Christ, not this as well. Lily, get me that blue box. You know where it is.

I roll out of bed and run across the lino. It's freezing and stings my feet. I find the blue box and throw it at Mummy.

—Don't nose, Lily. Go look at the sky.

Mummy hides under the sheets with the box and she wriggles about. I put my head through the gap in the curtains. The window's rainy. I rub a circle in it. The sky's grey. Aunty Chris and Tom and Bethany live on the ground floor. They've got grass but I can't see any today. I can't see the playground or down to

2

town. I can't see Aunty Sheila's house either, or Mrs Meadows' house or Pizza Hut. There's too much cloud in the way.

—LINCOLN, HUP!

—Lily, Mummy's voice wobbles. —Go tell Grandad it's the weekend. Tell him DECENT, TIRED, HARDWORKING PEOPLE GET A LIE-IN AT THE WEEKEND!

I nod my head.

—YOU'RE NOT DECENT . . .

I run across the bedroom and open the door.

—YOU'RE A STUDENT . . .

I step on the flowery carpet that's in the hall. It's warm on my feet.

—YOU'RE ALWAYS BLOODY TIRED! shouts Grandad.

I give Mummy a wave.

—IS IT ANY WONDER? WHEN YOU'RE ALWAYS AT IT WITH THOSE BLOODY RABBITS! she shouts.

I shut the door.

There's our bedroom, then a bit of the hall, then Grandad's bedroom that he used to share with Granny. Mummy keeps out of his bedroom. It's her rule. A rule's a rule. She keeps out of his room and he keeps out of ours and everyone shares everywhere else but sometimes Mummy stays out of the front room if Grandad's in there and sometimes Grandad stays out of the kitchen if she's in there. It's because they argue too much. Grandad is kind and Mummy's my mummy so they shouldn't argue but they do because they have personalities and they don't match like pairs, like the pairs game we do at school with Mrs Meadows. She's my teacher and

Mummy's friend and she jumbles up pictures and then we have to sort them out, putting the pictures of the lemurs together, and the chipmunks, the pussy cats, the rabbits, and the gerbils. It's not hard. A rabbit can't go with a gerbil, that's wrong. A rabbit goes with a rabbit, that's right, that's a pair and that's matching. But my mummy and Grandad don't go together, that's what Aunty Sheila says. They're different, not the same.

I look at the handle on Grandad's door. The handle's silver and long and thin and shiny and I can see my face in it. I'm all eyes. Doe eyes, Grandad calls me. A doe is a lady rabbit. I open Grandad's door. He's got Lincoln by her neck. His other hand's under her bum.

—Morning, Lily, he says.

—Morning, I say. —Morning, Lincoln.

I like Lincoln; she licks my face.

—Aah, I say.

Lincoln's eyes are scared and frightened.

—Was Mummy too screamy? I say.

Rabbits don't like screamy. They've got supersonic ears. They can hear whispers and people creeping with no shoes on. They hate telly. They enjoy peace and quiet.

Grandad shakes his head and his falsies clack.

—If your mother was one of my English, he says. —I'd have her put down.

—Where? I say.

—For a nice big sleep, he says, and he holds Lincoln up high and coos at her. —Let's try her again.

Lincoln twitches her nose.

—The triple this time.

—I need a wee, I say.

—Well, hurry yourself then. Go on. Scoot!

I run across the hall and into the loo. I wee as fast as I can. It comes out hot and splashy. I pull my 'jamas up too soon and piddle a bit inside them but I don't care. This is exciting. The triple. I can't miss this.

Grandad's brushing Lincoln. He's got a mitten on his hand and he strokes her fur with it. It's what you have to do. It gets the rabbit going.

—Right, says Grandad.

—Yes, Sergeant, I say.

—No messing about, he says.

—No messing, I say.

—Right. Fix the last jump, will you?

—YESSIR! I say and put my hands on my head like they're rabbit's ears and flap them. My secret sign.

—Lily.

—Soz, I say.

I pick up a stick and Grandad nods.

—Now, he says. —Put it on top of those magazines.

—*Fur & Feathers*, I say.

—Yes, he says.

Magazines are for grown-ups not children. Children have comics. Comics are called *Dandy* and *Rosie & Jim* and names like that. They have cartoons and big writing in. Magazines have little writing and photos. Grandad's *Fur & Feathers* are full of photos of guinea-pigs and rabbits and budgies and men in white coats and ladies wearing giant glasses.

I put one end of the stick on one pile of *Fur & Feathers* and the other end on the other pile.

—Now, out the way, says Grandad.

I do my secret sign and walk backwards. Grandad coughs and slowly bends and puts Lincoln on the floor. Lincoln sniffs, then looks about.

—That's it, Lincoln, says Grandad. —Take your time.

I'm good at walking backwards. I don't trip or anything. I put my hands behind me and feel for the hutches. I don't need eyes in the back of my head, peeping through my hair. I'm a natural. See. Here we are. I lean on the hutches and my bum presses on the holey wire and the rabbits inside thump up to say hello. One rabbit nudges and paws me.

—That's it, Lincoln, says Grandad.

It nudges and paws and makes me squeal. —OW!

—Lily, says Grandad. —Keep it down.

—Soz, I say.

Grandad straightens and he flaps his hand. He doesn't take his eyes off Lincoln. —Focus, Lincoln, Grandad whispers. —Focus. Find those jumps.

This is dead serious. I mustn't breathe.

—That's it, Lincoln.

I mustn't breathe. I mustn't giggle. I mustn't put her off.

—Now.

The rabbit's really at me. It can smell my wee. I mustn't giggle. It's nibbling my bum through the wire.

—Now ready, steady.

I mustn't. Grandad'll be cross.

—HUP, LINCOLN! HUP! HUP! HUP! YEES! YEES! SHE'S CLEARED THEM! ALL THREE!

—YIPPEE!

I jump a hundred miles and the rabbit's off my bum.

—YIPPEE! YIPPEE!

—SHE'S CLEARED THEM! YEES!

Grandad thumps the air. His old-age hands thump the air and Lincoln hops around and I do a happy dance, wiggling my arms and legs like that.

—SHE'S DONE THE TRIPLE!

Grandad stops his thumping and he coughs. Then he crouches and cuddles me and his bristles scratch my skin.

—Sweden, here we come, he says.

—Yes? says Mummy. —When?

She's in the doorway. She's hugging her belly and staring at us. Lincoln hops by her feet. Mummy looks at Lincoln and pulls a horrid face.

—Close the door, says Grandad.

He lets go of me.

Mummy stands on tiptoes.

—Close the door, says Grandad, and he sticks out his chin like Chesterfield does when he's facing up to Tamworth.

Those two rabbits are always at it. Grandad says it's because they've not sorted out who's boss. I think it's Chesterfield. He's the biggest and he chewed up Mummy's college book. He wins BOBs easily. Tamworth doesn't. BOBs are prizes and Tamworth doesn't win any prizes, not any more.

—Do you want me to close the door? asks Mummy.

Lincoln hops by Grandad.

—For God's sake, Donna, says Grandad. He picks Lincoln up and strokes her with his thumb on the soft bit near her ears.

Mummy watches Grandad.

He strokes Lincoln, and Lincoln's nose twitches.

Mummy hugs her belly.

—Well, spit it out, says Grandad.

—You know she enjoys the shows, says Mummy.

Shows?

I look at Grandad.

—So it'll be for her benefit, will it? he says.

—What? I ask.

I don't know what he means.

—There's a show today, Lily, says Mummy.

Grandad makes a tut noise.

—Grandad's thinking of taking you.

—YEES! I shout, and I jump up and down. I really want to go the show. I love the shows. I hope I can go. I pray to God.

—Stop messing about, Lily, says Grandad, and he turns and puts Lincoln in her hutch and fusses with the bolt and chain. I try to stand still but my legs keep jiggling.

—I need to finish my essay, says Mummy.

She stares at Grandad's back, his knobbly shoulders, his spiky hair.

—Yes, Mummy needs to finish her essay, I say.

Grandad turns from Lincoln and rubs some shavings off his hands.

—She needs . . .

He unplugs his heater and puts it by the wall.

Mummy needs . . .

I look at Mummy and she moves her mouth. She's doing the dumb game. The dumb game is when

Mummy moves her mouth but no words come out and I have to guess what she's trying to say. It's like spy-code. It's like passing secret messages. A secret's a secret. I smile. I've got it. Mummy is her own person. Mummy needs . . .

—Mummy needs *time* and *space*, I say.

Mummy smiles and nods at me.

Grandad coughs.

—Lily, he says. —See to the rabbits' hay. I need to talk to your mum in the kitchen, in private. Give them all a bit of new. Can you do that? And put away those jumps.

—OK, Sir, I say, and he ruffles my hair and then he leaves and Mummy leaves and the bedroom door goes click, and Grandad's shirts and trousers flap against the door, the coat hangers jangling.

I put the sticks and magazines near Grandad's sheets and pillows and his folded-up camp bed. He doesn't have a proper bed. He did have one but he gave it away, before me and Mummy came to stay. It was a big bed and he shared it with Granny. Mummy shared our big bed with Daddy, that's what Grandad told me. But it's a secret because we're not supposed to talk about him. Mummy gets upset. Grandad says our bed was Mummy's and Daddy's marriage bed. True-life!

Daisy, Daisy, give me an answer do.

Mummy isn't called Daisy. She's called Donna.

I'm half crazy all for the love of you.

Crazy is like mad. It's when you have a poorly brain.

It won't be a stylish marriage.

Grandad taught me this song.

I can't afford a carriage.

La la.

But you'll look sweet.

I open Granny's wardrobe.

Upon the seat.

It's next to the camp bed.

Of a bicycle made for two.

It's white with gold leaves and gold handles and it used to smell of flowery perfume, so Mummy says. Now it smells of everything to do with rabbits: shavings and mix and hay. I pull at the big bag of hay. It's stuck. I pull harder and it shoots out and I fall on the floor.

—Bugger.

I crawl to the bag and plips get stuck on my knees.

—Bugger. Bugger.

I stop my crawling.

—That's your fault, Lincoln.

I flick at the plips and the biggest gets stuck on my nail. I sniff it. Yuk.

—That's horrid. That's like baby poo.

I tell all the rabbits this because I can't remember which hutch Lincoln went in and now I can't tell which rabbit is Lincoln because all the rabbits look exactly the same. Some are big like Chesterfield and Tamworth and sometimes I can spot them but most are medium-sized and all of them are white with black pointy ears and noses and a black stripe down their backs and black spots on their sides. They're called English rabbits and their tails aren't round and fluffy; they're sort of square and stiff.

Mummy thinks it's creepy, all these rabbits looking the same. She likes the rabbits that Grandad sends away; the ones that aren't proper English, that have wobbly stripes or joined-up spots or funny teeth. Mummy doesn't understand. Grandad says it's because learning's turned her head, it's puddled her. Learning means brainwork and puddled means putting your vest on back to front and things like that.

Grandad wears big vests with holes in but he puts them on the right way. He's not puddled. He clips rings on the rabbits' legs, and the rings have numbers and letters on. The numbers and letters tell Grandad things about the rabbits, like their names and stuff. He sticks the rabbits' names on their hutch doors too but that's no good for me because I'm no good at reading. It's to do with my fidgeting, Mrs Meadows says. I don't stay still enough to learn. But it's not like I'm stupid. I can find the longest name, the one with the most letters. I can find Newbiggin-by-the-Sea.

Mrs Meadows has a hairy chin but Mummy likes her. She says she's the best teacher in the school because she wears trousers and isn't dead posh. Mummy goes to the pub with her and she wants to live in the same house as her, that's what she told me, and they have long talks in the classroom when Mummy's supposed to be reading to me or helping me sort my PE bag. My plimsolls are too small. I keep telling Mummy they're too small. She was going to use some of her Post Office money to buy me new ones. She promised ages ago. A promise is a promise. Mummy never keeps hers.

I shake my hand. I want Lincoln's poo to drop off my nail but it won't budge. It makes me feel shivery.

—Yuk.

I scrape my hand on the floor.

—Yuk. Yuk.

The poo falls off and I gob at it. I can do that. Grandad won't be cross. I can gob, I can wee, I can do anything on this floor because he's pulled the carpet up. Rabbits chew carpet till they get stuffed and then their hearts go pop! So Grandad pulled it up. He put it in the lift and it vanished just like that. He thought it would. —I've done someone a good turn, he said.

—He could've done us the good turn, Mummy told me. She was ever so cross. —It could've gone in our room. All we've got is that bloody lino.

I stick my head in the hay bag. It smells lovely like when the man on the mower cuts Tom and Bethany's grass and it's a sunny day and the grass bits shoot everywhere. Me and Tom and Bethany like rolling in the bits but Aunty Chris shouts at us to get up because of the needles, the injecting ones. Grandad sometimes comes down and puts on his big gloves and picks up the needles and puts them in the bin. Then we can roll while he gets the rabbits and the rabbit run. Uncle Paul normally helps him with the run. Uncle Paul is married to Aunty Chris. He's big and strong and he loads everything onto Grandad's special trolley. He puts the run on first and then the rabbits in their travel boxes. The run's like a giant hutch but without a top or bottom. It just has sides and it goes on the grass and the bunnies go in it and pretend they're in the countryside. It's good for them. They nibble the grass and sniff the air and feel the sun on their fur. Aunty Chris has a deckchair and she lets Grandad sit on it to watch his rabbits, and me, and Tom and Bethany too.

—Here rabby, rabby, rabbits. Here rabby, rabby, rabbits.

I make a squashy sound with my lips and pull some hay from the bag and wave it. Some of the rabbits are already looking out of their hutches, through the holey wire. Some run up when they hear my squashy sound.

Some stay in their sleeping bits. The does with their babies stay near their nest boxes. I have to be careful with them because mummy-does can nip.

—Here rabby, rabby, rabbits.

I wave the hay and move closer to the hutches. There's tons of them along one wall. They're in rows on top of each other and they look like our flats where we live and the rabbits inside them look like people moving about inside the flats, furry people peering out their windows. See, there's furry Aunty Chris and Uncle Paul and Tom and Bethany on the bottom, and there's furry Aunty Karen and Uncle Ben and Mickey and Layla above them, then there's Aunty Pam and Uncle Leslie and Danny and Pod, and then there's us, the three of us living near the top where the sky is grey and it's really cold.

It's the most cold here, in Grandad's room. His window doesn't shut that well and lets in the wind and rain. He's put some hutches under the window but only his biggest rabbits live in them. That's because they have fat and fat stops them being shivery, that's what Grandad says. There's ten fat rabbits; two of them are Chesterfield and Tamworth. They're men, bucks, and they're greedy and have goes at me when I try to feed them. I don't like them much but I start with them because they're easy to reach.

I open the first hutch.

—Get out the way you.

I push the fat rabbit with my hand and I try to shove the hay in the special basket. But the rabbit won't keep out the way. It jumps at me and tugs at the hay. So I drop the hay in his wee-corner. I know it's his wee-corner because the shavings there are orange, not white, and look wet, not dry. Rabbits wee a lot, loads more than guinea-pigs.

—Serves you right, I say.

I close the hutch door. Rabbits need new hay every day or else they get bellyache, and they have to have new mix and water too, and their shavings need to be changed. They're a lot of work. I do a few more hutches, then I put the hay bag on the floor and sit on it for a rest. I wiggle my toes. My friend, Finbar, has got a pet snake called Zippy. Zippy hangs off this twig all day. He's not a lot of work. He's green with yellow eyes and he eats scratchings from the pub.

BANG!

A door goes bang!

It makes me jump and the rabbits jump. They kick their shavings. Some of the shavings flutter out of the hutches. They're like butterflies, the white sort that eat all the cabbages in Mrs Meadows' garden. A few land on the floor near the hay bag and my feet.

I wiggle my feet and the rabbits stare at me. They look scared. Their ears are hurting, I'm certain sure. Rabbits have supersonic ears and I do too because I hear it all.

One time I tested my ears. I did an experiment on them in class. It was in the morning when the mummies and children were still coming in and some mummies were sorting PE bags and lunch boxes and stuff like that and my mummy was wanting to speak to Mrs Meadows.

—Join your group, Lily, said Mummy. —I'm just going to have a word.

I did as I was told.

Mrs Meadows has put our class into groups and my group is the Tortoises. There's six of us: me, Ben, Finbar, Wilma, Cathy and Kelly. We do activities together, like reading and writing and sums. I don't want to be a Tortoise. I want to be a Rabbit. But Rabbits are cleverer than Tortoises, and so are Chipmunks, Pussy

Cats, Lemurs and Gerbils, and I'll only get to be in the Rabbit group when I can read a Kipper book all the way through and when I can write my name and lots of other words and when I can do my tens and units. I hate tens and units. They don't make any sense to me.

Mummy tapped Mrs Meadows on the shoulder. I sat next to Wilma and her mum. Wilma's mum was reading to Wilma and Ben. The best mummies do this to settle their children in, if they have time, if they don't have to speak to Mrs Meadows. Settling in means calming down, sitting on your hands and no fidgeting. Wilma's mum was trying to get Wilma to read with her. Wilma doesn't like reading. She likes football. She's got big strong legs, like a rabbit. She looks like a rabbit but Mrs Meadows says she's a tortoise. Mrs Meadows thinks Wilma will always be a tortoise.

—What's this word? said Wilma's mum to Wilma the Tortoise. —Come on, Wilma, you know.

—Don't, said Wilma the Tortoise.

I could hear them and I wondered about Mummy and Mrs Meadows, if I could hear them too. I wiggled my fingers in my ears and poked out some of the sticky stuff. Yuk. It was brown. I wiped it under the table. Then I popped my ears. There was a whizzing in my head, then zero, nought, nothing. I listened.

—My husband wanted a family, said Mrs Meadows. —Three children.

—Three? said Mummy.

I could hear them, yes!

—Yes, said Mrs Meadows. —He didn't have a clue.

—It's c-h-o-c-o-l-a-t-e, said Wilma's mum.

—That's hard, said Wilma.

—But you like chocolate, said Wilma's mum.

And I could still hear Wilma and Wilma's mum! It was amazing.

—Never pair up with a scientist, said Mrs Meadows. —They're very controlling.

—There aren't that many where I live, said Mummy, and she laughed.

—Try this, said Wilma's mum.

—No, said Wilma.

—Just try, said Wilma's mum.

—Leave her alone, said Ben.

I could hear Ben too! It was fantastic-elastic.

—Pardon?! said Wilma's mum.

My experiment worked.

—So, will you be able to make it on Thursday? asked Mrs Meadows.

—Pardon? said Wilma's mum.

—Yes, I hope so, said Mummy.

It showed me I've got brilliant ears. Not tortoise ones but rabbit ones. True-life!

Pad. Pad. Pad.

That's Grandad coming down the hall. I know it's him and not Mummy because he sounds different to her. My ears work it out for me. Mummy walks fast and sighs a lot. Grandad pads in his slippers and he coughs. I wriggle on the hay bag. Sometimes he coughs so much he has to stand still and put his hand over this bit on his body, where his heart is. He's got a wobbly ticker, he says. Ticker's something to do with time. Time ticks and my Bugs Bunny alarm does too. You have time in your body that ticks and ticks and it makes you grow old. We're doing time at school. Bedtimes and proper growing-old time; minutes and hours and years.

Pad. Pad. Stop. Cough. Quiet.

Grandad's at the door. Not the one to this room but the bathroom door. He's going in the bathroom to run my bath. He always gives me a bath in the morning when I'm not going to school. I wriggle on the hay bag. I'm not that comfy. He turns on the taps. I hear them squeaking and the water gushing out. The water sounds like heavy rain but bouncy and light too. That's because it's daytime. Daytime sounds are different from nighttime ones. Nighttime ones are more scary. They're dark and black and blurry. They sound not quite right, like God's made a mistake with them.

I don't hear many nighttime noises normally because I go to bed at 6 just after *Pet Rescue* finishes on telly. Mummy puts me to bed then because she wants to be a solicitor and she needs to do her college work. She won't let me stay up to watch *Animal Hospital* like Wilma. Wilma goes on and on about Rolf Harris and the lady with the red hair who gets excited about kittens but Mummy won't change her mind. It's not fair. She won't let me go to other children's houses for tea even because it means I'll be late back and my hotty bottle will be cold and her essay won't get finished. She's a dedicated hard worker, that's what Mrs Meadows says. Dedicated is the same as dead. My granny's dedicated. Mummy's a dead hard worker.

Mrs Meadows is doing a graph about bedtimes and she worked out my time and everybody else's in the class. She pinned a big piece of paper to the wall and she marked the times down and mine's definitely 6, true-life. Mrs Meadows put my name above the 6 in a little box and now I've got to draw a picture of my bed so she can stick it by the box too. That's one of the things I have to do. It's like a project. I told Mrs Meadows it'll take me ages because it's got to be a big picture because I sleep in a big bed with Mummy. —Lucky you, she said.

I'm first on the graph and Finbar's last because his bedtime's the latest. —10! said Mrs Meadows. —No wonder your eyes have circles round them, Finbar Rex Smedley.

Rex is Finbar's middle name, I haven't got a middle name, and 10 is proper nighttime and Finbar hears all its scary sounds. He hears owls and dads smashing glasses in the pub and swearing and everything, and he's seen stuff too. He's seen the cheesy Man-In-The-Moon shine his cheesy rays on Zippy. He's seen an alien saucer and a witch and a giant bat with purple eyes. I don't believe about the bat. I asked Mummy if I could stay up and watch for it. —Nope, she said. —You know the rules.

Bedtime is bedtime is bedtime.

A secret's a secret.

A promise is a promise is a promise.

A rule's a rule.

I'm good at experiments. I did my ear one and I do other ones for Mrs Meadows too. I do them with the Tortoises. We use magnets and rulers and balloons. One time we had to rub balloons on our jumpers to make them hairy and hot so they'd stick on walls. I stuck mine by the weather board and it stayed up ages. It was a white balloon. Mrs Meadows was ever so pleased. She gave me a good work star.

Mummy does experiments too. She made a soap from leftovers, not leftover sandwiches or carrots or stuff but leftover soap bits. She wet the bits and rolled them in a ball, then she wrapped material round the ball and put it in the fridge. This made Grandad angry because he said it ponged the fridge and spoilt the milk and his special fat sausages. He said his sausages tasted horrid like Parma Violets.

Grandad turns off the taps. —Hop in, Lily.

The bath is steaming.

—It's hot, I say.

He flaps his hand in the water. —It's fine. Come on, it's nice and bubbly.

I lean against the bath and look in. The steam heats my face. He's used my Matey, loads of it; not the Matey man but the lady that Aunty Pam gave me for my birthday ages ago. The Matey man makes dark blue bubbly water and the lady makes pink, the girl-girl pink that Barbie likes.

—Come on, Lily, says Grandad. —Will you get in?

I look at him.

—Flannel? I ask.

He shakes his head and sits on the bathroom stool. He fusses with his dressing gown. Then he coughs and sighs and opens the cupboard under the sink.

—You'll have to find it, Lily, he says. — I can't get down to sort through that lot.

I do as I'm told.

I stick my head in the cupboard. It's full of dusty dark and it smells of mud. I blink my eyes and feel around. There's all kinds of stuff in here: soap and toothpaste and the powder Grandad puts on his feet when they're scabby and sore, and the scrubber and my flannels. I've got three. I'm lucky. I find my favourite, with Barbie's face on.

—Done? says Grandad.

I nod and stand up and he pushes the door shut and I chuck the flannel in the water. It floats round with Barbie smiling up at me. She's telling me the water's not that hot, not really.

—Ready, I say to Grandad.

I hold out my arms.

—Sorry, Lily, he says. —I don't feel up to it today. I was fine first thing but now . . .

—Ah, I say, and I give him a cuddle.

Poor Grandad. Sometimes he's up to it and sometimes he's not.

—Thank you, he says.

—Have you had your medicine? I ask.

He's got runny stuff in a bottle and tablets in a packet that he keeps in the kitchen, in a special cupboard that's got a plastic thing inside to stop me opening it. A safety thing. Safety means safe. You hide money in a safe to stop robbers getting it and policemen keep you safe from stranger-danger and Grandad's tablets are safe because they have to be, because they're only for him and I mustn't eat them.

—It's not time for my medicine yet, he says. —Now, in you pop.

I shake my head. I don't want to. I cuddle him. He feels soft and warm like Tamworth and Lincoln and Newbiggin-by-the-Sea.

—Please, he says, and he pushes me away, and his mouth is straight, not smiley.

I get in.

—OW!

The water burns my feet.

—OW! GRANDAD! OW!

It's burny flamey hell-hole. Barbie's a liar! The water's not OK!

—OW!

I want to get out. I hop and jump.

—No, says Grandad. He stands and stops me. He puts his hands on my shoulders.

—IT'S BOILING!

My feet are red and my ankles are too. I'm wearing shiny red skin socks.

Grandad turns on the cold tap and swirls the water round.

I puff and pant.

—There, says Grandad. —Happy now?

He swirls the water round. It's getting better. That's better. Not burny but warm like the ripples that come out the ripple machine at Splash World. I like Splash World.

—Ah, I say.

It's better than Megadeath. Finbar likes Megadeath because you do shooting there. You have guns and you run round a forest that's pretend and your face is painted green and you shoot children with the guns and this spray stuff comes out that's red and really sticky. Splash World's got a flume and rapids and the ripple machine. It doesn't have guns. I don't like guns. Finbar says that's because I'm a girl and girls are scaredy-cats. Sometimes he's horrid like that; he calls me a girl; he doesn't call me Lily.

I sit down and grab my Barbie flannel. The pink water laps over me, over my legs, my bum, my belly, and I screw up Barbie. I screw her silly smile right up.

—Peace at last, says Grandad.

—I'm all worn out, I say.

—Yes, he says, and he coughs and plops Mummy's soap in the bath. —There, use that.

The soap hits the bottom, then bounces up and floats by my feet. It's hard and round and I kick at it. I watch it spin and its colours mix and whirl.

—Don't kick it, says Grandad. —Wash your neck, behind your ears, your feet . . .

—You wash me, I say.

—No, he says. —I've got to start breakfast.

I look at him. He's cross, I think.

—What's wrong? I ask.

It could be the fridge. Maybe it's still pongy.

—Is it . . . ?

—Never you mind, he says, and he leaves the room and shuts the door.

—Oh, I say.

The door handle's long and shiny. It points up and clicks. Then it all goes quiet. The room. Everything.

Mummy gets cross about not getting her college work done and not having time and space. She gets cross about Grandad's rabbits and she gets double-cross when blood comes out her bum. Double-cross is like ordinary cross with lots more cross on top. It's like extra cross. Mummy gets extra cross because her bum-blood hurts; it gives her bellyache.

Blood doesn't come out of Grandad's bum. It comes out of his nose, I think, because it's on his hankies, big red spots and little ones too. Grandad doesn't have tissues made of paper. He has hankies made of material and he washes them all the time because of the spots but he doesn't get cross about that, he just gets sad. He gets sad about being poorly and he gets sad about Granny because he misses her, that's what he says.

I miss her too. Miss means not being married, it means you're a girl and a lady who's not got married, and it means being sad because someone's gone away; they're missing. Granny's missing. She's never been here with me. I've not touched her skin or held her hand or sat on her knee. She's not cuddled or kissed me. She's not given me presents or taken me to the play-park because she can't, because she's missing under the ground. She's in a box under the ground and she can't come out, honest to God, and I miss her because she's my only granny. She's in photos and Grandad talks about her but that's all. Other children have loads of grannies that are on top of the ground and are running around and laughing and everything. Finbar's got four. It's not fair. They take him on holidays in caravans and to Pizza Hut and everywhere.

Grandad says Granny was nice. Her name was Grace and she had curly hair and she was a good hard worker and she got up with the birds. There were tons of them in the olden days. They were little and brown and they sat on wires and went chirp. They pulled worms out of grass and pecked at snails and Granny had a special table for them, that's what Grandad says. It was when they lived in a house. The house had an upstairs and a downstairs, and outside at the back was the table for the birds and a toilet with a cold seat, and outside at the front was a doorstep that was joined to the door.

Grandad misses Granny and he misses his doorstep too. It was made of grey stone but Granny painted it white and kept it clean. Grandad used to sit on it with a cup of tea and watch the world go by. The postman left parcels on it and the milkman put milk on it early in the morning, ready for breakfast and more cups of tea. The milk wasn't runny all over the doorstep. It wasn't in boxes either. It was in bottles and the bottles had shiny metal tops. Milk-bottle tops, that's what they were called.

Grandad takes my knife and fork off my plate and puts them on his. Then he puts my dirty plate with the yellow egg mess under his dirty plate and he takes everything to the sink. He makes a lot of noise. The plates smash on each other and his metal knife and fork go clink as they drop in the bowl but my knife and fork don't make any sounds at all because they're made of plastic. A long time ago I had a knife and fork with Peter Rabbit on the handles. He's a famous rabbit from the olden days and he wears a little coat with sleeves and buttons and everything. But then my Peter knife and fork went missing. It was ever so sad. They disappeared – poof! – like that and Mummy said she couldn't find them anywhere and she gave me some grown-up metal ones like Grandad's but they were too heavy for me and my food kept dropping on the floor. So I got middle-sized plastic ones that came free through Aunty Chris's door. They're blue and sort of OK.

Grandad washes his hands and stares out the window at the sky. It's full of clouds that are dark and light and middle-sized grey. The clouds are squashed up together and they're moving across the window like that. It's because the wind's blowing them. I know. It's the weather. We're doing the weather in class. We've done the sun and now we're doing clouds because we can't do rain until we've done clouds. It's ever so hard and sometimes it confuses me. Confused means when your brain turns to mashed potato and nothing makes sense. There's confused old-age people at the church. There's a lady in a wheelchair, Finbar says; she's dead confused. She dribbles and shows her knickers off to the vicar and he has to wheel her where nobody can see. I think Granny went confused too but I'm not sure.

Grandad dries his hands on the tea-towel and fetches his rabbit book. He keeps it near Mummy's jars with the funny food in, the white beans and hard black peas and the yellow powder that he doesn't like. Mummy buys her food from Mr Azad's near the flats. Grandad calls it fancy but Mummy says it's good and cheap and it's better than sausages. She doesn't like sausages much. She likes chicken, she eats that a lot, and sometimes she says she likes rabbits in pies because that's where they should be, dead in pies and not alive in hutches in Grandad's bedroom doing smelly plips. She likes dead rabbits in pies. Yuk. She makes me feel shivery and sick.

—Right, where are we up to? says Grandad.

He sits by me, at the table. He smells of eggs and coffee, and he licks his lips. He runs his wrinkly hand down the middle of the book and he smooths the pages flat. There are no pictures in this book, just writing. That's because it's an important book, a manual. There are manuals for all kinds of things: lawn-mowers, potatoes, germs, cars, rabbits. Grandad's explained it to me. He's good at explaining. He's patient.

—Where's Mummy? I ask.

—Back in bed, says Grandad. —I expect she'll sur-
face later.

He shakes his head. He looks messed-up. His face-skin
is flaky, his hair's not combed or shiny with his special
grease, and his nose is purple with see-through snot
dangling from the end.

—Your nose is dripping, Grandad, I say.

He wipes the snot with the back of his hand and
he sniffs.

—Thank you, Lily, he says.

He needs a grown-up to tidy him like Aunty Chris
tidies Uncle Paul. Granny used to do it. She washed
his clothes and polished his boots and she made his
sandwiches for work. She cut them into triangles and
put them in a metal box and he ate them at the tyre
factory. He's still got his box. He keeps his tweezers
in it now, his long silver tweezers which he uses to pull
white hairs out of the rabbits' black spots, making them
show perfect. Perfect means just right, spot on. Grandad
makes his rabbits' spots spot on. He told me that. It's
like a joke. Grandad says Granny enjoyed his jokes and
she enjoyed staying at home with Mummy and Aunty
Sheila and everyone.

—Shall we do show-jumping? he says. —This section
here.

—Yes! I say.

—Ahem, he says, and he moves his finger under some
words and he reads them. He's clever like that. —The
first rabbit-jumping championship took place in Sweden
in 1987. That's ten, nearly fifteen years ago, Lily; well
before you were born.

I nod and smile because I'm thinking about Sweden. Sweden. Sweden. Sweden.

The best place in the whole wide world on this planet Earth. It's got mountains and snow and blue sky, not grey, and it's far from here and people from Sweden have yellow hair and they are very lucky because they live in Sweden.

—Sixty rabbits jumped in that championship, says Grandad. —Are you with us, Lily?

I nod. Yes. Because I am. I can listen to stuff and think about Sweden all at the same time.

—Sixty, I say. —That's a lot.

—Yes, says Grandad. —And now there are even more. Here . . . Currently, there are as many as fifty clubs that cater for the sport and 2,000 rabbits that are registered to jump in Sweden alone. There are also clubs in Norway and Denmark. Now, here's a little bit about the actual jumping. The average rabbit can clear fences of up to three feet.

—Oh, I say.

—Yes, says Grandad. —That's some height and the problem is we've not got the space to see if Lincoln can jump that, not in this flat.

—Oh, I say.

I don't know what he means.

—I've been putting it off, Lily, he says. —But I'm going to have to find somewhere to lay out a proper course. The church hall's a possibility but the floor might be too slippy. I think they buff it up. I'll have to ring the caretaker, have a chat.

He turns a page and I look at him. Sometimes grown-ups do this. They go on and on and I hear it all but there's too many words coming out too fast and they don't make any sense to me. It's because I'm a Tortoise and I'm dead slow.

—Here's a little bit about handlers, says Grandad.
—Do you know what a handler is, Lily?

I shake my tortoise head.

Grandad coughs.

—Well.

He swallows.

—Hang on.

He coughs again.

—Well, a handler's someone who races a rabbit, someone who puts the rabbit on the course and holds it and keeps it steady until it's time for the off. It says here that any handler seen pushing, jerking or kicking his rabbit will be disqualified. Now do you know what disqualified means?

I shake my tortoise head.

—I think you do, he says. —It happened to my friend Ernie at the Desborough show. Remember? There was a big lady judge and Ernie said something rude about her and so he was disqualified. He had to withdraw his rabbits. It was only a couple of years ago. Can't you remember all the shouting? You got upset.

—Was I crying? I ask.

I don't cry much. Mummy doesn't like it.

—No, says Grandad. —You clung to my legs, you wouldn't let go.

—That's babyish, I say. —Bethany does that, not me. I'm not babyish.

—OK, says Grandad.

—Bethany's babyish, I say.

—She's four, Lily, says Grandad.

He closes the rabbit manual and straightens its shiny cover.

—I'm nearly six, I say.

—I know, he says. —Time flies.

There's a photograph of rabbits jumping on the shiny cover. The rabbits' legs are stretched and their ears are flat and pushed back and their faces are thin and pointy and excited. Grandad's face is thin but it's not pointy and excited. It's sad.

I touch his dressing-gown. I stroke it like I stroked Beamish when she was off her hay. Poor Grandad. I don't love him like I love Finbar. He's not my best friend and he's not the same size as me. But I do love him because he's my grandad. You have to love your grandad. Finbar loves his. He's lucky. He's got three. He's got three grandads and four grannies and they're all alive and I've only got one and one, and one's alive and the other's dedicated, and that's not fair. Finbar says it's not fair too because his grandads don't keep rabbits. Finbar's greedy. He's got all his grandads and he wants my one too and the rabbits. Finbar's a greedy greedy boy.

—You know Lincoln, Grandad? I say.

Finbar loves Lincoln. He loves Zippy the snake but I think he loves Lincoln better. He's jealous about her.

—Mmm? says Grandad.

—Why's she your jumping rabbit?

—Why did I choose her and not one of the others?

I nod.

—Well, he says. —There's something about her, Lily. She's restless, spirited.

—What's that? I ask.

—Spirited? It means she wants a lot out of life, she's fiery and determined. That's very unusual for a doe. Bucks have it but does are generally calmer, especially English ones. I'll not be mating her, that's for sure. She'll not be having babies. She'll either eat them or they'll ruin her.

—Oh, I say.

Baby rabbits are born with no hair and they can't see anything.

—Come here, says Grandad, and he cuddles me. —Lesson over.

Grandad gives me tons of lessons. I like his lessons. I learn lots from them. Like.

Baby rabbits can't see anything because their eyes are shut.

Baby rabbits only open their eyes when they are ready.

When they've opened their eyes they can explore the world. Then they grow up fast.

Grandad gives me a kiss.

—Ow! I say.

—Sorry, says Grandad. —Need a shave.

A baby rabbit can grow into a man rabbit or a lady rabbit.

A man rabbit is called a buck and a lady rabbit is called a doe.

Does are fussy and quiet and bucks are greedy and angry.

Does and bucks mustn't share the same cage because they'll fight.

Does and bucks have to play with each other to make more baby rabbits.

They'll only play if they feel sexy.

Sexy means ticklish.

It's better if the doe visits the buck for a play because then her cage won't get messed-up. If her cage gets messed-up she'll feel sad and unticklish.

Small does can have four or five or six babies in one go and giant does can have ten or eleven or twelve.

Some does eat their babies.

Cousins are cousins. They're not brothers or sisters. They're cousins and I've got tons of them. I've got Pod and Danny, I've got Tom and Bethany, and Kylie and Joe, and Mickey and Layla. Tom and Bethany belong to Aunty Chris and Uncle Paul. Mickey and Layla belong to Aunty Karen and Uncle Ben. Kylie and Joe belong to Aunty Sheila and Uncle Brian, and Danny and Pod belong to Aunty Pam and Uncle Leslie. My aunties and my mummy are all sisters. They make a big family. I'm part of this family, that's what Grandad says, but I'm not really because I'm an only-bonely. I haven't got any sisters and I haven't got any brothers. I've just got cousins and they're not the same. I want Mummy to have a baby so I'll be like Danny with Pod. I wouldn't be an only-bonely. I'd be the grown-up child, the eldest, and the baby would be the youngest. Pod is my youngest cousin. He's two and he's dead sweet.

—Are you being careful, Lily? asks Grandad. —We don't want any breakages.

I smile at him and nod. I'm being very careful. I've got the tea-towel in one hand and the plate in my other hand and I'm holding the plate tight. I'm using all of my fingers and I'm holding it so tight my knuckles aren't pink any more, they're white.

Knuckles are the hard bits on the top of your hands. Some boys at school want to give Finbar and me knuckle sandwiches. I don't know why. They keep wanting to give us them and we keep telling them no because we have hot dinners. Finbar buys his dinners and I get mine free because I haven't got a daddy. They're cool. I like Loopy Loops and Crocodile Snaps and Barnyard Burgers; they're my favourites.

I show Grandad how I'm holding the plate. I'm holding it a bit like Pod holds his shaker, the one that's got beads inside and makes a rain noise. He won't let go of it, not even when he's in the bath or his cot. I don't see Pod so much, not now. Aunty Pam's too busy to bring him round and she's too annoyed with Mummy, I know. Aunty Pam's nice but she doesn't care about Mummy. She doesn't care that Mummy's got thinking to do and she can't do it when people are chatting to her. Aunty Pam chats a lot. She practises it at work, when she's washing the knives and forks for Pizza Hut. She chats and chats and she chatted at Mummy but Mummy was thinking. This was ages ago in the front room. I was with Grandad and Pod in Grandad's room looking at the rabbits. I was cuddling Newbiggin-by-the-Sea and Pod was talking to her. He was saying baby things and dribbling and his dribble was sticky and Grandad had to use his hanky to wipe it up. We were having a nice time. Then Aunty Pam shouted —EXCUSE ME! PARDON ME FOR BREATHING!

It was dead loud. We all heard. It made Newbiggin-by-the-Sea wriggle in my arms and Pod whiz round like a helicopter. He looked ever so funny but suddenly he toppled over and started to cry. Aunty Pam came into the room then. She picked Pod up and told Grandad she was sorry.

—What for? said Grandad.

Aunty Pam shrugged her shoulders and hurried away.

—Christ, said Grandad.

—Jesus Christ who died to save us all, I told him.

Then I held out Newbiggin-by-the-Sea because I wanted Grandad to take her from me because she was too wriggly. I held her out and she wriggled some more and dropped from me and went splat! on the floor. Grandad stared. He was double-cross, I could tell. He didn't smack me, Mummy does that, but he leaned over and put his shadow on me and he said my name over and over. It was like he was a wizard putting a spell on me and I thought I was going to turn into a frog and I didn't want to be a frog. Frogs are dirty. They live in muddy water and burp a lot. They're not furry and soft and kind like rabbits.

I dry the plate with the tea-towel and Grandad watches. I get all the bubbles off.

—Well done, says Grandad. —Now put it on the table and maybe your mother'll clear it away.

I do as I'm told.

I put the plate near Mummy.

She's in the kitchen with us now but she doesn't want to be, I know. She's eating cornflakes and reading her college book and she's hunched over the book and her black hair flops forwards so we can't see her face, and she slurps her cornflakes and she turns the pages of the book and she doesn't say one thing to Grandad and me.

She's thinking and that's OK but she's doing it like she's on her own and we're not here and that's rude, it's bad manners. It's like not saying please and thank you. It's like pinching people's bums.

I push the plate closer to her.

She's wearing her dressing-gown. It's old with a rip in the sleeve where her elbow is and her elbow's poking through.

I don't want her to be rude. I want her to be nice.

I push the plate so it touches her elbow skin.

—What? she says.

She looks up and stares at me.

Her eyes are dark and squinty and her hairy eyebrows are scrunching like Angelica's do in *Rugrats* when she's cross with Tommy Pickles.

I don't know what to say.

Angelica is horrid.

—Well?

She teases Phil and Lil and makes fun of Chuckie and bosses Tommy Pickles.

—You know Mrs Meadows? I say, because I don't know what to say. —She thinks I'm lucky.

—She said that? says Mummy.

—Yes, I say, and Mummy smiles at me.

Top marks. Top marks. Yes!

I smile too.

I'm being brilliant.

—Why did she say that? says Mummy.

Mummy likes Mrs Meadows. That's so brilliant of me.

—Because I sleep in the big bed with you, I say.

—Ah, says Mummy, and she looks at Grandad. She stares at him. I don't know why.

He's hunched over the sink, like a statue. His shoulders are dead still.

—So you were talking about our bed? says Mummy, and she touches me with her finger. —Why was that, Lily?

She strokes me like I'm a rabbit.

I want to be a rabbit.

—Lily, says Grandad.

He turns on the taps.

—Come and dry, please, he says.

He rattles stuff in the sink, his plate and his metal knife and fork.

—So why were you talking about our bed, Lily?

Mummy speaks louder.

—Come on, tell me.

Grandad rattles. He's being noisy. He stares out the window at the grey swirly sky.

—Lily, he says.

—Lily? says Mummy.

—WHEN THE RED RED ROBIN COMES BOB BOB BOBBING ALONG ALONG.

—Oh! I say.

It's our doorbell!

—Bugger, says Mummy. —Who's that? It's only half past nine.

Grandad turns off the taps.

—THERE'LL BE NO MORE SOBBING WHEN HE STARTS SINGING HIS OLD SWEET SONG.

The World's One And Only Singing Doorbell!

—GET UP! GET UP! GET OUT OF BED!

Granny bought it from QD. Mummy hates it.

—CHEER UP! CHEER UP! THE SUN IS RED!

She wants Grandad to get one that doesn't sing but he won't. He's keeping this one for his memories, that's what he says.

—Will you get that please, Lily? he says.

—LIVE, LOVE, LAUGH AND BE HAPPY!

—Why? I say.

—Because, he says.

I shake my head. I don't want to. Getting it means opening the door and there's corridors outside the door and the person who's ringing the bell. Oh God.

—Lily, says Grandad and he turns and looks at me and his lips are straight again, not smiley.

—Go on, Lily, says Mummy. —Who knows, it might be Mrs Meadows.

—True-life?! I say.

—Donna, says Grandad.

—What? she says. —What's wrong with that?

—It won't be Mrs Meadows, Lily, says Grandad. —I can assure you of that.

I don't know what assure means. Sure means certain sure and Finbar's certain sure there's horrible men outside our flats who hide in dark corners and growl like lions and wait for you to walk by. They're after bags, any kind of bags, shopping bags, PE bags. They'll scratch and claw and bite you and steal your bags away.

One time, I opened the door and I thought I could hear them. They're crazy-on-drugs. Say NO to drugs, that's what Finbar says.

Another time, I opened the door and no one was there and I thought I could hear them and I got scared, then out jumped Uncle Ben.

—TARRA! he shouted.

—NAA! I said.

He wasn't wearing a shirt or a jumper or any trousers. He was just wearing pants and a vest. His vest was holey and his pants were pulled right up over his belly. He was being silly with too much beer in him. He was asking where Aunty Karen was and he was singing a song about her coming round the mountain.

She'll be coming round the mountain when she comes.

She'll be coming round the mountain when she comes.

She'll be coming round the mountain, coming round the mountain.

I had to sing it with him and keep my eyes on him while Grandad fetched a blanket. He fetched the scratchy one and he threw it at Uncle Ben and told him to cover himself up and go home.

Another time, this stranger was there, a man. Stranger-danger outside the door. He wasn't growling and he had some clothes on, posh blue trousers and a posh blue jacket. He stared at me. He said I had to fetch my daddy.

—I've not got one, I said.

My mouth was wobbly and my legs.

—Well, who's Jim Phillips? he said.

—Grandad, I said.

That's his name. Jim Phillips. Mine's Lily. Lily Garner.

—Well, that's who I want to see, he said. —Would you fetch him for me, please.

—What's this about?

Grandad was in his 'jamas. He'd been seeing to his rabbits. The man looked at him.

—Sorry, said the man. —Did I wake you?

—Have you come to read the gas? said Grandad.

The man shook his head. He had a board and he showed it to Grandad. There was lots of paper on it and a photo. The man said somebody from the flats had complained about Grandad keeping rabbits. Complained means moaning and groaning. Unhappy people do it a lot and stressed-out people like my mummy.

—Was it next-door but one? said Grandad. —Mrs Ahmed?

Mrs Ahmed wears rings on her toes and she bashes her doormat against the corridor wall to get the dust and fluff out. She's not very nice. She doesn't say anything to us and she bashes her doormat when we're walking by and we get covered in the dust and fluff and some of it gets stuck down Grandad's throat and he starts choking. Choking's like coughing but worse. When Grandad starts choking his face goes purple and red and he bends like a really old-age person not the normal kind and he thumps his chest lots, here, there, and over his ticker.

—Mrs Ahmed's a busy-body, said Grandad. —A trouble-maker.

—We have to respond to every call, said the man.

Grandad tutted.

—So, may I come in? said the man.

—I don't think so, said Grandad. —We're not up for visitors.

—I do need to check, said the man. —The law's on my side.

—You're Animal Welfare, said Grandad. —Not the Police. Besides, there's no law against keeping rabbits.

—Depends how many we're talking about, said the man, and he smiled.

—I need to get some clothes on, said Grandad.

He closed the door. He wouldn't let the man in.

—Who's he? I asked.

—He's a spy, said Grandad.

—True-life? I said.

Grandad nodded.

—This is important, he said.

He bent down and stared in my doe eyes.

—Listen, Lily. That man wants to know about my rabbits. He wants to know how many I'm keeping and whether I'm breeding them, all those kind of things. But the trouble is he doesn't really like rabbits and so I've got to tell him some lies, otherwise he could take the rabbits away and we'll never see them again. Understand? He could take Lincoln and Tamworth and Chesterfield away. Do you understand?

—YESSIR! I said, because I did understand. The man was a spy. He wanted to take the rabbits away.

—No messing about, Lily, said Grandad. —This is very important.

He went in his bedroom. I could hear his coat hangers jangling.

—WHEN THE RED RED ROBIN COMES BOB BOB BOBBING ALONG ALONG.

The man was ringing our doorbell again.

—GRANDAD! I shouted.

—Don't answer it, Lily, he said. —Let him wait.

—THERE'LL BE NO MORE SOBBING WHEN HE STARTS SINGING HIS OLD SWEET SONG.

Grandad came out the bedroom. He had his vest and trousers on and he was holding a rabbit.

—Grandad! I said. —He doesn't like rabbits!

—He'll like this one, said Grandad. —It's my plan.

Just keep quiet, Lily, and everything will be OK. Promise.

—Yes.

A promise is a promise.

—GET UP! GET UP! GET OUT OF BED!

—Good girl, said Grandad. —Now I've given you Wigan. Hold her tightly.

—CHEER UP! CHEER UP! THE SUN IS RED!

—I'm going to open the door.

—LIVE, LOVE . . .

Grandad opened the door.

—LAUGH AND BE HAPPY!

—Ah, said the man, and he looked at me.

God. He was a bad man, a spy. I prayed to God and held on to Wigan but she was being wriggly. She was pushing me with her big head. She was scrabbling and digging her claws into me.

—OW! I said.

—Lily, said Grandad.

—Sorry, I said. —Soz.

I had to keep quiet. God.

—So, you do have a rabbit? said the man.

—It's her pet, said Grandad.

That was a lie! Grandad said he was going to tell lies. That was Lie Number One.

—I'll need to check her over, said the man.

Grandad nodded and the man put his hand on Wigan's head and pulled the skin round her eyes so her eyes sort of popped out, like that. It was horrid. He poked her back and he felt her belly and he pulled her ears.

—Well looked after, he said. —A proper English Spot. You could show her. Any more?

Grandad shook his head. —Just the one.

Another lie! Lie Number Two!

—Where's it live? said the man. —Not in the girl's bedroom?

—Oh no, said Grandad. —We know about that.

—It can be a health risk, said the man.

Grandad nodded. —I'd let you in to see, he said. —But we're busy today, my eldest daughter's getting married.

That was Lie Number Three! One, two, three! That was a big lie! Mummy wasn't getting married because she's done it once and she's not doing it again, that's what she told me.

—She's in bed, said Grandad.

That's Number Four! She wasn't in bed. She was out doing our washing, in the laundry place near Mr Azad's. She'd complained about going. Grandad had given her his special trolley to put the washing on, to wheel it down but she'd still complained because she'd had to get up early to get a machine because there's only five and lots of people want to use them. They like to sit and watch their washing go round, their knickers and bras and stuff. They think it's like telly. Some people watch their washing go round all day.

—It was her hen night, last night, said Grandad. —I wouldn't want to disturb her.

That confused me. There's daytime noises and nighttime ones and there's daytime animals and birds and there's nighttime ones too. Hens are daytime and bats are nighttime, and they don't mix up, no way.

—Well, I could come back, said the man.

—If you have to, said Grandad.

The man wrote lots of words on his paper.

—OK, he said. —That'll be all for now.

Grandad closed the front door.

—I'll bloody kill that woman, he said.

—Grandad, I said. —That's swearing! Bloody! That's a swear word.

Grandad wasn't listening.

—Bloody, bloody, bloody, I mumbled.

Grandad stomped into his bedroom and I followed him.

—Bloody, bloody.

He put Wigan in her cage and Wigan ran in a circle and bashed her head on her water bottle and she thumped her feet. She was frightened. Rabbits always do that when they're frightened. I know. Rabbits do lots of things when they're frightened.

What do rabbits do when they're frightened?

Run rabbit, run rabbit.

Thump their feet.

Nip you.

Run rabbit.

Stare with their eyes open wide.

Run rabbit.

Growl and grumble.

Rip up the paper in their cage, tear it up with their big front teeth.

Run, run, run.

What do children do when they're frightened?
Run baby, run baby.
Feel sick.
Go la la la.

—La la la.

I'm at the front door.

—WHEN THE RED RED ROBIN COMES BOB BOB BOBBING ALONG ALONG.

The doorbell's singing.

—THERE'LL BE NO MORE SOBBING WHEN HE STARTS SINGING HIS OLD SWEET SONG.

I stare at the door.

—La la la.

It's blue and it's got a letterbox but I can't peep through the letterbox because there's a cage over it, not a rabbit cage but one to catch the letters in.

—GET UP! GET UP! GET OUT OF BED!

I'm a scaredy-cat girl, that's what Finbar says, but I'm not, I'm a tortoise and I want to be a rabbit and I wish I had Superman eyes. I wish I had X-ray eyes that can see through people's clothes and see their bones and everything. I don't want to see through clothes but I want to see through the door, I want to see who's in the corridor, waiting to come inside.

—La.

It won't be Mrs Meadows, that's what Grandad says.

—La.

It's a warren out there, that's what Grandad says.

Warrens are made by wild rabbits in the countryside. They're under the ground and wild rabbits find their way round them by sniffing with their noses. Rabbits have supersonic ears and supersonic noses. The wild ones and the other ones.

—WHEN THE RED RED ROBIN COMES BOB BOB BOBBING ALONG ALONG.

If Grandad's rabbits tried sniffing in our corridors, he says, they'd be knocked out by the stink. He hates the corridors and so does Mummy. She calls them hell-holes and death-traps. Hell is hot and burny and isn't very nice. Death is what happened to Granny; it's not very nice either.

Poor Granny.

—THERE'LL BE NO MORE SOBBING WHEN HE STARTS SINGING HIS OLD SWEET SONG.

She's in the churchyard.

—GET UP! GET UP! GET OUT OF BED!

But she's ever so hard to find.

—CHEER UP! CHEER UP! THE SUN IS RED!

The grass is too long.

—LILY! shouts Mummy. —GET A MOVE ON!

—LIVE, LOVE, LAUGH AND BE HAPPY!

—ANSWER THAT DOOR!

I do as I'm told.

I close my eyes. I pull down the handle and I open the door and the cold air goes whoosh and hits me in the face and someone puts their hands on me.

—NO! I shout.

—THERE'LL BE NO MORE SOBBING WHEN HE STARTS SINGING HIS OLD SWEET SONG.

—Lily! says Aunty Sheila.

Phew! It's her, I know.

—It's me.

Her voice is kind and soft, and I know her flowery perfume too. I sniff it. It's like sunshine and big white daisies.

—CHEER UP! CHEER UP!

—Aunty Sheila, I say, and I hug her legs.

—Who's a silly sausage? she says.

Aunty Sheila lives in a house. It's a number three. That's a little number, an odd. There's odd numbers and even numbers. 2, 4, 6, 8 are evens. 1, 3, 5 are odd. We're doing them at school. Aunty Sheila's house has a yellow odd number 3 on the door and two even number gardens, one at the front and one at the back, and it's got trees and a pond with some gnomes round it. One of the gnomes is fishing in the pond. He's called Brian because he's got white hair and fat red cheeks like Uncle Brian, that's what Aunty Sheila says.

One time we went to her house; it was when I got my Bugs Bunny alarm at Christmas. Aunty Sheila invited Mummy and Grandad and me round for Christmas turkey sandwiches and Grandad couldn't come because he had to put Beamish to sleep because she couldn't hold her head up and was off her hay. I wanted to see Beamish's special bedroom but Grandad wouldn't let me.

—Off you go to Sheila's, he said. —Go on. Scoot!

It was miles. Mummy and me had to cross some roads and we went through this play-park with a swing and a bouncy elephant that wasn't covered in scribbly teenager writing and drawings of ladies' cracks like our park is near the flats. I wanted a bounce on the elephant but

Mummy wouldn't let me. She said we had to hurry or the sandwiches would go off.

—Where they going to? I asked.

She laughed. I like it when she laughs.

—Never you mind, she said.

Aunty Sheila's house looked lovely. There were no corridors. I could only hear quiet and I could only see nice stuff like the big Christmas tree in the front garden with flashing lights and a fairy on the top and the doormat with Santa's face on that was lying on the doorstep. You could wipe your feet on Santa's face, true-life! And you could stand on a doorstep that was stuck to the front door like Grandad's and Granny's used to be. It was fantastic-elastic.

—Why can't we live in a house like Aunty Sheila? I asked Mummy. —Why are we in flats?

—It's not her house, said Mummy. —It's Brian's and he lived in it with Kylie and Joe's Mummy, ages ago, long before he met Sheila.

—Oh, I said.

I know about Kylie and Joe's Mummy. She had big feet and she worked in the shoe factory. She put shoes in their boxes and closed the lids but the shoe glue made her go funny in the head and one day she went in the fruit shop and got all the apples and pears and threw them up in the air, then she stamped on the bananas with her big feet. Kylie told me. It was when she was being nice to me before she got her boobies. She said a police car came and took her mummy away, and nobody knows where she is any more, and it was sad to start off with but now it doesn't matter because Uncle Brian loves

Aunty Sheila and Joe likes her much better and Kylie did too before she got her boobies. Joe's nine and he fiddles with his willy.

Kylie and Joe weren't at the house when we visited. They'd gone to Splash World with Uncle Brian. It wasn't fair. They hadn't asked me. I got upset then and Aunty Sheila said she was sorry but Uncle Brian had wanted to do something with Kylie and Joe alone. I didn't understand. It didn't make sense to me.

—Oh, don't be sad, said Aunty Sheila and she cuddled me and promised I'd go the next time.

A promise is a promise.

—OK? she said. —Now, come and see my kitchen.

It was as big as the hall at school and there were shiny saucepans and tinsel and flowers hanging from the ceiling. Aunty Sheila said the flowers were magic ones and they would last for ever. She was being a liar. Bum's on fire. The flowers were ordinary. They were yellow and red and they had ordinary leaves.

We sat down and she gave me a Ribena and Mummy had some wine that was red like Ribena. Then she put this plate of turkey sandwiches on the table. There were lots of sandwiches full of turkey. Yuk. Turkey comes from turkeys, I know, and turkeys are birds that make funny noises in their necks and their necks are wobbly and dangly-down like the necks that old-age people have. I looked inside my sandwich. There was lots of turkey. I didn't want to eat it.

—It won't bite, Lily, said Mummy. She was speaking with her mouth full and I could see her gums and teeth and the turkey falling about.

—That's horrid, I said.

—What? said Mummy with her mouth full.

I looked at Aunty Sheila. Perhaps she'd tell Mummy.

—There's something I want to ask you, said Aunty Sheila to Mummy. —It's about the wedding.

—Ah, said Mummy.

—Aunty Sheila, I said.

—In a minute, Lily, she said.

—Sorry, said Mummy, and she swallowed the stuff in her mouth. —But I'm not doing any sewing.

Aunty Sheila looked at her.

—But it wouldn't take long, she said. —The speed you go on that machine.

—Sorry, said Mummy.

—Aunty Sheila, I said. —Mummy was speaking with her mouth full. That's rude.

—Not now, Lily, said Mummy.

—Mummy's expert at sewing, I said.

—Lily, said Mummy. —Shut it. Please.

I did as I was told.

I shut it. I didn't say anything more. I didn't say that expert means super clever and Mummy's super clever because she made curtains for posh people before Daddy put me in her belly and hurt her front teeth. I didn't say how she had a big machine in a factory and her own front teeth and how she's got a little machine at home now and plastic teeth that are yellow and match her other teeth like pairs, except they've got this black line at the top touching her gums.

I did as I was told.

I shut it. I was good.

Aunty Sheila picked up a shiny magazine.

—I'm not after anything fancy, she said.

She opened the magazine and showed it to Mummy and me.

—I want something simple and classy, like this, she said, and she pointed to a picture of a lady in a white nightie swinging on a swing. The lady was smiling and there were pink hearts floating in the sky around her head.

—Sorry, said Mummy. —I've packed the machine away.

That's true. Mummy made my stripy 'jamas and my PE bag and then put her machine in the cupboard under the telly.

Aunty Sheila looked at her.

—But you made Pam's . . . she said.

—Sorry, said Mummy.

—And you made Karen's, and Christine's, and she had a twelve-foot train and a veil. I'm not asking for anything like that.

—I've no time for sewing, Sheila, said Mummy. —Not now.

She put her crusts on her plate.

—But I thought you could do with some cash? said Aunty Sheila.

—Of course I could do with some cash.

—So?

—So, it's not about cash! said Mummy.

—You're being unreasonable, said Aunty Sheila.

—I want to be a solicitor, said Mummy. —Not a seamstress.

—Making one wedding dress is not going to stop you becoming a solicitor, said Aunty Sheila.

—It won't be one dress, said Mummy. —It'll be that, then something else and something else. I'm sorry, Sheila, but I'm saying no.

—Here you go, says Grandad, and he coughs and puts a mug of tea on the table in front of Aunty Sheila.

The mug's special. Grandad bought it from a show. It's got a picture of an English rabbit on. Grandad always gets stuff from the shows. He gets food and medicines for his rabbits and he got a tie once. He wears it for parties and he's going to wear it for Aunty Sheila's wedding. It's red with English Spots jumping on.

Aunty Sheila puts her hands round the mug and she smiles.

—Look at you lazy lot, she says, and she winks at me. —Still in your dressing-gowns.

I smile and I try to wink my eye back at her. I like Aunty Sheila. Grandad does too, I know, because his mouth's not so straight and he's stopped watching the grey clouds go by and he's given her his special mug. He likes her, I think, because she's nice to him and she looked after him one time when he was rubbish at sleeping. He was tired and grumpy and so Mummy looked after the rabbits and me, and Aunty Sheila looked after Grandad and made him loads better.

Grandad puts his arm round Aunty Sheila's shoulder and sort of squeezes it.

—Sit down, Dad, she says, and she pats his hand, then she pats the chair next to her. —You look shattered.

—Well, thanks, he says, and he does a little laugh, and Aunty Sheila copies him. They laugh together. It sounds nice.

Mummy slurps her cornflakes.

—So? says Aunty Sheila. —How's things?

Mummy looks at her college book. She doesn't look at Aunty Sheila or anything because she's jealous. True-life. She's jealous because she doesn't have curly hair and Aunty Sheila does and she's jealous because Grandad's given Aunty Sheila the special mug and because Aunty Sheila lives in a house near Mrs Meadows and she's going to marry Uncle Brian.

Grandad sits down. He takes his tablets out of his pocket and puts them on the table.

—Are those your new ones? asks Aunty Sheila. —Are they doing any good?

—Haven't a clue, says Grandad.

He opens the packet and takes out a silver bit of card and he presses the card and two blue tablets fall on the table. He picks them up and presses them on his tongue. His tongue's grey like his hair. My tongue's pink. It's the same colour as Lincoln's.

—Well, I hope they're helping, says Aunty Sheila. —Don't you, Donna?

Mummy stares at her college book. She doesn't say anything. She slurps her cornflakes. She gulps! them down her throat. That's what happens. Food goes in your mouth and down your throat and then in your belly and then it poos out your bum. I hate poos. They're worse than squits. They're brown and smelly and there's always loads floating in our loo.

Aunty Sheila stares at Mummy. —Are you all right, Donna?

—I'm fine, says Mummy.

She turns over a page of her college book.

—And the course? says Aunty Sheila. —Any essays?

—She has to finish one today, says Grandad. —I'm taking Lily to the show, to give her some time.

—That's kind of you, Dad, says Aunty Sheila.

Mummy turns over another page. —I'm not making you that dress, Sheila, she says.

I don't know why.

—I don't need you to, smiles Aunty Sheila. —Brian's bought me one from the internet. It's made by a French designer, and, no offence, the cut and the stitching are . . . well, it's just so much better than home-made.

Mummy sighs.

Aunty Sheila holds the special mug carefully with her fingers like posh people do and she sips her tea. She does it ever so well.

—It was expensive, mind you, she says.

Expensive means lots of money, and designer . . .

Mummy sighs again.

I don't know what designer means, or no-offence, but the internet's inside computers and it's inside Uncle Brian's at work and he buys Pokémon stickers for Joe from it and scary skeleton rings for Kylie and carrots for Grandad's rabbits. They're brilliant. I like them. They're pretend, not real, and they're for the rabbits to chew, to stop their teeth from growing pointy and sharp like Dracula ones. They're made of orange wood.

Nobody likes me.

Dracula's stranger-danger.

Everybody hates me.

He wears a coat with bat wings and he flaps round and looks for grown-ups to stick his teeth into, my cousin Mickey told me.

Think I'll go and eat worms.

Big fat juicy ones.

Long thin skinny ones.

Dracula sticks his teeth into grown-ups' necks, that's what Mickey told me.

See how they squiggle and squirm.

Dracula sucks blood up the teeth-holes, that's what he did to Granny, that's what Mickey told me.

Bite their heads off.

Suck all their juice out.

Throw their skins away.

Dracula sucked up Granny's blood and she went all floppy and died and Dracula threw her skin away and Grandad looked for it everywhere and when he found it he cried and cried and put it in a box under the ground in the churchyard.

It's not very nice to die. It's better to be born and to get married.

Aunty Sheila's getting married.

She picks up the plastic bag that's on the floor by her

feet and I stick my head under the table and watch her lift it. Sometimes she gets me presents. It's bulgy, full of stuff. Maybe she's got me a present today.

—Stop messing about, Lily, says Mummy.

She tugs my arm. She's hurting me.

—Ow! I say.

—Well, sit up, she says.

I do as I'm told, and she lets go of me, and I stick a bit of my tongue out at her, just the end. Her face is squashed up like a toad's.

—I hope you're not doing what I think you're doing, she says.

I put my tongue away.

Aunty Sheila looks inside her bag.

It's plastic with an elephant on. The elephant's skating but that's not allowed because elephants are animals and animals have to walk if they're big, or run if they're fast, or hop and jump if they're rabbits and frogs and kangaroos. Skating's only for human beings like my cousin Kylie. She skates at Cooller Rollers all the time. It's because human beings have got arms that can stop them falling into walls and ponds.

Aunty Sheila takes something out of her bag.

—What's that you've got? says Grandad.

A present for me. Dear God, I pray to God, please let it be a present for me.

—Stop fidgeting, Lily, says Mummy with her toad face.

Aunty Sheila holds up a photo.

Bum.

—What do you think? she says.

—It's a photo, I say, and my face goes like a toad's too.

—But do you know what it's a photo of, Lily? she says.

—A dress, I say.

It's a photo of a dress and it's boring, it's not a present for me.

—My wedding dress, she says, and she smiles. —Well, what's the verdict?

—You'll look lovely in it, Sheila, says Grandad.

—They gave me a little emergency bag too. Here it is. It's got spare buttons and thread and a piece of fabric in case of accidents. I hope there's no accidents. Touch wood.

Aunty Sheila taps her nails on the table. Her nails are painted pink and they sort of shine. Then she pushes a see-through bag over to us. Inside is some white material. Mummy stares at the bag.

—Real silk, says Aunty Sheila. —Go on, take it out, have a feel.

—I know what silk feels like, Sheila, says Mummy.

—Oh, says Aunty Sheila.

—I'm going to the bedroom.

Mummy picks up her college book and pushes back her chair.

—Well, I've got a present for Lily too, says Aunty Sheila.

—YEEHAH! I shout, and I jump up and I bash my nose on Mummy's arm. She hurts me. It's an accident. She doesn't mean it. It's an accident and my nose is runny. I rub it. There's blood! There's blood on me!

—MUMMY! I shout. —MUMMY! MUMMY!
—Calm down, she says.
—MUMMY!
—CALM DOWN! she shouts. —ENOUGH!

Accidents are things that hurt you by accident. I know about them. We have them at school. They have to go in the book with the green cover with a white cross on it that dangles from a string in Miss Musters' office.

Miss Musters' office is at the front of the school, near the big brown door, so she can watch everybody come in and go out. She watches for strangers and child-catchers and willy-weirdos. Willy-weirdos are men with willies who are weird and they do strange things. They're stranger-danger. They're the same as strangers and child-catchers, I think. They're not very nice.

There was a child-catcher in the film about the flying car. We saw it in the holidays. There was the flying car. There was a boy, a girl and a dad. There was no mum but there was a pretty lady called Truly Scrumptious who sort of became their mum. And there was the child-catcher. He was the worst bit. He had black hair and a long nose that sniffed out children and he wore a black coat with bat wings and he flapped and swirled and showed his pointy teeth.

—He's 'tend, isn't he Mummy? I asked.

—Well, *he* is because he's an actor, in a film, said Mummy.

She was sitting in Grandad's easy chair by the fire. She

was having a rest from her reading and she was eating a minty Aero. She sucked her Aero. She always sucks her Aero because she likes the minty bubbles to tickle her tongue.

—But there are some real child-catchers about, Lily, she said.

—Oh, I said.

—Mmm, she said.

—True-life?

—Yes.

—Where?

Grandad came into the front room.

—Where's my latest *Fur & Feather*? he said.

—Where's the child-catchers? I said.

I felt sick.

—On our estate . . .

—*Fur & Feather* anyone?

—. . . in the corridors, outside school, at the shops, said Mummy.

—What's this? said Grandad.

—She's aware, said Mummy, and she put more Aero in her mouth. —I'm telling her nothing new. There was that policeman who came to your school. He talked to you about stranger-danger, didn't he, Lily?

I nodded. Don't talk to strangers. Don't take sweets off strangers or get in their cars. Don't believe anything strangers say to you, not even if they say your mummy is dying and she's sent them to collect you, to take you to hospital to see her, so she can kiss you bye-bye.

—I'm just reinforcing the message, said Mummy.

—You're scaring her, said Grandad. —She'll be having nightmares.

—No, she won't, said Mummy.

—She'll be waking you up.

—She won't. Will you, Lily?

I shook my head.

—Promise? said Mummy.

I nodded my head.

—A promise is a promise, said Mummy.

But I couldn't help it.

—OH MUMMY! I cried.

It made me all sweaty and shivery in bed.

—Mummy, Mummy, MUMMY!

—Christ! she said. —What is it? What's going off?

—Truly Scrumptious gobbled them up! She was the child-catcher and they didn't know! She was licking her lips, like this, over and over and over!

—Bugger, said Mummy.

I held on to her nightie. I gathered up the scratchy cloth with my fingers.

—Lily, she said. —Stop it now.

—Can't, I said.

My teeth were chattering.

—That's enough, she said, and she whacked my fingers away.

Miss Musters once had a fight with a blue-faced man in a raincoat. He was a child-catcher, a stranger-danger, and he had a willy and a knife! The knife was a dagger one and he jabbed it at Miss Musters and she punched him and he fell down and sicked all over her shoes. She saved us, that's what Mrs Meadows says, and we sang a special song in assembly to thank her. She was ever so pleased. She was a Super Hero and a newspaper man came and took her photo. But she had to have a rest from school for ages after. She got shaky hands and her hands shake now especially when she sees blood and there's lots at school because we get ripped-up knees and scratches and stuff and the blood squirts out and we have to show it to her because it's her job to wipe it up, that's what she has to do. She puts on plastic gloves and dabs the blood with cottonwool and her hands are so shaky sometimes she drops the cottonwool on the floor. She writes about our blood in the accident book. I've been in that book. Miss Musters showed Mummy. It was when Ben hit me with a skittle in the playground and crackled my head like Humpty Dumpty. Mummy couldn't read Miss Musters' writing.

—What's that? she asked.

—Sorry, said Miss Musters. —Shaky hands.

—Ben Cley did what?

—Ben got overexcited. He threw a skittle and caught Lily on the head. He split the skin, just a little, near the hairline. He's been told off. Lily was upset but she's fine now.

—Don't you have playground monitors? asked Mummy. —Or dinner ladies or something? Boys can be little buggers. They need watching.

—We have a volunteer rota for dinner-times, said Miss Musters. —I can put your name down if you like. Lot of mums do it. It breaks up the day for them.

—I'm not a mum, said Mummy.

—She's a mummy, I said.

—No, I'm not, Lily, said Mummy. —I'm a single parent and a student and I don't need to break up my day. My days are broken up enough as it is.

—It was just a thought, said Miss Musters.

—Come on, Lily, said Mummy. —Home now.

Mummy dabs my nose with the tea-towel. I'm bleeding. My nose is bleeding but I'm being brave, I'm not crying. I'm like Mummy. She's not crying and she's bleeding, except she's not doing it from her nose.

—Am I pouring, Mummy? I ask.

She's pouring, that's how blood comes from her crack.

—No, Lily.

—Flooding? I ask.

—Lily! says Aunty Sheila, and she shakes her head and her curls bounce up and down.

—But Aunty Pam floods, I say. —She told me.

—You're just dripping, says Mummy.

The blue tea-towel's covered in red spots.

—Oh, I say.

Mummy bends her knees and stares at me. Her eyes are dark and squinty and they look up my nose, I don't know what they're looking for.

—You'll live, she says, and she tucks the tea-towel in my hand.

—Let's see Lily's present now, shall we? says Grandad.

He nods at Aunty Sheila.

—Yes, right, she says, and she opens the elephant bag and fumbles around inside it. —This is for the

71

wedding, Lily, because I know your mummy can't make you anything because she's so busy . . .

—Well, says Mummy quietly. —She has ears.

That's right. She does. She has little pink ears and she's got earrings too, dangly ones that twinkle like stars.

Aunty Sheila smiles at me.

—She can't sew you anything, and I know she can't afford to buy you anything new because she's on a grant . . .

—We manage, says Mummy.

—So . . .

Aunty Sheila flaps something in the air.

It's a dress! I've got a dress!

I drop the tea-towel. I clap my hands. I feel like crying. I feel like singing.

—ALL GOOD THINGS AROUND US . . .

—Lily! says Mummy.

—ARE SENT FROM HEAVEN ABOVE . . .

—Christ, laughs Grandad.

—THEN THANK THE LORD, OH THANK . . .

Mummy grabs my hands. She holds them tight and still.

—Sit down, she says.

Aunty Sheila puts the dress on the table.

I sit down and Mummy does too.

—Have a proper look, go on, says Aunty Sheila, and she pushes the dress over to me.

I don't wear dresses. Dresses are girl-girl. Kelly wears girl-girl stuff all the time. She falls over in the playground and her girl-girl dresses fly up and show off her knickers. She wears frilly knickers and she squits them. I wear boy-girl clothes normally, leggings or shorts and tops.

—Brilliant, I say, and I sniff. There's still blood up my nose, I can feel it. I sniff so it doesn't drop and splash on my dress.

—It's Barbie pink, says Aunty Sheila.

—It's got a pocket, I say.

—Mmm, she says.

It's got a pocket with a crinkly edge and white stitching round, and it's got extra white stitching on the neck and sleeves, and the sleeves are short and puffy.

—You're allowed to touch it, says Aunty Sheila.

—Go on, says Grandad.

I do as I'm told: I move my fingers. I walk them over the dress. It feels soft and furry like a rabbit, like Lincoln and Barnsley and Newbiggin-by-the-Sea.

—Oh, I say. —Brilliant.

—Velveteen, says Aunty Sheila. —But it's for my wedding. Understand?

—Weddings are for men and ladies who love each other, I say.

Mummy makes a tutting noise.

I stroke the velteen.

Daisy, Daisy give me an answer do.

I'm half crazy all for the love of you.

It won't be a stylish marriage.

I can't afford a carriage.

Aunty Sheila can. She's having one with ribbons and bells and a black horse with a white star on its head to pull it. She told me.

I stroke the pocket, the neck, the sleeves.

—There'll be extras too, nearer the time, says Aunty Sheila. —Pink socks, black plimsolls.

Plimsolls!

—At least they're useful, says Mummy.

—And I've got something for you too, says Grandad. —Lily.

I look at him. He's staring at me and he raises his spiky eyebrows and he smiles.

—A surprise! he says.

—YEEHAH! I shout.

Today is Saturday and Saturday's normally normal. It's not normally surprise! surprise! day. Surprises are fantastic-elastic. I pray to God for them but he doesn't listen to me, he listens to Tom and Bethany. They get surprises all the time, little and big ones. Once they even went to Disneyland. They went in this train under the sea. They didn't get wet or anything. It was dark but there were no sharks or whales. Aunty Chris said it was ever so good. She dreams about it every night.

Uncle Paul sorted it. He got tickets from the newspaper and one morning he put Aunty Chris and Tom and Bethany in his lovely blue car. Tom and Bethany fell asleep and when they woke up they were in a tunnel under the sea going to Disneyland. They couldn't believe it. Disneyland. True-life! They saw Aladdin and Peter Pan, Thunder Mountain and It's A Small World, and they got Mickey Mouse to write his name on some paper for me, and they gave me a Goofy key ring, which was stupid because I've only got my Barbie key and that goes under my hair bobble collection that's on the table near the bed. I've got loads of hair bobbles.

They're all different colours and they're in a big pile with the red-and-white stripy bobbles on top because they're Manchester United, Finbar's favourites.

Grandad said Tom and Bethany should've got me a Bugs Bunny present, a mirror or a drawing book, something to go with my clock. Mummy said Bugs Bunny's nothing to do with Disneyland and really they shouldn't have got me anything at all. She said they should've kept Disneyland a secret from me. A secret's a secret. She talked to Aunty Chris about it.

—You're unbelievable! Aunty Chris snapped. Then she said something about cramping, I don't know why, because cramps are what you get when you go swimming with lots of food in your belly. Cathy got cramps at Splash World. We went with our class and Mrs Meadows had to jump in the pool and save her. Mrs Meadows was wearing her trainers and they got soaking. Cramps are dangerous and annoying. They don't have them in Disneyland.

Mummy stomped out the flat. She was dead angry and forgot about me.

—Oh dear, Aunty Chris sighed. She pushed her hands through her hair and crouched down and cuddled me. —I'm sorry, Lily. I'll take you to Disneyland one day, I promise. Cross my heart.

—Doesn't matter, I said. —I'm going to Sweden with Grandad.

Sweden. Sweden. Sweden.

People who live in Sweden are called Swedes, that's what Grandad told me. You can eat swedes with chicken and potatoes too but that's swedes the vegetable. It's a funny vegetable because it's orange. Mummy likes it but I'm not sure. I think peas are better. They're more normal. They're round and small and green.

—Here we are, says Grandad.

He's got a paper bag from his medicine cupboard and he's rustling it in front of me. My surprise is in there. Grandad sits down. It's so exciting. My God. Grandad opens the bag and pulls something out and passes it before my eyes. It's a red circle with . . .

I jump up. —YEEHAH!

—LILY! Mummy shouts. —STOP THIS SHOUT-ING!

It's a judge's badge! My favourite judge's badge! A red circle with a black rabbit in the middle! I jump up and down. I can't believe it. Judges are at the rabbit shows. They give prizes to rabbits and they wear white coats covered in badges and their mummies and girlfriends have to sew the badges on their white coats using the in-out in-out in-a-straight-line stitch. The badges are made of material and they're different sizes and shapes and colours, and I like the red circle ones with pictures of black rabbits on best.

—There's more, says Grandad, and he empties the paper bag on the table.

—Grandad, Grandad, I say, and I sit down and shake my head and look at the badges.

There's triangles, squares and stars, all with pictures of rabbits on. I turn them so they face the right way up, every one of them. I want to cry. I'm like Aunty Sheila when Uncle Brian asked her to get married. She told me. She told Mummy. —I was so happy, she said. —The tears were rolling down and Brian couldn't get off his knees to give me a tissue, he was laughing so much, the silly man.

—So you think they'll be OK? asks Grandad.

I nod.

—Oh, yes, says Aunty Sheila. —They're nice.

Grandad smiles and Mummy stares at him, I don't know why. She stares at Aunty Sheila too.

Grandad leans across the table and smooths out my dress.

—I'll just take this one, he says, and he picks up a badge and puts it on the dress, near the neck.

It's a blue badge with yellow writing that goes round in a circle. I can't read the writing, I don't know what it says, but it doesn't matter. The yellow and blue look brilliant on the dress.

—Cool! I say. —Can I do some?

—Take your time, says Grandad. —Nicely now.

I put millions round the frilly hem.

—They shouldn't take much stitching, Donna, says Grandad.

—I'm sorry? says Mummy.

I look at her. I look at Grandad too.

—I'd like your mummy to stitch them on the dress, Lily.

He speaks slowly like Mrs Meadows does when she's talking to daft-bat Kelly.

—YES! I say and I thump the air.

—You're not serious, says Mummy. —Sheila?

Aunty Sheila smiles.

—So, what happened to the classy wedding?

—Oh, it'll still be classy, says Aunty Sheila. —But with a twist. The kids'll have badges on their clothes and some of Dad's rabbits will come to the reception . . .

—Oh very novel, says Mummy, and she snorts through her nose like a pig and she folds her arms and looks out the window at the clouds.

—What's that? I ask.

The clouds are dark grey and they're squashing and pushing each other like they need more room, like they want to rain, to really chuck it down.

—What's reception? I ask.

My heart is beating.

—The party afterwards, Lily, says Aunty Sheila.

—A party! I say.

I don't go to many of them.

—Are we having jelly?! I ask. —Can Lincoln do her jumping?! She can do the triple, Aunty Sheila. She's practising for Sweden.

—Oh really? she says. —That's clever.

—Isn't he? says Mummy.

—She, says Grandad. —Lincoln's a she.

—A doe, I say.

Lincoln's a prize doe. She's not won prizes for jumping, not yet, but she's won prizes for being show perfect. Her eye circles are perfect and her spots, and her back is perfectly curvy.

She's brilliant, that's what Grandad says; and he writes about how brilliant she is in his special book. He writes about all his other rabbits too, about what prizes they've won and how old they are and what babies they've made.

Lincoln's not made any babies because she's a spirit and she'll eat them, she's not the same as other does. They have babies all the time. They have to, that's what Grandad says. They have to have loads so he can pick the best ones, the ones he wants to keep. He looks at twenty or thirty or forty babies before he picks just one. True-life! Then he clips a ring round that one's leg and when it's ready to leave its mummy he puts it in a hutch, all on its own, and that's a bit sad because the baby bunny's like me then. An only-bonely-lonely.

Grandad puts the babies he doesn't want in some hutches near his window, not right under the window where the bucks are, but near. They cuddle up to each other so they don't feel the cold so much and they lick each other and everything. Some have got shiny eyes and big muscles and OK spots. They're almost perfect and Grandad sells them at the shows. Some are runts. That's what they're called. I'm called Lily and I'm a Tortoise and they're called runts because they're the weedy wimps. They've not got much energy and they're the weeny and shivery and Grandad gives them to the pet man. He's got a pet shop in a van and he drives to Scotland where there's snow and ice and penguins and to Devon where it's creamy. Scotland and Devon are in our country, England and Britain where we live. The pet man goes all over our country to sell his pets and he sells Grandad's runts too, that's what Grandad says. The pet man fusses the runts and makes them strong. Then he sells them to people who don't care about perfect.

Grandad says the pet man's nice but he won't let me have a ride in his van or see him or anything, I don't know why, because he lets my cousin Mickey see the pet man all the time. It's not fair. Mickey's horrid and ugly with a squeaky voice but Grandad gives him the runts and he puts them in his cat basket and he carries them down the corridors and he delivers them to the pet man. Deliver's like what the postman does and the people who push free things through Aunty Chris's door. My friend Finbar says you can only deliver things that are flat, you can't deliver rabbits, and anyway he doesn't believe about the pet man because we had a pet man come to our school and he had a shop in a street, not in a van, and that's a proper pet man, that's what Finbar says, and anyway he says he's seen Mickey take the rabbits down to the garages and throw them at the garage doors, cross-his-heart-and-hope-to-die, and I think Finbar'll die because Mickey can't hurt the rabbits, no way! Grandad wouldn't let him. He can't throw them at the garage doors or splat! them off the top of the flats. He can't be scary. He belongs to Aunty Karen; she's nice, and scary doesn't come from nice; it comes from stranger-danger and crazy-on-drugs. That's right. I'm sure.

Aunty Karen is Mummy's sister. She lives in our flats, on Floor 1, with Uncle Ben and Mickey and Layla, and she works in Hot Pies. We don't see her so much but one time she rang our doorbell and Grandad answered and she burst into tears.

I could hear her with my supersonic ears.

I was in the front room looking at Grandad's magazines, the travel ones he gets from town, that are all about Sweden. I was looking at the shiny pictures of airplanes and mountains and people with yellow hair, and I could hear Aunty Karen crying and I wanted to see, so I ran into the hall.

I could see.

There were tears dribbling down her face. There were too many tears, and I could see them, and they frightened me.

—La la la, I said.

—Karen, said Grandad.

—I'll . . . I can't . . . she said, and she rubbed her eyes.

Grandad looked at me.

—Go feed the rabbits, Lily, he said. —Go on. Scoot!

Grandad put his arm round Aunty Karen and took

her to the front room. He closed the door. I looked at the door. I was supposed to feed the rabbits but it was dinner-time and normally rabbits only have breakfast and tea. I didn't know what to do. Grandad had made a mistake, I was sure, and I wanted to tell him but I daren't go in the room because Aunty Karen was crying and talking too much. I could hear her because Grandad hadn't closed the door properly and there was a gap, and I stuck my supersonic ears near the gap, first one ear, then I turned my head and gave the other ear a go.

Aunty Karen was really fed up with Uncle Ben, that's what she was saying. She was crying because of him. He was doing nothing but watching telly and drinking beers, and she was having to work for Hot Pies and do all the stuff at home and everything. She was having to cook and clean and look after Mickey and Layla, and it was whacking her, and Layla wasn't happy and was pooing her pants, yuk, all the time. Aunty Karen said Uncle Ben was getting on top of her every night too. He was climbing on her. I don't know why. Grandad made a funny noise then. He said some things should be left in the bedroom. It didn't make any sense to me but I listened some more and it got better. Aunty Karen was telling a story, a true-life one about when Uncle Ben took Layla up the park in town and she got stuck on the slide. She was screaming and Uncle Ben didn't hear, he didn't do nothing, because he was snoring on the bench. He'd drank loads of beer and he was snoring and Layla was screaming and some lady had to rescue her.

—I've had enough, cried Aunty Karen. —I've had . . . Is this supposed to be my life?

—It could just be a bad patch, said Grandad. —Grace and I went through a few, most couples do; and Ben did lose his job and that wasn't his fault.

—I can't see an end to it, said Aunty Karen. —If I could only see the end . . .

Grandad's got a photo of Aunty Karen where she's on her own, not with her sisters, so she looks like me, like what I do in photos. She looks like an only-bonely. She's holding a rabbit and I do that in photos too. But the rabbit's not an English. It's just ordinary and black. Aunty Karen is wearing a T-shirt with criss-cross laces at the neck. She's a teenager and she's looking down at the ordinary rabbit. It's small and its eyes are wide and scared. Aunty Karen's eyes look wide and scared too. Grandad says the rabbit belonged to the family that lived next-door. That was in the olden days when him and Granny were in the doorstep house. Grandad says Aunty Karen loved the rabbit but was frightened of it scratching her. She was frightened of Liverpool scratching her as well.

Grandad gave Liverpool to Aunty Karen because he was an old rabbit and couldn't make babies any more, he didn't feel ticklish. He was a present for Aunty Karen's birthday. Grandad gave Aunty Karen a hutch too and she put it in her hall. But Liverpool's nails were long and Uncle Ben chopped them with some scissors and cut the red bit you're not supposed to cut and blood came out and Liverpool's heart went pop! and

he died. It was horrible. Aunty Karen cried then too.
She's always crying, except when she's doing her work
for Hot Pies.

—BYE!

That's Aunty Sheila. She's in the hall. She's answering the door because someone's banging on it. They want to come in and she wants to go home. She's going back to her house with the gnomes and the doorstep, back to Uncle Brian and Kylie and Joe.

—BYE SHEILA!

That's Grandad. He shouts and coughs.

—BYE AUNTY SHEILA!

That's me.

—I'd better get dressed.

And that's Mummy.

She picks up her college book and she doesn't say bye. She just picks up her book and leaves the room.

—Mummy's not very happy, I say.

—No, says Grandad, and he takes a rabbit badge off my dress. —She needs to lighten up.

—Oh, I say.

He takes off some more badges, one by one, and he opens the paper bag and drops them in, and I'm like Mummy, I'm not happy. My rabbit badges are going away.

—Grandad, I say, and I hold my hand out for the bag but he tucks it in his dressing-gown pocket and my cousin Mickey walks through the door.

—Hello, says Grandad. —Thought it might be you.

Mickey nods.

I gulp.

I don't like Mickey.

He makes me sick. I can taste the sick. It's in my mouth.

—Well, how're you doing? asks Grandad.

—OK, says Mickey in his squeaky voice.

His voice is squeaky and crackly. It's not normal. He's not normal. Everything was brilliant and now it's not. It's like the shivery stories that Mrs Meadows reads on Fridays. It's like Batman Dracula has flapped his wings and made it dark and gloomy over me. Brr. I shiver. I look at Mickey.

He's wearing baggy trousers. His hair is orange and he's got his cat basket for the baby rabbits, the ones Grandad doesn't want.

—How's your mum?

—OK, says Mickey.

—Good, says Grandad, and he puts his old-age hand over his mouth and he coughs. He does it like that because it's good to cough in your hand and it's bad to do it, huh-huh, in the air because cough germs can float through the air and make other people cough too.

I look at Mickey.

I want to be a cough germ. I want to germ him right up, germ him into hospital, germ him dead.

Mickey stares at my dress. He smiles a naughty smile.

I pull the dress near me. I hold it in my arms. I cuddle it. It's warm and soft like a rabbit. I want to be a rabbit.

I want to hop from here to all the good places, to the rabbit show and Sweden.

I know tons about Sweden, much more than Mickey. I know about the mountains and the blue sky and the blue flag with the yellow cross on it, the flag that belongs to Sweden.

Grandad puts his hands on the table and pushes himself up.

Mickey stares at my dress.

—Well, Mickey, says Grandad. —You'd better come and get them.

—OK, Grandad, says Mickey, and he stares at my dress and he makes his fingers into scissors.

He pretends he's got some scissors and he goes snip snip snip like that in the air.

It's quiet in here. It's nice. Mickey's in Grandad's room with the rabbits and I'm in here with Mummy, in our bedroom. I'm sitting on the big bed with my legs under the covers and my dress safe on the pillow beside me, and Mummy's by the window, and we're doing our work. I'm doing my diary and Mummy's huddled over her books, learning to be a solicitor.

Solicitors are clever. They make up rules and earn lots of money. Mummy's good at making up rules but she's not good with money. She keeps pinching 2ps and 5ps from the Treats Jar and spending them on bread and milk, ordinary stuff. It's a good job Grandad doesn't put money in his Treats Jar or she'd be pinching that too. His Treats Jar's got special sweeties for the rabbits. The sweeties look like chocolate drops and Finbar and me tried them once. Grandad doesn't know. We had six each and put them in our mouths all in one go. They were horrid. Finbar spat his out but I was brave and swallowed mine. They gave me green squits.

I've stuck a rabbit sweetie in my diary but I've not put in a squit, no way! I've put in a dried-up rabbit plip that doesn't smell and I've drawn Lincoln and I've copied some photos from one of Grandad's *Fur & Feather*s and I've put a bit of rabbit fur in and a shaving and a weeny map of Sweden and a picture of the flag with the cross on it. That's in the front of my diary and at the back I've done my secret pages about Grandad. A secret's a secret. I can keep these pages secret because I've got a padlock on my diary.

Padlocks are metal with keyholes and they lock things up. The padlock on my diary is tiny and gold. It's got a shiny gold key to undo it with.

Aunty Sheila gave me my diary for my birthday because she had one when she was a little girl and she wrote in it every day about what she did at school, what made her happy or sad, that sort of stuff. She keeps her diary in her special room that's like a box, that's got shelves in for her memories and photos and Grandad's prizes, the BIS shield and the cups he wins for Best Fancy.

I looked at the diary. —Thanks, I said.

—You don't sound very enthusiastic, she said. —What's wrong?

—I can't do nothing in it, I said. —I can't write, my letters aren't good, I can't read, and I'm rubbish at tens and units.

—Maybe this'll get you started, Aunty Sheila said. —Try to put your name in it first. One step at a time. Try. Go on.

Aunty Sheila gave me her best pen. It was heavy. My fingers couldn't hold it properly.

—I don't like pens, I said.

—No excuses, she said. —Now, what's the first letter of your name?

—'L', I said.

—Very good. So write it down. Go on, Lily, she said.

It took me ages. It looked wavy like a worm.

—Is that a capital 'L' or a little 'I'? asked Aunty Sheila.

—Don't care, I said.

—Well, you should care, she said.

—Not me, I said.

I didn't look at my diary for ages after. It was like school. I hate school. I'm a Tortoise. But then I started to play with the key and the padlock, and now I click it open and do my work in it all the time. It's special to me, and my grandad pages are the most special because they let me know about him, about his coughing and his wobbly ticker and everything. They're sort of sad but they're good because they help me know. So it's like I know lots about rabbits and lots about Grandad.

Here's what's in my grandad pages.

Page 1: A photo of Grandad and Mummy and me. We're in the front room and Grandad and me are on the sofa and Mummy's standing by the window. She's hugging her belly and Grandad's hugging me and his eyes and mouth are smiley. My cousin Danny took the photo. It's not blurry.

Page 2: A drawing of Grandad with his ticker inside that I did with my crayons. There's his arms and legs and head and then he's sort of open so you can see his ticker inside. His ticker's his heart and it's a clock too. I've done it ever so well. It's a pink heart with a long hand and a short hand and numbers and the long hand is pointing to the 12 and the short is pointing to the bit between the 5 and 6 because that's the same age as me.

Page 3: One of Grandad's medicine spoons that are white and made of plastic. I found it in the kitchen bin and washed it, then squashed it with Mummy's cookery book to make it nice and flat except it's cracked a bit down the middle which is not so good.

Page 4: A photo of Grandad's hospital that was in the newspaper. It's a big hospital with lots of towers and Grandad visits it sometimes and once he had to sleep there when I was three. I can't remember that but he was there true-life, he told me, and he had to wear this dress because that's what everybody wears when they sleep in hospital, I don't know why.

Page 5: A drawing of Grandad's doctor, Doctor Whitworth, who visits us and is really tall like a giant. Poor Doctor Whitworth. He has to watch out in case he bangs himself on ceilings and lights and doors and stuff. He has to scrunch his shoulders and droop his head. He wants to be small like me, that's what he says. He wants to be like me and he wants to be like Grandad too because he wants to show rabbits. He talks to Grandad about rabbits when he's testing Grandad's ticker. He tests with his fingers. He sort of taps them on Grandad's chest and Grandad doesn't like this because Doctor Whitworth's fingers are cold. That's why I've coloured them blue in my drawing because that means cold: hot taps are red, they have red dots on, they're burny, and cold taps have blue dots on and they're cold.

Page 6: A drawing of my sad face when Grandad went away to Aunty Sheila's. He went to get some rest and he stayed ages and that upset me. I couldn't see him or anything and I was missing him more than I miss Granny.

Page 7: A bit of hanky. I cut up one of Grandad's hankies that had blood on and I put a corner in my diary, then I threw the rest away. Grandad doesn't know. He has lots of hankies and he forgets about them. He leaves them in the kitchen by the salad stuff and on top of the loo and everywhere and Mummy gets cross and tells him off. His hankies are made of material. They're white and grey and some have got letters on, a J and a P, because they're the letters for his name. Jim Phillips. That's my grandad's name.

I touch the bit of hanky. It's stiff like cardboard but it's nice. I can see Grandad's blood on it and it's like mine, like what came out of my nose on the tea-towel, lots of little drips.

I get my Barbie mirror off the table by the bed and I put it under the holes in my nose. I want to see the blood. I can't see anything. Only dark, going up and up into my head. It's like a warren up there. I press my warren nose with my finger.

—Ow! I say.

It's sore and painful. It's like my leg when Finbar did his Jesus thing on me. Jesus Christ was put on a cross. He died to save us all. He didn't have Batman Dracula sucking his neck and his heart didn't go pop! He died to save us all on a cross. It wasn't nice. Soldiers put him there. They didn't tie him to the cross and they didn't use staylers; they banged big nails in him and Finbar tried that on me. It was an experiment. I'm good at experiments. I do them with the Tortoises. Finbar does too but his aren't so good, his ones hurt.

He put his policeman's handcuffs on me and squashed a hanky in my mouth, I don't know why, and then he got this nail. It was silver and it had a dead sharp end and he pressed it in my leg. He pressed and pressed and it really hurt and I wanted to scream. I pushed the hanky with my tongue but it wouldn't fall out. I couldn't breathe. I wriggled my hands in the handcuffs. I wriggled my head from side to side like that but Finbar kept pressing on my leg till water came out. True-life. There's water in my legs. Finbar touched it with his finger and said it was miracle water and he dabbed it on his funny eye, the one that doesn't see so well, but it hasn't done anything, not yet. Finbar says it will. He says it'll happen when he's a teenager because teenagers need their eyes more than us because they have hard-ones and sexywexy to do in the dark; they have to have good eyes to see in the dark.

—Is Mickey a teenager? I ask.

I put down my Barbie mirror and look at Mummy.

She stretches out her arms and turns her head and looks at me.

—I suppose it couldn't last for ever, she says, and she gets up, and I close my diary quick and lock it with the key and hide it near my hair bobble collection. I've got hundreds. People give me them even though my hair's short like Finbar's.

Mummy comes across to me. She sits on the bed and it makes a creaky metal noise.

—I've got a thumping headache, she sighs.

—Oh, I say.

—Mmm, she says, and she fumbles in her tracksuit pockets.

She's wearing her black tracksuit with the white lines on, that's the same colour as English rabbits, and her face is white and there's little red lines under her eyes and her hair's messy. It always is. It's never straight and shiny like Aunty Karen's or yellow and curly like Aunty Sheila's. It's black with grey bits and it sticks up and everything. It was probably the same when she got married to Daddy in the office that was full of chairs. She whispered about it to Mrs Meadows in class. I heard. Ladies don't get married in offices normally. They do work in them and they have to look posh to do the work. They have to wear frilly blouses and do their faces with blue eyeshadow and bright red lipstick. Aunty Sheila worked in an office. She counted money and put it in piles. The money made her skin go green, she told me.

Mummy pulls a little bottle from one of her pockets. She clicks the lid and shakes it and two white tablets fall on her hand. She swallows the tablets and gulps dead loud.

—Well, she says. —I'd better get you ready for Tom and Bethany's.

—Aren't I going with Grandad? I ask.

It's gloomy again. It's the spell.

—Aren't I going to the show?

—Later, she says. —In the afternoon.

—HURRAH!

There isn't a spell. I thump the air like they do in *Hey Arnold!*

—Lily, calm down, says Mummy.

She puts the bottle back in her pocket and gets off the bed. She opens my cupboard. It's empty. I can see. There's nothing in there. No jumpers, no socks, no panties, nothing, because all my clothes are dirty. They're in the washing box. They're waiting to go to the laundry place near Mr Azad's.

—I can wear my dress, Mummy, I say, and I hold it up.

—Don't push it, Lily, she says, and she opens the washing box and pulls out a T-shirt and leggings. The T-shirt's got Barbie on the front but I can't see her face, there's a big splodge of tomato sauce covering it. Mummy picks at the sauce and it crumbles off. —That'll do.

She holds up the leggings and she sniffs the bum.

—I don't want them, I say.

They're my red ones. They're too tight for me.

—They're OK, says Mummy. —You're having them.

—I don't want them. They make me wee.

—You're having them. Get out of bed and put them on.

I shake my head and Mummy grabs me.

—I don't . . . OW!

She pulls my arm. Her fingers dig into my arm and she pulls and my feet are stuck under the covers and I'm going all twisty and tears fill my eyes. I blink. Mummy doesn't like tears. She lets go of me. I blink and blink until they've gone.

—OK, she says. —Come on now.

I do as I'm told.

I pull the covers off my feet and the cold air freezes me. I stand and the lino nips my toes.

Mummy kneels. She takes off my dressing-gown and my 'jamas. —Give us a hand. Honestly, Lily, you're old enough to do this by yourself.

She pushes me into the smelly T-shirt and I wiggle my arms but I'm not helping, not really.

—More effort, she says. —You're not trying.

—Am, I say.

Then I shut up. She hurt me. I hate her. I don't want to say anything to her. She pulls the leggings over my bum. She's forgotten my knickers. But I'm not telling, I'm not saying anything, not to her.

—OK, GRANDAD.

God.

That's Mickey, his squeaky voice. I can hear him coming down the hall.

I have a thought. I open my mouth.

—What is it, Lily? says Mummy.

Jesus. Mary.

—Lost your tongue?

—Mummy? I say.

—Ah, she says.

I have to say. —Who's taking me to Tom and Bethany's?

—Mickey, she says.

I look at her.

—I don't like Mickey, I say.

I feel shivery.

—He's your cousin, she says. —He's harmless.

—He scared me, I say.

He did the scissor thing and he did that other thing too.

I feel really shivery.

—He won't scare you again, she says. —He's been warned.

—Told off? I say.

—Hit with the slipper, she says.

Yes!

—Uncle Ben whacked him.

—When? I ask.

There's a knock on our door, and Mummy stands up.

—COME IN! she shouts.

One time Mickey scared me. He scared me more than the scissors. He really scared me.

It was when he was taking me down the corridors. I'm not allowed to go down them on my own because they're a hell-hole and death-trap. Someone has to be with me. Usually it's Grandad or Mummy. Sometimes it's Mickey.

—Which way shall we go then? he grinned. He nodded at the corridor. He pointed up it. —This way?

He pointed down it.

—Or that way? Come on, hurry up, tell us.

—Don't know, I said.

—You don't know? said Mickey, in his squeaky voice. —Eeny meeny miny mo. Come on, thicko. Which way to the lift?

—Stop it, I said.

—YAH! Mickey said, and he walked off.

I followed him. My jellies made a squelching noise on the floor like suckers.

—Wait for me, I said.

Mickey was walking fast. He was wearing his trainers that have lights in the heels and flash when he runs. I didn't want him to run. He was carrying his basket. There were five little rabbits in it. Grandad had given him five white runts to take to the pet man. Grandad doesn't show all white. Mickey started to run.

—WAIT MICKEY!

I started to run.

—YAH! he shouted.

—WAIT! WAIT! I shouted. —MICKEY!

—YAH! YAH! he shouted.

He was swinging the basket and the little white rabbits were crashing around inside it.

—THE BUNNIES! I shouted.

—FUCK! shouted Mickey, and he threw the basket down.

—NO! I said.

I dashed to the basket and fell on my knees.

—Bunnies, bunnies, I said.

I looked through the wire. They were huddled in a corner. Their noses were twitching. They were OK.

—Fuck, said Mickey.

He pushed his hands through his orange hair.

Gingernuts, Gingernuts, Copperknob and Carrot-top.

Gingernuts, Gingernuts, Copperknob and . . .

—What you smiling for? Mickey said. —You've got nothing to smile about. We're lost. I've fuckin' lost us.

—What? I said. I stood up.

—Yes, he said.

He looked scared.

—Jesus, Mary, fuckin' Joseph, what're we going to do? I've lost us. We're doomed! We're going to be stuck in these corridors for ever, walking round and round. Nobody'll help us. Nobody'll care. We'll starve and die of thirst, and our skin'll drop off and our skeletons will be chucked down the rubbish shoot.

—You're messing, I said. Boy skeleton, girl skeleton, little baby rabbit skeletons! My mouth was wobbly. —No messing, Mickey.

—Who's messing? grinned Mickey.

—You.

—Me?

He laughed and shook his head. Danny says they get Mickey in the showers at big school and bash his head against the wall and hold his nose and fill his mouth with water until he's sick. Danny says Mickey's sick stinks.

—Your sick stinks, I said.

—You what? said Mickey. —What did you say?!

His face was red. I looked at my jellies.

—See these rabbits, he said. —I'm taking them to the top of these flats and I'm going to drop them off one by one. Splat! Splat! Splat! Splat! Splat!

—I'll tell Grandad, I said.

—Scare me, said Mickey. —Why don't you? BYE!

—MICKEY! WAIT!

Mickey ran.

—MICKEY! MICKEY!

His trainer lights flashed.

—WAIT FOR ME, MICKEY!

He went round a corner.

—MICKEY!

He ran and ran.

I ran and ran.

—OW!

I tripped.

—MICKEY!

I was on the floor, the dirty grey floor. The floor was dirty grey and the walls were white and there was a rubbish hole with a red door. It wasn't our rubbish hole. Someone's drawn a heart on ours. Not me. I can draw hearts. I'm good at hearts. But it wasn't me. I didn't know where I was. The corridor was long. There was no Mickey. The flats had red doors with little glass windows. Some had frilly curtains and some had cardboard on the windows, and there were numbers and names on the doors but I couldn't read them. There was no Newbiggin-by-the-Sea. I didn't know where I was. I listened with my supersonic ears. I couldn't hear anything. I sniffed with my normal nose. There were smells but too many, all jumbled up and I couldn't work out the right one, the one to follow, the one rabbits know will lead them from the warren. I thumped the floor.

Oh God.

I thumped the floor again.

I wanted a clever rabbit's nose.

I thumped and thumped the floor.

Dear God, please God.

I put my hands together.

I couldn't sniff my way out.

I sent a prayer.

Nobody'd care and nobody'd help. I was going to starve.

My eyes were wet.

—Our Father. Jesus Christ who died to save us all.

I thumped and thumped the floor.

I was going to starve.

—Lord God.

And die of thirst.

—Amen.

Because I wasn't a rabbit.

—I want to be a rabbit!

I thumped the floor really hard.

—Please let me be a rabbit!

I thumped. I shouted. I screamed.

—I WANT TO BE A RABBIT! I WANT TO BE A RABBIT, GOD! I WANT TO BE A RABBIT!

Mickey's trainers kicked me.

—Shut the fuck up, he said.

There are hundreds of buttons in the lift. Some are green with numbers on, some are black and there's one big gold one for emergencies. Mummy had to press the gold one once when the doors started eating the bottom of her motorbike jacket. She hasn't got a motorbike but that doesn't matter. The man in the shop said she could buy one later. —Don't make me laugh, said Mummy.

Mickey presses the o button. Zero. Ground floor. Going down. I like going down. It makes my belly go funny. It's like the flume at Splash World. I like the flume. It's a helter skelter with water. A good idea for children.

—Do you like the flume? I ask Mickey. —The flume at Splash World? It's a good idea for children.

Mickey doesn't answer. He's been warned. He has to be nice and he is; he's being nice and quiet. That's why I'm chattering to him. He's not played any more tricks on me.

—The flume's great, I tell him as the lift goes clunk and the doors slide open.

I see a bag of chips someone's dropped on the floor, and half a battered sausage.

—Do you like chips? I ask. —And sausages?

Mickey doesn't answer. I follow him down the corridor to Aunty Chris's.

—Hot dogs? I say. —Do you like hot dogs? With onions? And ketchup?

Mickey coughs.

—I'm hungry, I say.

He walks slowly. He's slouching. Slouching's bad for you. It's not fit and healthy. The nurse at school says you have to watch out for slouching, and nits, and sugary sweeties that rot your teeth. She says it's OK to poo your pants because that happens sometimes, especially when you're sad. It happened to me once when Finbar told a lie about my mummy, about how Daddy doesn't come to see me or send me presents or anything because Mummy killed him with a dagger. Mummy stuck the dagger into Daddy's heart, right there, that's what Finbar said, and Daddy fell on the floor and blood squirted out his mouth and everything. It made me cry. I cried and pooed my pants. I didn't want to, I hate poos, but it was all right, the nurse was nice to me. She cuddled me and said Finbar was a naughty boy, he told a lie, and she wiped my bum and she gave me new pants to put on, she called them fresh, and I put them on and she promised she wouldn't tell anybody about my poo, cross her heart. It was our secret. A secret's a secret. Mummy didn't realise. She didn't notice my new pants, so that was good.

—You're slouching, I say to Mickey. —Slouching hurts your body.

It does too. It curls your body right up and you can't wear nice clothes when you're a teenager. Mickey doesn't wear nice clothes. He wears baggy trousers.

—Are you a teenager? I ask, because Mummy didn't tell me, and I don't know because sometimes my big cousins have their birthdays and they don't say, they don't invite me to their parties or anything.

Mickey coughs. He doesn't answer me. He coughs and his cat basket jiggles up and down and the baby rabbits fall about inside it. Grandad's given Mickey three rabbits today. They look like proper English but something must be wrong with them, they can't be perfect. Maybe their fur is falling out or maybe they've got too many spots or maybe they've got poorly bellies or dried-up brains.

—Where's the pet man? I ask. —Is he outside in his van?

Mickey doesn't answer me.

—I believe about him, I say. —He's nice, I think. Do you think he's nice?

Mickey coughs.

I think he is. I think he looks after the rabbits and cares for them in his pet van and I think he probably takes the poorly ones to the animal doctor to get them mended. I think that's what he does.

—You know *Pet Rescue*? I say to Mickey. —There was a rabbit on *Pet Rescue* and he had sticky eyes and the animal doctor had to clean them with this special medicine.

Mickey stops and puts down the basket and coughs and coughs. He's got a bad cough like Grandad. He looks at me. He's got freckles on his nose. Perhaps Grandad's germed him. God.

—Mickey, I say.

Perhaps he'll cough and cough and blood'll go on his hankies and down his clothes and everywhere.

—Oh dear, I say. —You've got germs.

Perhaps he'll go to hospital.

—Oh dear, I say, and I shake my head. —Oh dear. Oh dear.

Mickey's eyebrows are orange. They're scrunching and frowning at me.

—What? I say. —Oh dear, Mickey.

—Shut it, he says, and he puts his hands over my mouth and he pushes my head back and presses on my mouth and hurts me.

—THAT'S ENOUGH! somebody shouts, a lady, Aunty Chris!

She's in her doorway.

—Shit.

Mickey lets go of me.

—AUNTY CHRIS! AUNTY CHRIS! I cry.

I run from Mickey and my jellies go squelch and my leggings rub at me.

I puff and pant.

—Here, sweetheart, she says, and she opens her arms and hugs me close.

Soft and squidgy. Her body feels like jelly. Wibble wobble. Wibble wobble. Soft and squidgy.

Aunty Chris is Mummy's sister.

—MICHAEL! she shouts. I can hear her voice booming in her belly. —I WANT A WORD WITH YOU.

She's my aunty and Mickey's and she's my pretend mummy too, but she's not Mickey's pretend mummy because he's bigger than me and he doesn't need one.

I'm not so big and I need Aunty Chris especially because my real mummy wants some time and space. I like Aunty Chris. I like her lots.

Some baby rabbits have pretend mummies because their real mummies aren't any good for them. Their real mummies squeeze them out and get them born and then they just close their eyes because there's too much blood pouring from their bums. It pours and turns the fluffy stuff in the nest boxes soggy and red, and it makes a horrid pong that smells like mouldy meat. Poor mummy rabbits. They can't stop the blood or do anything except close their eyes and let Grandad take them for a nice long sleep to the Isle of Skye. He took Beamish there and she's not woke up yet. Sometimes they never do, that's what Grandad says. Every bunny, all things bright and beautiful, all creatures great and small have to go to sleep, that's what Grandad says, and sometimes they wake up and sometimes they never do.

If a mummy rabbit doesn't wake up then her babies are in trouble because they need her milk to drink and her furry body to cuddle up to. She has to keep them warm because baby rabbits don't have no hair, they just have ugly chicken skin.

Boo hoo.

What can you do,

If Mummy Bunny dies?

You can look after her babies, that's what you can do. You can give her babies to another mummy or you can be their pretend mummy. True-life! It's called adopting, that's what Grandad says. But it's hard work like tens and units and reading and writing. It'll make you really sweaty.

Here's how you can be a pretend rabbit mummy:

Get a hotty bottle and put it under the baby's nest box to keep her warm.

Buy thick milk in cans and get an injecting needle from the animal doctor.

Fill the needle with the thick milk.

Get the baby rabbit and hold her safe in your hand.

Make her lie on her back with her paws sticking in the air.

Tickle her tummy because that will make her feel hungry.

Put the needle in her mouth and squirt in the thick milk. You do this at breakfast-time, dinner-time and teatime.

When the baby rabbit is more grown-up you can squash some oats or carrots and put it in the thick milk for them and this will make them strong and then they'll turn into a proper rabbit.

You can be a pretend mummy for any kind of rabbit. It doesn't matter because baby rabbits don't know the difference really, they've not got very big brains.

Aunty Chris is my pretend mummy and sometimes Aunty Sheila is too because she buys me presents. But I like Aunty Chris better because she doesn't get sad about Granny. Aunty Sheila gets sad about her all the time, more than Grandad, lots more than me. She really misses her, that's what she says.

One time we went looking for her in the churchyard in all the long grass. There was just me and Aunty Sheila. Kylie wasn't with us or Joe or Uncle Brian because they've got another granny and she's not dead, she lives by a busy road and she can't cross it because she's not got speedy legs.

It was windy and the long grass was blowing about and getting in our way. I was wearing my jellies and Aunty Sheila was wearing sandals with high heels and lots of straps. Her skin was showing and the grass irritated it. She kept stopping and itching her feet.

—Where's the man with the mower? I asked. —We need him, don't we, Aunty Sheila?

—There's no mower man, Lily, she said. —They're keeping the grass long for the dormice. Disgusting if you ask me, putting dormice before people.

—Will we see some dormouses? I asked.

—Mice, said Aunty Sheila. —Dormice. Plural.

—Mice, I said. —Plural. What's plural?

—More than one, said Aunty Sheila.

There was an angel in the grass. A stone angel with broken wings. She had mouldy green on her face.

—Did Granny know she was coming here? I asked. —Did she have to do her suitcase like I've got to when I go to Sweden?

—No. You don't pack your suitcase to come here, said Aunty Sheila. She looked about her. She was holding a bunch of flowers. They were yellow and white, really pretty, like her dress. Aunty Sheila always wears dresses, not trousers. —She got herself ready though. She was prepared. She had to be.

I looked at Aunty Sheila.

—She was very sick. Now, where's that monument?

I didn't understand, and I stuck up my hand, like you do in class, when you don't know anything, but she didn't notice, she wasn't interested in me.

—Ah, she said. —Got it. Come with me, Lily.

She grabbed my hand and we went by some crosses that were grey and cracked and boring and a shiny white book with a picture of an ugly man on it with no hair and we stopped at a thick black pole sticking in the sky.

—This belongs to the bird man, said Aunty Sheila. —Do you know about him, Lily?

I shook my head.

—He was a pigeon fancier, she said, and she patted the pole. —He used to keep lots of pigeons and he loved them almost as much as your grandad loves his rabbits, and when he died the other fanciers paid for this monument for him.

—Oh, I said.

It had pictures of grey birds flying up it and there were long grey feathers lying on the ground around it.

—Now, where's your granny? She should be here somewhere, said Aunty Sheila.

She let go of me and I picked up a feather. It was stiff. I sniffed it and it smelt like wee. Yuk. I threw it away and I ran to Aunty Sheila. She was standing by a stone that was white and flat like a doorstep, that had three black letters on it.

—Mum, she said.

She crouched so her head was the same height as me and she put her flowers at the bottom of the doorstep-stone and she sighed.

—Hello, Mum, how're you doing?

She was talking to the stone. She was calling it Mum but it wasn't her mum, it was a stone, and she was scaring me.

—I want to go home, I said.

Aunty Sheila stroked the stone.

—Can we go home now?

She looked at me.

—What is it? she said.

—I want to go home, I said.

—But we've only just got here, she said. —What's the matter?

—La la la, I said, and I kicked the stone.

—Don't do that, Lily, said Aunty Sheila. —It's disrespectful.

I looked at her.

—Do you know what that means?

I shook my head.

—It means you're being rude.

—Oh, I said.

—You wouldn't be alive if it wasn't for your Granny buried here, she said. —She's a part of you.

—Oh, I said.

I didn't understand. I stared at my hands. She's a part of me.

—La la la, I said.

—Here, just say hello. Go on, said Aunty Sheila.

I shook my head. I didn't want to speak. The stone didn't have a mouth. It wouldn't answer me.

—Silly, said Aunty Sheila. —I always have a chat. It feels nice. It's helpful. You'll understand when you get older.

There were some dandelions by the stone.

—This is a mess. Shall I tidy it for you, Mum?

Aunty Sheila pulled them out and threw them over her shoulder and I picked them up for the rabbits because rabbits like their stalks and yellow flowers. They don't like the dead dandelions that have turned into clocks, the ones you can blow and say 1 o'clock, 2 o'clock until the dead feathery bits disappear, the ones you can make a wish on because they're magic like those bones you get from chickens. I wish. I wish I had a daddy. I wish Mummy would turn into a solicitor. I wish Grandad would hurry up and take Lincoln and me to Sweden.

Sweden. Sweden. Sweden.

—Put those down please, Lily, said Aunty Sheila. She was staring at me. —They'll make you pee.

—Oh, I said.

—Down, please.

Her voice was strict and I did as I was told. I dropped them by my feet.

—That's better.

I squashed them with my jellies, and Aunty Sheila stroked the stone and chatted to it about how I was with her, how I'd come along because Mummy was at college. She chatted about Mummy, and Grandad, and all my aunties and cousins, and about Uncle Brian too. She said he'd finally asked her to marry him and she was so happy and then she sniffed and got her hanky out and wiped her nose and eyes.

—Why're you crying? I asked.

—Sorry, she said.

She wiped her eyes and hooted her nose.

—Oh dear, she said.

She scrunched up her hanky.

—I do miss her, Lily, and it doesn't get any easier. She's getting further and further away from me.

I looked at the doorstep-stone.

—She was lovely, sniffed Aunty Sheila, and she grabbed my hand and held it like daft-bat Kelly does in the playground sometimes, grabbing my hand and holding it tight and hurting me.

—OW! I said.

—Sorry, she said, and then she pulled me down, so I was by the stone, so my hands touched the white cold stone, and she kissed and cuddled me.

—He's a naughty boy, I say.

—Isn't he? says Aunty Chris.

She closes the door on Mickey and his coughing, the red mark on his face and the little baby rabbits in the cat basket. —I don't know what's got into him. What set him off this time, Lily?

There's a frilly curtain on Aunty Chris's door. It's pink and lacy. It's her summer curtain. Her winter door curtain is woolly like a blanket. I go to touch the frilly curtain and she pulls me from it, down the hall.

—Lily?

She squeezes me, with her hand, on my shoulder.

—Why was Mickey being rough with you? What was it about?

Her flat is the same as Grandad's except it's prettier, like the summer curtain. It's got carpet and pictures and there's a nice smell in the toilet. We pass the toilet. The door is closed. Someone's in.

—Where's Tom and Bethany? I ask.

—Watching *Super Ted*, Lily. You'll see them in a minute.

—Who's in the loo?

—Uncle Paul.

—Oh, I say, and I pull at my leggings.

They're in my crack. They make me want to wee.

—He's set up home, says Aunty Chris. —He'll be there all morning.

—Oh, I say.

We're at her bedroom. She shares it with Uncle Paul and she shares the bed with him like I share the bed with Mummy. Except Aunty Chris's bed is bigger. Everything about Aunty Chris is bigger. I like her. I'm busting. She squeezes me again.

—Lily, I want to know what Mickey was doing because I'm going to have to tell Aunty Karen.

I nod.

—I need a wee, I say.

—Oh, she says.

—I'm really busting.

—That bad? she says.

She stops and looks at me, and the wee starts trickling out, down my legs and into my jellies. There's lots of it and it's very warm.

—Oh my God! she says. —I'll get a cloth!

She runs off down the hall. Her pink skirt wobbles and her fluffy slippers go pad pad pad. I kick off my jellies.

—Bugger.

I tug at my leggings.

—Bugger. Bugger.

My leggings are sopping and tight. I pull them out my crack. I peel them off me. They've made a red line on my belly. I drop them on the floor.

—Lily! says Aunty Chris.

She's on her knees. She scoops the leggings up.

—Soz, I say.

—I don't know, she says.

She looks at the leggings.

—My crack hurts, I say.

—Where's your pants? she says.

—Don't know, I say.

—Christ, she says, and she hands me the leggings and rubs the carpet with her cloth. —Let's clear this up and then we'll get you sorted.

Aunty Chris is a housewife. Housewife means a lady who likes to clean and Hoover and stay at home and look after her children for pocket money. Her husband gives her the pocket money. Her husband's Uncle Paul.

Mummy isn't a housewife. She doesn't like cleaning or staying at home, and she doesn't look after me much, only sometimes, and she hasn't got a husband, not any more. Mummy's a student. Students are big grown-ups who go to school and don't have any money. Mummy worries about money.

One time Aunty Chris took me to town with Tom and Bethany. We went in a taxi and she bought us Happy Meals. I had chicken nuggets and chips and Tom and Bethany had burgers and we all got dinosaur toys. My dinosaur had a yellow belly and you had to balance it on a blue mountain. I showed it to Mummy but she wasn't very pleased. I think she'd wanted to take me for the Happy Meal. She'd been saving up for it, putting 2ps and 5ps in her Treats Jar. She'd almost got enough.

I didn't go to Tom and Bethany's for ages after. I had to stay with Mummy and Grandad and annoy them. I got under Mummy's feet especially.

Then Aunty Chris came up with a cake and some free

things, shampoo and cleaning stuff and my plastic knife and fork and round tea-bags that'd been posted through her door. She gave them to Mummy and they had a cup of tea and Mummy even went in Grandad's bedroom with Aunty Chris to look at the rabbits. Grandad was weighing the babies and Mummy helped to put one on the scales.

—Are you and Aunty Chris back in love? I asked Mummy after Aunty Chris had gone.

Mummy did up my 'jama top. —Sisters can't be in love, she said.

—Oh, I said, and I looked at her.

—Time for bed, she said.

—Why don't we get free things posted through our door? I asked.

—Into bed, said Mummy.

—But why? I said.

—Because we're too high up and the delivery people forget about us.

—Really? I said.

—Really, she sighed. —Now, into bed.

—Finbar's a liar, I said.

—Lily, I'm in a good mood, said Mummy. —Don't spoil it.

Mummy tucked me in and then she put on her special lamp and sat at her desk with her books. Her shoulders were hunched and I stared at them and tried to send the message through the air and into her head without moving my lips and saying the words out loud. It's true. Finbar's a liar. A magic message. Finbar says we don't get free stuff because of the crazy-on-drugs men that hide in the corridors and growl like lions. Finbar says they rob the delivery boys and steal their free stuff away. He's a liar. Bum's on fire. Burny. Burny.

—Lily, you're pissing about. I can feel it, said Mummy.

Pissing is rude. It means rude whispering. Psst. Psst. I wasn't doing that.

—Close your eyes and get to sleep, right now!

I was being a rabbit. I was being quiet and I was sending a message without saying the words out loud.

Rabbits send messages all the time. They send them with their bodies.

How does a rabbit send a message to say it's happy?
It rolls.

How does a rabbit send a message to say it's tired?
It lies down on its side.

How does a rabbit say it wants a kiss and a cuddle?
It nudges your hand with its nose.

How does a rabbit say thank you?
It licks your hand.

How does a rabbit send a grumpy message?
It pushes your hand away.

How does a rabbit send a very grumpy message?
It nips you hard.

How does a rabbit say it's frightened?
It stares with its eyes open wide.

Super Ted is flying. The sky is blue. A bird sits on his head and I sit on the floor next to Tom and Bethany. I'm wearing a girl-girl skirt, the one Aunty Chris keeps for me just in case. It's got a pocket and some frills. I cross my legs like I'm on the mat at school, and I push the skirt down to cover Tom's pants. I hate boy pants. They've got stupid holes in for their stupid willies. I hate willies. So does Finbar. His keeps dripping.

Super Ted flies through a cloud. There's a strange thing in the cloud. It's ugly and big. It might be an alien.

—LOOK! I say. —It's an alien. True-life!

—Yes, LOOK! says Tom.

He's nearly six like me.

—LOOK! says Bethany.

She's four and copies Tom.

—I saw an alien, I say.

—When? says Tom.

—Last night, I say. —Out the window. He waved at me.

—Liar, says Tom.

—Liar, says Bethany.

—SHUT UP, BETHANY! says Tom.

—ENOUGH! shouts Aunty Chris.

We all turn round. Aunty Chris crosses the hall. Her slippers go pad. She's got her serious face on.

—Right, she says. She comes into the front room. —Where's the remote?

We shake our heads. Something's happened to Super Ted. He's shouting, behind us.

—GERROFF! he's shouting. —GERROF . . . F . . . F!

—The alien's got him! I say.

Aunty Chris presses the remote. It all goes quiet.

—Aaah, we say.

—Never mind aaah, says Aunty Chris. —I don't want any more shouting or bickering. Give the telly a rest now and go and play nicely in your bedroom. And, Tom and Lily, I want you to understand that Bethany is younger than you and has to copy because copying helps her to learn. OK?

—OK, we say.

—Hmmm, says Aunty Chris, and she watches us leave the room.

—What are we going to play? whispers Tom.

We walk down the hall together. Me, Tom, and Bethany. Tom is holding my hand. He likes me.

—Let's 'tend I'm boss, I say, and I let go of his hand and do my secret sign.

Tom and Bethany don't know anything about my sign. They see me do it and Bethany copies it sometimes. But they don't know it's about rabbits and I'm not going to tell them.

—I want to be boss, says Bethany.

She stares at me.

—NO! I say.

—You're too babyish, says Tom.

—NOT! says Bethany.

—ARE! says Tom.

—CHILDREN! shouts Aunty Chris. —I'LL BE SEND-ING SOMEONE HOME!

We look at each other. Tom puts his finger to his lips. That means shush, zip-up-your-mouth, I know. Tom opens the bedroom door.

—Password, he says.

I unzip my mouth.

—Bum, I say.

—Bum's correct, he says. —You may enter.

Tom and Bethany share a room like Mummy and me, and Aunty Chris and Uncle Paul, but they don't share a bed. Tom's got his own bed, it's in the blue corner, and Bethany's got hers and that's in the pink and black corner.

Tom's bed is a car. It's very good. Uncle Paul made it. It's got wooden wheels. Uncle Paul likes cars. His true-life one is big and blue with a horn that sounds like the police. He wants a flashing light to go on the top that's like the police too. I asked Mummy if we could buy Uncle Paul the light, because Mummy doesn't give Aunty Chris or Uncle Paul anything, except me. Mummy pointed to the Treats Jar. It was empty. The 2ps and 5ps were gone. —We're not made of money, she said.

Tom sits on his bed and swings his legs. Bethany watches him and so do I. One time Tom fell off his bed and bashed his bum on one of the wheels. But he was ever so brave. He didn't cry. He held his mouth shut and he didn't tell Aunty Chris, no way, because he thought she'd chop up the wheels and throw them in the bin. So we made it a secret. A secret's a secret. We know about it and no one else, not even Bethany because she was watching *Pingu*. She likes *Pingu*. She's got a *Pingu* quilt.

—Let's play *Pingu*, says Bethany.

I look at Tom and shake my head.

—No way, I whisper.

—Go on then, says Tom to Bethany. —Go and play *Pingu*.

—All of us, says Bethany. She's got *Pingu* slippers too. They're big and black and furry and they're on her feet staring at us.

—You're babyish, I say.

—Not, she says.

—Zip, I say. I put my finger to my lips. —Sit on the floor.

Bethany sits on the floor and stares at Tom and me. She's got sticky-up hair and a big round head. I close the bedroom door.

—Bethany, I say. —This is an emergency. You've got a big round head. It needs an operation.

—Yes! Tom says.

He jumps off the bed and runs round the room. He's driving an ambulance.

—Nee nah. Nee nah.

—I'll be doctor, I say.

I run for the bits bag. I know what I want.

—I'm scared, says Bethany.

I want a tube and a box. A toilet-roll tube. A cereal box. Yes!

—I'm scared, says Bethany.

—Silly, I say. I push the box on her head. —This won't hurt.

She squeals.

—Nee nah. Nee nah. EEEEE!

Tom slams his brakes.

—I'm Super Ambulance Man, he says. —Has she got a big round head?

—Yes, Super Ambulance Man, she needs an operation.

I slap Bethany's hands. She's pulling at the box.

—This is an emergency! says Super Ambulance Man. —Patient's going to die!

Bethany squeals and Super Ambulance Man pushes her over.

—She's dying! Look, she's dying!

—Hole in the box! Hole in the box! I say.

I run round the room. I want some scissors. Bethany's kicking. Super Ambulance Man sits on her. She's going wild.

—Stupid patient, I say. —Cut holes in the box.

I give the scissors to Super Ambulance Man. He looks at them.

—For breathing, I say. —Saving her life.

—Yes! Yes! he says.

He cuts the box and Bethany spits.

—Yuk! he says, and he punches the box and Bethany jiggles her legs like she wants a wee and her hands open and shut, open and shut, and then she starts to cry.

—Naughty girl, she's a naughty girl, I say, and I pull up her skirt and jab her with the tube. I make red circles on her skin. She's squit her knickers but I don't tell.

—Take off the box, says Super Ambulance Man. —Patient's crying.

We pull and pull. Uff!

—There! I say.

I look at Bethany. She has Frosties stuck in her hair and snot's dribbling to her mouth.

—Congratulations, patient, I say. —You're cured.

—Mummy, cries Bethany. —I'm going to tell MUMMY!

—Shush, says Tom.

We look at the door.

—I will, cries Bethany. —I'll tell MUMMY!

—No, I say. I get up off the floor. I do a wobbly penguin walk. —Look, I'm Mummy Pingu.

—Mummy Pingu, says Bethany, and she sniffs and the snot goes slurp! back up her nose.

We are the Pingu Family. We live in an igloo. Our wee comes out like ice-cubes. We are the Pingu Family. We laugh and sing and skate. Daddy Pingu has a deep voice. Mummy Pingu wears boy's knickers. Baby Pingu drinks her fish milk. Baby Pingu finds a fish eye in her fish milk. Yuk. It's so disgusting.

—HIYA KIDS!

—AARGH! we say. —YOU SCARED US!

—Sorry, kids, says Uncle Paul.

He stands in the doorway. He's big and fat and he's finished his poo.

—Little Lily here again? he says. He smiles. —We're going to have to adopt you.

—Oh, I say.

I look at Uncle Paul. I like him lots. And I like Aunty Chris and Tom. And sometimes I like Bethany too.

How many people live in your house?

One my mother.

Two my father.

Three my brother.

Four my sister.

And one other.

Let me see.

It must be me!

How many people live in your house?

—Can you adopt? I say. —True-life? Can you adopt me?

Uncle Paul pushes his fat hands through his hair. His hair is brown and floppy. It sticks up, falls down, sticks up.

—True-life? I say.

He shakes his head.

—I was just being silly, he says.

—Oh, I say, and it all goes quiet. The room. Everything. Like it happens in school, sometimes, in class, when everything stops and I don't know why, when there's no talking, no sounds. Nothing. Only breathing. In out. In out. Horrid. —La la.

I stare at my skirt.

—La la la.

I fiddle with the frills. I put my hand in its pocket.

—Well, says Uncle Paul.

I can see him out the corner of my eye.

—La la la.

Eye corners are very small but you can see lots from them if you know how to use them right. I can see Uncle Paul bending down and tickling Bethany.

—And how are you, my little princess? he says.

Bethany giggles, and I pick at a frill.

—La la la.

I wish I was a princess, a rabbit princess, all furry with lots of money. I'd eat golden carrots and Grandad would keep me in a silver hutch, and I'd travel on a velteen cushion to Sweden.

—We played *Pingu*, giggles Bethany.

—*Pingu*! says Uncle Paul.

He looks at Tom.

—Good lad, he says.

Aunty Chris gives us pizza and chips and salad stuff. Mummy likes salad stuff. She says it's good for you. It's good for rabbits too. Grandad gives them loads every day, not the best stuff for humans but leftovers, manky, from a man in the bottom flats who feeds the old-age people at the church. The old-age people get the nice leaves and Grandad's rabbits get the stalks and the bits with caterpillars on. Mummy says she can't wait till she gets old-aged because she'd love to eat nice leaves every day as well, not just on Saturdays and Sundays like now which is all she can stretch to. Stretching is exercises and stretch to means doing arm exercises. You swing and bend your arms and lift heavy things with them so they grow long enough to reach down to very low shelves. Salad stuff's on a very low shelf in Mr Azad's.

Me and Tom and Bethany eat at the table and not in front of the telly. That's because we watch too much telly and it makes our mouths drop open and the food fall on Aunty Chris's orange carpet. Bethany doesn't like her pizza because it has square bits on and Tom's fiddling with his chips. He pokes one in my ear because I'm talking about my dress and Lincoln and my sore nose and everything.

—Stop it, he says.

—No, I say. —It's interesting.

—NOT!

—IS!

Tom pokes the chip in my ear and I whack it away.

—TOM! LILY! shouts Aunty Chris.

Tom kicks me on the ankle.

—OW! I say.

—THAT'S ENOUGH! shouts Aunty Chris.

—But Tom hurt me!

—You're both as bad as each other, she says.

Uncle Paul comes in the kitchen. —What's going off? he says.

Aunty Chris nods her head at us. —Bethany won't eat her square bits, she says. —And Tom and Lily are squabbling over Lincoln.

—Well Lincoln's not worth squabbling over.

—He did the triple, I say. —And I got a dress for Aunty Sheila's wedding and I . . .

—Lily.

Uncle Paul holds up his hand.

—Quiet now.

I do as I'm told. I zip my mouth. I always zip my mouth when a daddy tells me to because daddies are important. They're like the boss.

Uncle Paul looks at Bethany.

—So what's wrong with your square bits, madam?

—They're square, Daddy, says Bethany.

Uncle Paul smiles. —Well pretend they're round then, he says.

—Like circles? says Bethany.

Uncle Paul nods.

—I like triangles, she says.

—Well triangles then, whatever helps, Uncle Paul says, and he pats Aunty Chris's belly. Uncle Paul does this a lot. He likes Aunty Chris's belly; he's fond of it. Fond means caring for something soft. Granny was fond of her dressing-gown. That was soft. I know. Grandad keeps a piece in the pocket of his best trousers. It's purple and pink. Grandad let me touch it once.

Aunty Chris whispers something in Uncle Paul's ear and he laughs ho-ho like Santa, and he unhooks his keys from the peg near the fridge.

—We've got to go soon, Lily, he says.

—Mmm, I reply.

I munch my pizza crust.

—Soon like very soon, he says.

Aunty Chris fetches my leggings off the heater.

—Finish what you've got in your mouth, Lily, she says. —Then you'll need to get changed.

I crunch and swallow the crust. It's jaggy and scratches my throat. I cough and take a sip of apple juice. I like apple juice, it's better than orange. Mummy always gives me orange though because it's cheaper, she says, about half the money. Half is a fraction. Fractions are to do with difficult sums. I take another sip, then I get down from the table.

—Catch, says Aunty Chris.

She throws the leggings and they land on the floor and I stare at them.

—Pick them up, she says. —You haven't got all day.

—They hurt my crack, I say.

I don't want to wear them.

—You'll not get to where you're going, she says.

I pull a face. I don't know where I'm going.

—Where's she going? asks Tom.

I look at him.

—It's a secret, I say.

—Tell us, he says.

—A secret's a secret, I say.

—Lily, says Aunty Chris. —That's enough. It's no big deal, Tom. She's going nowhere special. Isn't that right, Lily?

I look at Aunty Chris.

She's sending me a message with her eyes. Watch yourself. Be careful what you say. Mummy sends this message to me too, all the time. Watch yourself or you'll be in trouble, you'll get a smack. Her and Aunty Chris open their eyes really wide and send the message through the air. Watch yourself.

I look at Aunty Chris.

Watch yourself, say her eyes.

I pick up my leggings.

—That's better, she says, and she stares at me with her big brown eyes.

Human beings have two eyes flat across their faces and rabbits have eyes on the sides of their heads, one eye on one side and one on the other, so they can look sideways that's all. Human beings can look sideways out of their eye corners and they can look forwards too and they can see colours. Rabbits can't. They can't see how green their green stuff is or how their wee turns their shavings orange. It's very sad but they do have whiskers so they can feel where things are, so they don't bump into stuff, and they have their supersonic ears, and their special noses that can work out smells. So they're better than us, I think.

I pull on my leggings.

I'm going to see lots of rabbits soon at the show. Yes! I'm going to the show. That's where I'm going. I remember.

—No, Lily, says Aunty Chris. —Skirt off first.

My legs are jiggly. I pull off my leggings. I'm so excited. I pull off the skirt. I tug at my pants. My hands are so wobbly. I'm going to the show!

—Keep the pants on Lily!

—Boy pants! giggle Tom and Bethany.

—Look, says Uncle Paul. —If you hurry yourself, Lily, I'll give you an ice-cream. Deal?

—Paul! says Aunty Chris.

—That's not fair! says Tom.

—Only trying to help, says Uncle Paul to Aunty Chris.

—Deal, I say.

Ice-creams are made of ice and cream and flavour like strawberry or chocolate or green. Ice is cold. It's freezing. Sometimes that's good, it can stop you boiling on a hot day, but sometimes it's dangerous. Lots of ice can turn you blue and it can upset rabbits too. It can make them feel sad and unticklish so they don't want to play.

One time Grandad and me were watching *Pet Rescue* on the telly. It was about a goat that couldn't wee. It was boring. We were eating crisps. Mummy wasn't in. She was drinking beers with some policemen. It was to do with her college work. She had to ask them questions about jails and robbers and naughty boys and girls. But Grandad and me weren't missing her, not one bit. We crunched our crisps and the animal doctor pressed the goat's belly and then suddenly we heard the stones. We didn't see them because the curtains were closed but we heard them on the windows.

—Christ! said Grandad. —Hail!

He jumped up and spilled his crisps. He moved like Wilma, like he had big strong legs, running from the room.

—Grandad! I said.

The noise wouldn't shut up. I scooped Grandad's crisps from the sofa and shoved them in my mouth.

I ran to the hall. It was quieter there. I chomped the crisps.

—LILY! shouted Grandad from his bedroom. —COME AND HELP!

I swallowed the crisps and did as I was told.

The hail was coming through Grandad's broken window, the one that doesn't shut so well. It was clattering on the bucks' hutches and bouncing off to hit the floorboards and everywhere. The bucks were jumping. They were kicking their shavings and bashing their heads on the holey wire. They were going barmy-bonkers.

—Their ears! I said.

—Madness! said Grandad, and he closed the window as good as he could, and he plugged in the heater and the bars went red.

—Poor rabbits, I said.

Rabbits hear everything, whispering, leaves dropping from trees, carrots growing.

Grandad shook his head.

Breath was coming from the bucks' mouths. It was hanging like frosty clouds in the perishing air.

Grandad fetched the little brush that Granny used to do her doorstep with and he swept some stones off the bucks' hutches and onto the floor. Then he gave the brush to me.

—Push it all under the wardrobe for me, would you? he said.

I got down on my knees. Everything was quieter now. The rabbits were still. I swept the floor. Lots of stones went down the floorboard cracks and I tried to pick them out but they freezed and hurt my fingers. I asked Grandad for help but he said he had to warm the bucks.

—Look at them, he said, rolling a newspaper. —I've never seen them like this before.

They were sitting huddled up. They looked thin and shivery and scared. Grandad laid the roll of newspaper on top of the hutches. He pushed it in the gap at the bottom of the window. Then he put his mitten on. The bucks stared at him.

—Kettering first, he said.

He opened Kettering's hutch and put his mitten in and Kettering pushed his head at it.

—There, said Grandad. He patted him. —We don't want your willy dropping off now, do we?

—Grandad! I said.

—Well, if it drops off, said Grandad. —He'll be no use to me. I'll have to get rid.

—Oh, I said.

I didn't understand.

—What? I said.

—I wouldn't be able to keep him, Lily, said Grandad. —I'd have to get rid.

—Where? I asked. —Would he go to the pet man?

—No, sweetheart, said Grandad. —He wouldn't want a worn-out old buck. Now, less of your chat, you're distracting me.

I lick my ice-cream. We're at Grandad's flat. I look at the door. It's blue. It's got a letterbox and some writing on and some odd number 7s. 7 and 7 and 7. The writing's under the 7s. It's made of metal and it spells Grandad's name. I know because he told me. He says it's there so everybody who comes to his door knows the flat belongs to him, it's his flat and nobody else's, not even Mummy's. All the flats have names on. All the flats in all the corridors. Some of the names are metal, some are wood and some are on bits of paper that are pinned to the doors like Grandad pins the names of his rabbits to their hutches. Some are pinned at the top of the doors and some are in the middle and I can see the middle ones better but I can't work out any, I can't read what they say. There's one made of pictures, that's good, and there's one with loads of letters but it's not Newbiggin-by-the-Sea.

Uncle Paul presses Granny's doorbell. I can hear the lady singing faint inside.

—When the red red robin comes bob bob bobbing along along.

I lick my ice-cream. It's chocolate and icy and stings my tongue.

—There'll be no more sobbing when he starts singing his old sweet song.

Uncle Paul taps his toes on the dirty grey floor.

—Get up! Get up! Get out of bed!

—Your grandad's taking his time, he says.

—Cheer up! Cheer up! The sun is red!

—What's he up to?

I shrug. That means you're not sure. I'm not sure. Maybe Grandad's getting his rabbits ready for the show, maybe he's putting them in their travel boxes, or maybe he's fighting with Mummy, or maybe he's the same as me. Maybe he's in there but he doesn't want to open the door because he's a scaredy-cat girl. He might be peeking through the keyhole. I bend to see.

—Live, love, laugh and be happy!

I can't see anything. I can't see Grandad's eye staring back at me. I can just see black, black nothing.

—Don't worry, Grandad, I say to the keyhole. —It's not the man about the rabbits.

Uncle Paul laughs.

—What's this? he says, and the door opens and I tumble in but I hold onto my ice-cream and don't drop it, no way!

I'm on my knees on the flowery carpet and my hand's in the air. I hold my ice-cream in the air like the liberty statue in America that's made of stone and wears a crown and holds a stone ice-cream. America's famous and lots of people want to live there but I don't, I want to live in Sweden.

—Grandad! I say.

He's next to me.

He's wearing his rabbit show trousers. They have patches on. I tug his trousers but he doesn't speak to me.

—Grandad!

He flaps his hand.

I look up.

He's on the telephone.

—No, he says. —It's Lily and Paul. Yes, Lily. No, not that Paul. Chris's husband, you know.

Uncle Paul helps me up. I'm on my feet. He hugs me.

—Who's that? I ask.

Grandad flaps his hand.

—Shush, says Uncle Paul. —He's trying to concentrate.

Grandad coughs.

—Hang on a minute, he says.

He puts his hand over the phone and looks at Uncle Paul.

—Can you take her to the front room? he asks, and then he opens his mouth and he moves his mouth and whispers something and I can't hear what but I do the dumb game and guess the words. There's two.

It's . . . Jed . . .

—Oh, I say.

One. Two.

It's Jed.

—No? says Uncle Paul. —Christ.

Grandad nods and looks at Uncle Paul and it's like he's sending a message with his eyes, the same message as Aunty Chris sent to me. Watch yourself. That's the message. Be careful what you say. Uncle Paul's got to be careful what he says, I don't know why. This is puddling me.

It's Jed.

Uncle Paul pushes me.

I don't know what Jed means.

—Come on, Lily, says Uncle Paul, and he pushes me again. —Your grandad's got business to attend to, let's watch telly.

—No! I say, and I stomp my jellies on the carpet and I hold my legs dead still. I make them straight and strong.

—Lily! says Uncle Paul. —Watch your ice-cream!

Uncle Paul's got to be careful and Grandad's whispering and sending messages with his eyes.

—What's wrong? I say.

—Watch your ice-cream!

—What's Jed? I say.

—What? says Grandad.

—Jed, I say.

—Oh dear, says Uncle Paul.

Grandad looks down the hall at Mummy's bedroom door. His mouth is straight, not smiley. —I didn't mention any Jed, he says.

—You did! I say, and then I hear it coming from the phone. A mumbly voice squeezing out past Grandad's fingers. And then I know. My brain works it out for me. —That's Jed!

—No, says Uncle Paul —It's not. That's Peter. You're getting mixed up, Lily. It's someone called Peter, not Jed.

—That's right, says Grandad. —It's Peter.

—Oh, I say.

—From the English Club, says Grandad.

—Peter Potter, says Uncle Paul.

—Yes, says Grandad. —Peter Potter.

—Oh, I say.

I got it wrong. I don't know nothing. I'm a Tortoise. I'm rubbish. I can't do the dumb game. I can't do anything. Nobody likes me.

—Come with me now, Lily, says Uncle Paul.

Everybody hates me.

—Come on.

The front room's empty. I lick my ice-cream and sit on the sofa and Uncle Paul switches on the telly.

—There, he says.

It's a picture of some ladies and children and they're screaming and they've got their hands on their heads and there's a man running round and there's blood on his face and he's got a gun.

—NO! I say.

—Christ! says Uncle Paul, and he makes the picture go away and another one come on.

—I want that! I say.

—Ah, says Uncle Paul, and he sits on the sofa next to me. —Batman and Robin. I like them. KERPOW!

Uncle Paul thumps the air, then he pats my back. He's excited because that's what Batman and Robin do to you. They get Finbar excited and me too.

Batman and Robin are Super Heroes. Batman isn't like Batman Dracula, no way. He doesn't suck your blood and make you die. He's just Batman and he wears tights and Robin does too, and their tights have hard pieces in to cover their willies.

Dudda-dudda dudda-dudda Batman!

Batman has a Batmobile in his Batcave.

Dudda-dudda dudda-dudda Batman!

Batman slides down a greasy pole to his Batcave.

Holy! Holy!

His Batmobile's in his Batcave and he jumps in his Batmobile and fire shoots out and the Batcave opens and he zooms.

Dudda-dudda zoom!

He fights the Penguin, the Joker, and Catwoman, but not Rabbitwoman, there's not one of them.

Kerpow!

Finbar wants to be Batman.

Smash!

He's got a Batman badge.

Batman's a Super Hero and a clever bat.

Wallop!

Bats are nighttime creatures and they're sexywexy, that's what Finbar says.

Sexy is ticklish. Wexy is double ticklish.

There were hundreds of double ticklish bats on *Pet Rescue*. This lady had them in her roof. They lived in her roof because it was clean, without any cobwebs, and it was on top of her house and it was dark. The lady took us up the stairs to see the bats. They were fluttering round. The lady whispered. She said bats are clever; they have good steering and their wings are giant hands, true-life! She said bats eat fruit and, this is horrid, they like blood too because it's sweet and warm.

Oh.

Batman and Robin are waving bye-bye.

—The end already, says Uncle Paul, and he slaps his legs at the top and gets up. —That was good.

He switches off the telly. He moves his head from

side to side. It's quiet and he's listening to the quiet, I know. His chin points in the air and his eyes twitch and that's how you listen. You hear with your ears and you listen with other bits because hearing's different from listening, that's what Mrs Meadows says. Everyone can hear, except for poorly deaf people, but not so many can do proper listening. It's like concentrating, that's why. You do it with your body but you mustn't move your body. Rabbits can do it but tortoises can't, that's what Mrs Meadows says, but that doesn't make much sense to me because tortoises never move their bodies, hardly ever.

—Right, says Uncle Paul. —I think you should fetch yourself a woolly, Lily. Then perhaps we can get to the show.

—Yes! I say, and I jump off the sofa. I do it dead easy because I've eaten my ice-cream and I've got two hands to help me. I push on the cushions and jump with my legs. We're going to the show. Yippee!

I run.

I've got to get a woolly.

I stop.

A woolly's like a jumper and I can't get one because Mummy's in the bedroom and she's having her time and space and she doesn't want me.

—Mummy's working, I say.

—It won't take two seconds, says Uncle Paul. He opens the front-room door and smiles at me. —Go on, princess.

He pats me.

He called me princess.

I'm a princess.

I do princess tiptoes across the flowery hall. I can do them much better than Bethany. I see Grandad. He's finished his call. He's putting down the phone. I give him a princess wave and he waves back at me. Then the phone rings again and he snatches it up and looks double-cross and turns away from me.

I push the bedroom door. It swings open and clunks! on the wall.

God.

I look at Mummy.

She doesn't look at me.

She's hunched over her books at her desk. The curtains are closed. The desk lamp's shining round her like cheesy yellow moonlight.

I lift my princess feet and step over the bump that's in the doorway. The bump irritates Mummy. Sometimes she trips over it when she comes back from the pub. She's tried to get rid of it; she's tried to tug it out and one time she even tried sawing it. She used Uncle Leslie's saw but there's metal in the bump and it wore the saw down. Uncle Leslie was cross. He came to look at the metal.

—Well, that needs to be there, he said. —It's a lintel.

They're what you have in pies. They're orange and beady and Mummy buys them from Mr Azad's because they don't cost much money.

—That's your theory, is it? said Mummy.

Theory's something to do with being puddled. Uncle Leslie's puddled.

—Don't get at me, he said.

I close the door.

—You fucked my saw.

I tread slow across the lino.

I need a woolly for the show because it's cold outside, that's what Uncle Paul says. The wind's blowing and the sky is grey. It's grey up here and it's grey down below.

I've not got many woollies. I've got a Teletubby one and a horrid black one with holes in and both of them are in the washing box because Mummy's not a housewife. I open the box. I try to do it quietly. I stick my tongue between my teeth and open the lid, quietly like a mouse. Eeek. Eeek. The lid goes eek and a smell comes out. I cough. Yuk. It smells like Wilma's plimsolls. They're muddy and bogging and she needs some new. I'm getting some new. Aunty Sheila's buying them for me. I'm going to wear them to her wedding with my girl-girl dress that's over there on the bed. I love my dress. It's velteen.

I pull my Teletubby woolly from the box. I sniff Tinky Winky, La la, Dipsy and Po. They're not OK. They need some perfume on them, some of that air that's on the telly. This lady catches it. She's in a flowery field and she jumps all around and catches the air in a packet, then she gives the packet to her friend who sprinkles it on her clothes. It makes her clothes flowery fresh. She sniffs them. She smiles. Mmmm! It works like magic, and I want some to go on my woolly jumper. I shake my woolly. I want the dirty smell to go away.

—LILY!

—Mummy! You scared me!

She did.

—Well stop it, she says. —I'm trying to concentrate.

—Soz, I say.

I shake my woolly, a tiny bit.

—Sorry, she says. —Not soz.

—Sorry, I say.

—That's better, she says.

She doesn't look at me.

I shake my woolly.

It's not fair. She should look at me because that's what mummies are supposed to do, they're supposed to look at their children and feel tingly inside with happiness and love, that's what Finbar says. Mummies and daddies are supposed to love their children. But I haven't got a daddy, I've got a mummy, that's all, and she only loves me lots when I tell her stuff about Mrs Meadows or when I ask about college or when I'm going away.

I can't go away.

Not yet. Grandad isn't ready.

I look at Mummy.

—Is it hard? I ask. —What you're doing?

I won't go away but I want her to tingle with love.

—Very, she says.

Yes!

She doesn't look at me but she's being nicer, I'm certain sure.

—Is it your essay? I ask. —About men solicitors and ladies?

—You know it is, she says.

I nod. That's true. I know it's about men solicitors and ladies. The men solicitors work with banks and factories and computers and the internet like Uncle Brian's got, and the lady solicitors work with unhappy mummies and daddies and children. It's because of quality, I think. It doesn't make much sense to me but Mummy says it will when I'm a big girl. She says I'll understand then because ladies fought for it in the olden days and they're still fighting for it now. They didn't use guns in the olden days or go to Megadeath. They did the fighting with handcuffs, I think. Mummy says the lady that Granny's great-aunty worked for, a lady in a big house, she wore a long skirt and marched up and down with a poster that was asking for it. She wanted to share it with men, I think. She didn't have any handcuffs. She was posh and she liked wearing purple and green. Granny's great-aunty wasn't posh and she wore brown and dusted stuff.

—Mummy, I say. —You're doing about quality.

—That's enough, Lily, she says.

—I'm right, aren't I?

—This really isn't fair.

—I am, I say. —I'm right.

I know. Because grown-ups do this all the time. They won't say you're right, they won't give you ten out of ten, because they're jealous that you're being brilliant. Mummy's jealous. She's jealous that I'm being brilliant and she's jealous of Aunty Sheila because Aunty Sheila's pretty. It's a shame.

I shake my woolly in the air.

—I'm going to count to ten, says Mummy.

—Why? I ask.

She sighs.

—Stop asking stupid questions, she says. —One . . .

They're not stupid.

—Two . . .

They're clever.

—Three . . .

They're clever rabbit questions, not stupid tortoise ones, and I can ask more.

—Four . . .

I can think of more.

—Five . . .

Like.

—Six . . .

—What's this, Mummy?

—Sev . . .

I move my mouth, I do the dumb game and Mummy turns in her chair and looks at me. I'm by the washing box and she looks at me, true-life! I move my mouth like Grandad did and Mummy stares. She doesn't say anything. She probably needs a clue.

—It's a name, I say. That's my clue.

—It's Jed, she says and her voice is shaky.

God.

She stares at me and her eyes aren't happiness.

—What're you playing at, Lily? she says.

Her eyes are dark and squinty and they've got no love and her eyebrows are scrunching like Angelica's. I don't know why. My heart is thumping. I can feel it here.

—What's this about, Lily? she says.

My heart is thumping like a rabbit's.

—It's Peter, I say. —Grandad showed me.

—What? she says.

She stands. The yellow light falls all around her. It's like she's covered in light and it's fizzing and sparking.

—Do it again, she says.

I hold my woolly and I move my mouth. My mouth is wobbly.

—It looks like Jed to me, she says.

I shake my head.

—It's Peter, I whisper. —Peter Potter.

I cuddle my woolly on my heart.

She comes across to me.

—Where's your grandad? she says.

My heart is thumping.

—On the telephone, I say.

I can hear my heart and it's like I can hear hers too. She's standing really close.

—Jed's a rabbit fancier, she tells me.

—Oh, I say.

—He's a very horrible man, she says. —And you're to keep away from him, understand?

She's fizzing and sparking.

I nod.

—He's got nothing whatsoever to do with you, or me. Understand?

I nod. I shake my head. I don't know. He's not been near me. I don't know who Jed is.

—Did you speak to Jed? she asks.

—Peter, I say.

My voice is wobbly.

—Peter then, she says.

I nod my head.

—You spoke to him?

I shake my head.

—Did you or didn't you, Lily?

149

I don't know. I shrug my shoulders.

Mummy storms.

—DAD!

The door swings back clunk! on the wall.

Nobody likes me.

I hold my woolly.

Everybody hates me.

Mummy's angry.

I don't know what to do.

I can see through the doorway.

—La la la.

Mummy's got the phone. She's taken it off Grandad and her mouth's right up against it and she's shouting.

—JUST KEEP AWAY! she shouts, and she slams the phone down.

Uncle Paul comes from the front room.

—What's going on? he asks. —DONNA, LEAVE HIM BE!

Mummy's got Grandad. They're in the corner and she's shouting at him and his face is purple and he's bending like a really old-age person. He's choking, I can see.

—GRANDAD! I say.

I drop my woolly. I run and pull on Mummy's arm.

—LILY!

I hold her arm.

—OFF ME!

Grandad's choking.

—LA LA LA! I say.

I can't stop me.

Grandad's hands are fumbling. Uncle Paul tries to cuddle him. —Let's get you in the front room.

—LA LA LA! LA LA LA!

I pinch Mummy's arm.

—BUGGER!

She whacks me.

—Wha . . . ? I say. My head is blurry. Then everything goes still. I sit on the floor. I look about me.

—Pleased with yourself? says Uncle Paul to Mummy.

She screws up her face. It's like she's going to cry but she won't because she doesn't like tears and I won't either, no way.

—She was making a show, she says.

I sniff. I'm sniffing.

—It was for her own good, she says.

—Oh please, says Uncle Paul.

Grandad coughs.

—It was, says Mummy, and her voice is tiny. —She was getting hysterical.

—*She* was getting hysterical? says Uncle Paul, and he helps Grandad to straighten up – then they walk to the front room. —You should do something about your temper, Donna.

—WHEN THE RED RED ROBIN . . .

—Fuck's sake, says Mummy, and she sighs and leans back on the wall.

It was for my own good. I was having a tantrum, making a show, and Mummy whacked me. She stopped me, and that saved me. It was for my own good.

That's what everyone says when they're saving you, I know, because Grandad said it about baby Totnes, hundreds of years ago. Totnes was a rabbit and it was for her own good. I remember. I told Mrs Meadows about it at school. I told my class.

We have to do that. Some days we have to stand on the mat by the weather board and tell a tale. Not a tell-tale-tit-your-tongue-will-split but a story tale. It can be about true-life or it can be about a dream. Cathy told a true-life tale about her mummy having a hair cut. It was good. Cathy showed us the hair. It was in a plait and she'd stuck eyes on it. It looked like Zippy the snake. We gave her a clap. —Well done, Cathy, said Mrs Meadows. —Now, Lily, your turn. Cathy sit down. Lily stand by the board.

I passed by Cathy and she wiggled her hair snake at me.

—What's your title, Lily? asked Mrs Meadows. —Quieten down please, class.

A title means Sleeping Beauty or Peter Rabbit or Kipper Gets Spots. It's like a name.

—Totnes, I said.

—Interesting, said Mrs Meadows. —A town in Devon where they make cream, you'll remember. Take a deep breath, Lily, then begin.

I did as I was told. I opened my mouth and I breathed in the classroom, the Wilma-wee and rubber and pencil smell. It was bogging. I coughed.

—OK, Lily, said Mrs Meadows. —Begin.

—Once upon a time, I said.

Once upon a time there was a nice fluffy doe rabbit called Bristol and a big buck called Wigston. Bristol and Wigston were feeling ticklish so Grandad put Bristol in Wigston's hutch so they could be ticklish together. They jumped about and tickled each other lovely. Then Bristol stopped feeling ticklish and went tired.

Grandad lifted Bristol. —Come on, lovey, he said. He put her back in her own hutch.

—What's wrong? I asked.

—Nothing, he said. —Nothing at all.

He stroked Bristol.

—Everything's fine, he said.

Wigston had put some babies in Bristol's tummy but not to worry, it was normal, he said. Bristol was going to need lots more love and understanding, and a nest box, and extra food and water. She was going to get grumpy and fall out with us but it didn't matter. It was normal. She was going to be a mummy. True-life!

I jiggled my legs. It was so exciting. Grandad told me to stop messing.

—Fetch a nest box, Lily, he said.

I did as I was told, and I found a nice yellow one and

put it in Bristol's hutch and she sniffed it and curled up in it. Then Grandad filled her food bowl with his special mummy mix and some frilly lettuce, and he tied this lump of salt to the holey wire for her to lick. He didn't know when she'd have her babies, he said, because mummy rabbits keep that a secret. But mostly they have their babies at night or early in the morning when nobody's supposed to be looking. Bristol had hers in the morning. Grandad was looking. She had four.

When the babies were old enough and started getting fur, I asked Grandad if he was going to pick names for them from his map.

—It's too early, Lily, he said. —I'm not sure if I'm going to keep any. I only name the ones I keep, you know that.

—Oh, I said. It wasn't fair. —Please, Grandad. Please.

He sighed. —OK. We'll choose a name for that one, he said, and he pointed at the tiniest baby. —I think she's a Totnes.

He decided to call her Totnes.

—That suits her, doesn't it? he said.

I shook my head. It wasn't making any sense to me.

—Suits are what people wear for posh, I said.

—That's right, he said. —You're on the right track, Lily. I've chosen Totnes because it's the right name for her, it'll not make her feel uncomfortable or awkward, it'll fit her like a good posh suit.

—Oh, I said.

—Look, he said, and he pointed to his map that Granny had given him ages ago, that's on a big piece of paper that's blue round the edges because that's the sea and yellow in the middle because that's the land, Eng*land* and Britain, where we live. The yellow is covered with red and green lines, they're roads. Then there are blue lines which are rivers, green circles which are forests, and black dots which are towns and big grey splodges which are huge towns. Grandad pointed to a black dot. —Look.

I looked at the dot. It was just a dot, a town, and there was some writing near it that I couldn't read.

—Carlton Scroop, he said. —Now, I saw that name and I thought I won't call her that because it won't sit on her right.

—Oh, I said.

—Yes, he said. —It'd be like dressing her in a sack. So, we'll stick with Totnes.

—Totnes, I said. —OK.

I looked at Totnes the rabbit. She was curled up with her mummy and her sisters in the nest box. She wasn't going to be called Carlton Scroop because it didn't suit her because Carlton Scroop's like a sack. Perhaps that's what it said on the map. Perhaps that's what the writing said. I don't know. I'm in the Tortoise group.

Totnes isn't a tortoise, she's a rabbit, but when she was a baby rabbit she was like a tortoise because she knew nothing and she had to be saved. She was a silly bunny. She was mad about Bristol's boobies. She was on them all the time and she wouldn't let go, not even when Bristol jumped out her nest box and had a walk round; Totnes still hung off Bristol, still sucking on her boobies.

—She's risking it, that one, said Grandad. —If she

falls, that'll be the end of her. Bristol won't notice she's gone.

—Oh, I said.

Then it happened. Totnes fell off Bristol. Grandad spotted her when I was in his room counting his rosettes and he was sweeping the floor. He tutted and dropped his brush and went over to the hutches.

—What you doing, Grandad? I asked.

—Just tidying, he said. He took something from Bristol's hutch and put it in his pocket.

—What's that? I asked.

—A piece of nothing, Lily, he said.

—Can I have it?

—No, it's nothing, Lily. You don't want it.

He opened Granny's wardrobe and I could see something sticking out of his pocket. There wasn't much fur and it was pink. Pink rabbit skin! There was a rabbit in his pocket!

—That's a rabbit! I said. —There's a rabbit in your pocket!

Grandad looked at me.

—Who is it? I asked. —Can I see?

—Totnes, said Grandad. He sighed and pulled her out.

—Aaah, I said.

She was curled in Grandad's hand and I touched her with my finger, ever so gently. She was shivery and a shaving was stuck in her eye.

—She's a poorly rabbit, I said.

—Mmm, said Grandad.

He let me hold her and love her while he got a bottle and some cottonwool from Granny's wardrobe.

—What you doing? I asked.

He shook the bottle. It looked like water inside except it wasn't, I knew.

—That's medicine, I said.

Grandad nodded.

—It's for her own good, Lily, he said. —Now, give her here.

He held out his hand and I gave him Totnes. I did it slowly and carefully. She felt light like Bethany's Pingu beanie, the weeniest one.

—Thank you, said Grandad. He stroked Totnes with his big fat thumb. She didn't care. —I'm going to give her the medicine now.

—OK, I said.

—I'll need you to leave the room.

—Oh, I said.

—Go on, he said. —Scoot!

He stared at me with his strict face, and I did as I was told. I scooted into the hall. But the door was still open and I looked at Grandad holding Totnes. He was cradling her in his hand, rocking her like Mother Mary rocked Baby Jesus.

—Close the door now, Lily, said Grandad.

We will rock you.

—Why?

Rock you, rock you.

—Because this medicine's very strong, it'll knock you out, so close the door.

—Where's the spoon? I asked.

I couldn't see Grandad's medicine spoon.

—I don't need it, said Grandad. —I'm using this.

He held up the cottonwool. It was white and fluffy, fluffier than Totnes.

—Oh, I said.

—I'm going to pour some medicine on it and then I'm going to put it over her nose, he said. —Now, close the door.

He stared at me again and I did as I was told. I closed the door. The coat hangers on the back of the door rattled like bones. Dem bones. Dem bones. And I thought about opening the door to take a peek but I daren't. The medicine was very strong. I put my ear to the door. I listened but couldn't hear anything. Only dem bones.

Then Grandad came out.

—Can I see Totnes? I asked. —Is she better now?

He closed the door behind him and he looked at me and shook his head.

—What's wrong? I asked. My mouth was wobbly. Then my knees. The medicine hadn't worked. I knew.
—TOTNES!

—Schh, said Grandad.

—TOTNES!

—Schh.

He put his arm round me and gave me a squeeze.

—Lily, Lily, he sighed.

—I don't . . . I gulped.

—Oh dear, he said. —Look. Tomorrow. In the morning. You can see her then. But knock first. I'll be very cross if you just barge in. OK?

—So, she's alive. She's alive?

I jumped, with my wobbly legs, jumping high. I knew

she was alive! Babies can't get dead. It's not allowed. No way!

—Fine, sighed Grandad. —Whatever you want. OK.

I was busting to see her and thought about sneaking in when Grandad was watching football on the telly but I daren't. The medicine was strong. It was dangerous. It'd do me no good. So I waited and knocked on Grandad's door in the morning.

—IS THAT YOU, LILY? he shouted, and coughed. —I'M IN THE KITCHEN.

He was in the kitchen, eating his breakfast.

—Can I see Totnes? I asked. —Please, Grandad, please.

—When I've finished this, he said. He was chomping his breakfast, speaking with his mouth full, being rude with his manners like Mummy is.

I sat at the table. He was getting on my nerves. Nerves are red lines inside your body that make you feel twitchy. I was feeling very twitchy. He chomped and chomped. He chomped three sausages and one egg and he drank two cups of coffee and then he said, —Don't follow me, Lily. I'll bring her out.

My legs were jiggly. Mummy came into the kitchen to make some toast.

—What's going off? she said.

—Totnes, I said.

—This little one, said Grandad.

He had her in his hands. Mummy wasn't pleased. She didn't want a bunny near her toast, specially not a poorly one.

—Honestly, she said. —Hold it over the sink.

My heart was thumping.

Grandad showed me Totnes. Wow! It was for her own good. We will rock you, rock you, rock you. He'd saved her. She was brilliant. Her nose was twitching. I touched her. She felt warm. She felt lovely and warm and furry, much more furry than before, and the shaving was gone from her eye, and her eyes were open and she was bigger too. She'd grown!

—Totnes, I said. —Aah.

Kylie stomps round the play-park. She's being dead annoying. She's stomping round and round and she's moaning and groaning because she wants Grandad and Uncle Paul to hurry up. She wants Grandad to finish his rest, and Uncle Paul to help bring the rabbits down, then give her a lift to Cooller Rollers. She wants a lift in Uncle Paul's bluey car. That's what she said when she rang Granny's doorbell and disturbed us.

I wriggle on my toadstool.

Kylie stomps past the feely wall for blind children. I don't know any blind children but I've seen some on *Blue Peter*. They have grey furry eyes and smile a lot.

—Yawnsville, says Kylie. —Yawnsville. Yawnsville.

She stomps past the bench that's covered in bird poo and the concrete tube you can hide in if it's raining. The tube's got naughty pictures inside. Ladies' cracks and dribbly willies. Hard-ones, Finbar says. Sexywexy.

I wipe my nose on my arm.

—Oh come on, fuck's sake, says Kylie.

I sniff. My nose is sore. It's not bleeding. It's sore like my whole face is sore.

Kylie kicks some mud. —Slow fucking cunts, twats. Cunts. Twats.

They're teenager words, I know.

Twats. Cunts.

Cunt cunts. Twat twats.

Kylie sits on the swing with the tyre seat. She's got skates round her neck and Monkey-bag on her back. Monkey-bag's brown and furry with a plastic monkey face. I can see him peeking over her shoulder. He's smiling at me.

Twats.

Kylie swings.

Cunts.

She watches me, but she's not smiling; she's keeping an eye. Mrs Meadows does that too. She keeps her eye on me and all the Tortoises because we need attention, that's what she says.

Attention means standing to it and watching and staring and Mrs Meadows' eye does that at us. It stares and it tells her if we fidget or stick pencils in each other or scribble on our maths books. She only uses one eye. Her other one is for the Chipmunks, the Pussy Cats, the Lemurs, the Gerbils and the Rabbits.

I wriggle on my toadstool. It's my favourite, pink and not so big. The other toadstools are red, green, yellow, and brown, and they're different sizes and they're all around the play-park. Some are for playing houses under, and some are for climbing on and running round and kicking and stuff. Men with spades planted them. They dug holes and poured concrete in and then they planted the toadstools in the concrete but they had to do it again and again because teenagers kept knocking the toadstools down. BEWARE WET CONCRETE, the sign said, Grandad told me. The teenagers stole the sign.

Aunty Chris was so annoyed. She said it was disgusting. Mummy said it was nothing new, remember the climbing frame? Aunty Sheila said she'd hung upside down off the climbing frame when she was drunk, showing her panties off to Uncle Brian. Mummy said that was nothing new either.

I wriggle on my toadstool.

It's freezing plastic and I'm freezing too. I've got freezing chicken skin. It's on my hands and ears and everywhere. Aunty Chris says it's still summer and she won't be changing her door curtain to the wintry one, not yet. But we've only had rain and wind and clouds and Grandad's bones have been creaking. Specially his knee. Sometimes he lets me listen to his knee. It sounds like a hundred years. It sounds like Dracula's box opening. CREEEEK. It sounds like Batman Dracula coming out his box.

I think it must be autumn.

—ALL GOOD THINGS AROUND US . . .

There's not just summer and winter, there's autumn and there's spring time too when Jesus died. I think it's autumn because we've been practising autumn songs in assembly.

—ARE SENT FROM HEAVEN ABOVE . . .

I have a lovely voice. Miss Baxter who plays the piano says so. She was encouraging me.

—THEN THANK THE LORD, OH THANK THE LORD FOR ALLLL HIS . . .

—SHUT IT! shouts Kylie.

She jumps off the swing and marches over to me.

—SHUT THE FUCK UP!

She flicks my knees.

—Ow! I say.

She's got rings on her fingers. Two scary skulls.
They're from Uncle Brian's internet, I know.

I rub my knees and Kylie takes off Monkey-bag. Kylie
helps out at Mr Azad's. She sweeps his floor for money
so she can buy things like Monkey-bag. I watch her.
She's a teenager, I think, because she says teenager words
and she's got boobies and they're nearly as big as Aunty
Chris's and she has those blue boxes like Mummy has.
Kylie can have babies.

—Kylie?

Kylie unzips Monkey-bag's belly.

—Do you want three babies or four babies? I ask.

—Oh, shut it, she says. —Please!

She feels in Monkey-bag's belly. She makes a growly
noise. She feels in her pockets. Her trousers have got
tons of pockets on her bum and legs and everywhere.
Some have zips and badges on, not rabbit badges but
silver metal ones, hearts and crosses and daggers.

—Are you wearing them to Aunty Sheila's wedding?
I ask. —Will she let you?

Kylie throws a chewy wrapper on the ground. She's
a litterbug. Her hair's in bunches like the girl in *Hey
Arnold!*

—Do you want to be the girl in *Hey Arnold!* Kylie? I
ask.

She makes another growly noise and she feels in
Monkey-bag's belly again and she brings out the phone
that Santa got her. It's black with red buttons and it
hasn't any wires. It's a mobile.

—Who're you going to phone, Kylie? I ask.

—Just your daddy, she says, and she smiles at me.

—What? I say.

I don't know what she means.

—Have I got one? Where's my daddy?

God. I pray to God.

—Is he coming here?

I look round the play-park. I can't see him. He's not near the feely wall or the yellow toadstool or the red one or the climbing frame or the bench. He's not in the concrete tube. I can't see no man curled up in there.

—Who do you think they were rowing about? says Kylie.

I don't know what she means.

—What? I say. —Who?

—Christ, she says. —Forget it. Uncle Paul says I've got to phone if it looks like a plane's going to crash on us . . .

—What? I say.

—Or there's a rapist, or a runaway train or what-ever.

Kylie stares at me.

—Do you know what rape is?

—No, I say.

—Evil fuckin', she says.

She presses the phone buttons.

—Fucks you up.

—Oh, I say.

—Shh! she says. —I'm dialling.

—Why?

I feel sick.

—Why d'ya think? Kylie says.

Oh God. I look for a plane, I look for a rapist, I look for a train. Nothing. I look again. Nothing. Zero. Nought. Where's my daddy?

—You're tricking me! I say. —Stop tricking me.

She's tricking me. She's tricking me about my daddy and everything. I don't like Kylie. I don't want to be with her. I don't want to speak to her or go to Splash World with her. No way!

—Yeah, who is it? says the phone.

—Michael, it's me, Kylie, says Kylie.

She walks down the path. She walks like Sporty Spice. She's going away from me.

—DO YOU WANT TO BE SPORTY SPICE? I shout. She shouldn't go away from me. —KYLIE?!

She sticks a finger in the air. Shiver on it.

—I'm shivering, I say.

True-life. I'm shivering because she's leaving me. She shouldn't do that. I cuddle myself. Stranger-danger might get me. The child-catcher or Batman Dracula or the smelly man. He's danger. He's a stranger. He wears a big black coat and he did some tricks and he frightened me.

It was when me and Mummy went to the laundry and the machines were full and we had to wait and I got fed up and pretended I was a rabbit. I did my secret sign and I jumped all over the benches and knocked some powder on the floor. It looked like sherbet dip. It was all over the floor and it was an accident but Mummy got cross with me. She didn't whack me. There were people and they were staring. She hissed at me like

Zippy the snake. —Play outside, she hissed, and I did as I was told.

I ran to the park. There was nobody there. I sat on my favourite toadstool. My eyes felt itchy like they were wanting to cry. I rubbed my eyes and then someone creeped up behind me.

—Hello.

It was a man. He had a growly man's voice and he smelled of fag-puff and I could smell him behind me.

—On your own?

He stamped his feet. He stamped and stamped until he was in front of me. Oh God, he was a stranger and he was looking at me.

—No one to play with?

I stayed very still.

—I can't see your mum. Where's your mum?

He was wearing a long black coat. He had curly hair and he was looking at me. He was all eyes.

—I've seen you here before, he said. —This is your park, isn't it? You live in the flats, don't you? Let me guess; top floor?

I nodded my head.

Oh God.

The smelly fag-puff man smiled at me.

Jesus.

He stared at me.

—You're a lovely-looking girl, he said. —You've turned out well.

—My grandad . . .

My voice was quiet. Grandad was in his flat with the rabbits. I wanted him to rescue me.

—Don't worry, said the smelly man. —I shan't hurt you.

I prayed to God.

—My grandad, I said.

—Here, the smelly man said, and he took his hands out of his pockets and I prayed to God he wouldn't rob me.

He rubbed his hands.

I looked around.

I did it quick.

I couldn't see Grandad or Mummy or anybody.

I could just see his hands. They were coming for me.

My breathing went whizzy and light. His hands were near my face. I closed my eyes.

—Open your eyes, he said. —Or you'll miss it.

He clicked his fingers and silver money came out of my ears and he gave it to me.

—Don't tell Mummy, he said. —It's our secret, OK? Spend it on some sweeties.

Then he waved bye-bye.

—Maybe see you again, he said. —There's lots more where that came from.

He waved bye-bye and he walked down the hill into town.

—KYLIE! I shout.

His coat was flapping, and I threw the money away. I didn't want it. It was warm in my hand and it was burning me and I didn't like it. I threw it away and jumped off my toadstool and ran to the laundry.

—KYLIE! KYLIE!

I ran to Mummy and she asked me if I was going

to behave and I promised. Then she smiled at me and I didn't tell her about the smelly man, no way! I didn't tell her about his hands and his coat and the silver money. She was being dead nice to me.

—KYLIE!

Kylie puts the mobile away.

—FOR FUCK'S SAKE! she shouts, and she shows me her finger and then comes up to me.

She's got a spot on her chin. Teenager spots are dangerous. She stares at me.

—A joke, she says. —What do you get if you pour boiling water down a rabbit hole?

I shake my head. She's upsetting me. You mustn't pour boiling water down a rabbit hole, down a burrow, into a warren. Bunnies can't swim. They'd sink in the water and it'd be too burny for them. It'd pop their hearts. It'd be a burny flamey horrid hell-hole.

—Hot cross bunnies! says Kylie. —Get it? Ha! Ha!

—Where's Grandad? I say.

I want Grandad.

—Where do you think? she says.

I look at her.

—Stuck in the lift, she says.

—Stop it, I say.

—What? she says.

—Where's Uncle Paul? I say.

—Stuck in the lift, she says.

—The rabbits? I say.

I want Chesterfield and Hull and Lincoln and New-biggin-by-the-Sea.

—Same place, she says.

—Oh, I say. My mouth's wobbly.

—They've got about thirty seconds and that'll be it, they'll suffocate.

—What's thirty seconds? I ask.

—Time, she says. —Not much time. Less than a minute.

Less than a minute. A minute's a minute.

—Suffocate? I ask.

—Oh come on, she says. —You can't be that thick. What's the worst thing you can think of, the horriblest thing?

I rub my eyes and I see Kylie and I see Dracula sucking Granny and I see Mickey throwing runts off the flats. Splat! Splat! Splat! I see Grandad and Mummy shouting and Daddy on the phone but I can't see his face and it's Jed, he's Peter and it's confusing me, the smelly man is coming for me.

—Thirty seconds, twenty-nine seconds, twenty-eight seconds, counts Kylie.

—La la la.

I feel dizzy.

—La la la.

—Twenty-seven seconds, twenty-six seconds, counts Kylie.

—Are they . . . ?

—What? says Kylie.

She smiles.

I gulp.

My mouth is dried up. I swallow.

—Dead, I say.

—Got it in one, she says.

Uncle Paul's car is big and blue. It zooms along. We zoom along. The seats have silver stripes. I love Uncle Paul's car. It's cool with music. There's a lady singing about a bad man, an old-age lady not a *Top of the Pops* lady.

—What's heart-yes? I ask.

Kylie makes a pig noise.

—Grandad, I say. —What's heart-yes?

Grandad doesn't answer me.

—Heart*less*, says Uncle Paul.

Grandad doesn't even look round at me. He's in the front seat next to Uncle Paul, and he's got a scarf and a woolly hat on, and he's scrunched up and being dead quiet.

—It means you haven't got a heart, you haven't got any feelings. It means you're cruel and wicked, like our Kylie, says Uncle Paul.

Uncle Paul's wearing black gloves. He's the driver.

—I'm not wicked, says Kylie. —She's just stupid.

—She's just five, says Uncle Paul.

—I'm nearly six, I say.

—She's still a baby, says Uncle Paul. —Which means you should've looked after her better, Kylie.

I look at Kylie. That serves her right. She was horrid

to me. Uncle Paul and Grandad weren't stuck in the lift. They weren't dead. She fibbed and made me cry. I stick my tongue out at her. She's writing things with a pen and paper that she got from Monkey-bag. She's ignoring me. I waggle my tongue at her. I waggle it so much it hurts me.

—Here, baby, she whispers, and she leans over and shows me her writing.

I don't know what it says.

She makes a silent laughing face and I turn away.

I look out the window. My eyes are sore. I rub a circle in the steamy blue.

The windows are blue and they make the outside world look blue too. There's people with bluey faces and hands and legs. There's blue babies and blue shops and dogs and vegetables and puddles and rubbish. There's a blue motorbike and a van and a blue fallen-down wall and bluey lines on the road. Some stuff's more blue than other stuff. It's like being in the swimming pool. It's like going under and opening your eyes, seeing everything all blue and wavy, bottoms and things.

Mrs Meadows takes us swimming and Mummy helped once. Lots of mummies do. Maya's mummy is mad for it. They walk us to Splash World and help us get changed. We have to walk in pairs in a crocodile. Finbar and me are a pair. He carries my bag for me. Finbar and me might get married. But it's a secret. A secret's a secret. Mummy went at the back of the crocodile but she got irritated with Susan D. Susan D's a slow walker. Mummy called her a snail. —Speed up, snail, she said.

Mummy's normally irritated; she's stressed out. Stressed

out means she needs a new life. New means shiny, not old. Mummy's life is old. It's given her grey bits. It's been heart-yes to her. Mummy doesn't like her life.

—You know a new life? How do you get one? Do you have to be dead first? I ask.

Uncle Paul does a weirdo laugh, not the proper kind.

—But do you? I ask.

—Shut it, wank, whispers Kylie in my ear.

—I'll tell, I say. —Wank's rude.

I know about wank. Wank's something to do with willies.

—Scare me, says Kylie. —Why don't you?

—JESUS! shouts Uncle Paul.

His car goes stop, start, stop, start.

—OW!

Kylie falls forward.

—OW!

I do too.

Stop, start, stop.

—DID YOU SEE THAT! shouts Uncle Paul. —THIS FUCKING JUNCTION!

Grandad fusses with his hat. It's gone wonky. —Paul, please.

Start.

—WATCH THE CAR IN FRONT!

—I AM! I AM! shouts Uncle Paul, and he puts on his horn that sounds like the Police. Nee nah. Nee nah.

Stop, start, stop.

—PAUL! THE RABBITS!

Grandad looks at Uncle Paul.

—They don't need upsetting, Paul, he says.

Uncle Paul taps his gloves on the steering wheel.

Grandad looks at us.

—Are the rabbits all right, back there? he asks. He's got a croaky voice. He fiddles with his scarf and pulls it off.

—Yeah, says Kylie. —Only me and Lily have broken bones.

—Will you turn that thing off, Paul.

Grandad wipes his mouth with a hanky. There's red spots on the hanky. Blood.

—PAUL!

Uncle Paul turns off the horn.

Start.

Grandad wipes his face with the hanky. Yuk.

—None of the boxes fallen over? he asks.

—Nah, says Kylie. —Just me and Lily smashed our skulls.

—Don't be cheeky, Kylie, says Grandad. —Are you sure about the rabbits? Take a proper look.

Kylie undoes her seat belt and takes a proper look. —Yeah, I'm sure.

—Positive?

The lady stops singing. Uncle Paul pulls her out the machine and throws her on the pile.

—I said so, didn't I? says Kylie, and she does up her belt.

There's children's tapes in the pile, Brum and Singing Kettle and Revolting Songs, that's about bogeys.

—Good, says Grandad, and he looks at Uncle Paul. —Right.

Uncle Paul stares out his bluey window.

—Everything's fine, says Grandad.

Uncle Paul drives round a blue roundabout.

The car's quiet. All the people and all the rabbits. The rabbits are behind me and Kylie, in their special boxes. They're near Grandad's trolley, in the bit where Bethany goes for a sleep and Aunty Chris puts her shopping. Rabbits are normally quiet. They're not guinea-pigs. Guinea-pigs are chatterers. Guinea-pigs are at the shows sometimes, and mice and hamsters and gerbils. Guinea-pigs are the noisiest. They go EEK EEK EEK EEK. Grandad hates them. He says they go EEK when they're sad, happy and angry, and what's the use of that? Rabbits, he says, are cleverer. They have real language. They're quiet when they're OK, they growl when they're annoyed, and they thump their feet when they're frightened. They send messages.

Our rabbits are very quiet. They're very OK. I look at Kylie. Kylie's staring out the window at a blue boy on a blue bicycle. She's smiling. God. Our rabbits are really quiet. More quiet than rabbit quiet. Rabbit quiet has movements and snuffles. There's no snuffling. Their boxes could've crashed. Kylie wouldn't care. She fibs. No movements. Their hearts could've popped. Rabbits have rubbish hearts. She only wants to get to Cooller Rollers.

I feel sick. Pizza sick's in my mouth. I pray to God. I press the silver button but it won't work. —Kylie, I say. —Help!

She's staring at a blue lamppost.

—Kylie!

—What?

She's staring at me.

—I want out, I say.

—You can't, she says.

—Why? I ask.

She smiles at me.

—Why? I ask.

—It's the law, she says. —Liddle babies have to wear straps.

—THAT'S NOT FAIR!

—Hey! says Uncle Paul. —What's going off?

—I feel sick, I say.

—You feel sick?

—Is this the truth? says Grandad.

—Really sick? says Uncle Paul.

—Oh no! says Kylie. —Lily's going to puke! She going to spew on your covers, Uncle Paul!

Once upon a time, when I was in Mrs Bagley's class in Year R, I sicked up in her rubbish bin and my sick was yellow and it was disgusting to me. Mrs Bagley phoned Mummy at college and told her to come quick. Mummy was doing different learning then, ordinary reading and writing and maths, but she left it and ran to my school because she was worried, I'd had my jabs and she thought they were hurting me. She took me home and phoned Doctor Whitworth and he told her I should be in bed. So she put me in my 'jamas and tucked me in. She gave me a glass of water. She wet my Barbie flannel and patted it on my head and she put a bowl for my sick on the table near the bed. Then she put Grandad in charge so she could go back to college to fetch her work. Grandad looked at his watch and made a tut noise. He read me a story about the Flopsy Bunnies. He looked at his watch again. It was no good; he had to see a man about some rabbits. —Won't be a minute, Lily, he said, and he went out the flat.

A minute's a minute. Grandad's minute went on and on and on. I started to shiver. The bed was icy. My teeth chattered. I couldn't find my hotty bottle. So I sneaked into Grandad's room and borrowed a baby doe. She was lovely and furry and we cuddled each other and it was great but then she weed and plipped and Grandad was angry when he got back. He changed my 'jamas and the sheets and I thought he was going to tell on me but he didn't, he was kind; he told Mummy he'd spilled my water and that was the whole truth and nothing but the truth so thank you God, Jesus, Mary and Joseph.

I went back to Mrs Bagley's the next day because I was much better. She said she was glad because we were going to collect leaves for the creative corner. Creative means *Art Attack* and stuff like that. Mrs Bagley took us into the playground and she showed us this big bag and she said she wanted it filled with the leaves that were lying on the ground, the papery red and orange leaves that drop from trees in autumn.

—Urggh!

That's me.

Mrs Bagley told us we were going to use the littlest leaves for pictures and the biggest ones for noises, crispy crackly sounds.

—Urggh!

There's little and big leaves down here, over this wall, but I'm not collecting them. I'm trying to be sick on them

and Uncle Paul's feeling sorry for me. He pats my back.
—Come on, sweetheart. We're only getting dribble.

I look at the leaves. I'm dangling over a wall near some shops and a wood. The wall goes round the wood. My belly's balancing on the top of the wall and my head and shoulders and arms are dangling over it, dangling in the wood. I stare at the leaves. Uncle Paul said it'd be the best place for the sick. Over the wall and out of the way. Like wee. Wee has to be out of the way.

—Urggh!

I feel dizzy.

—And again, says Uncle Paul.

—Urgggh!

It hurts my throat.

—Urgggh!

But I have to do it. I'm being Super Lily. Super Lily is like Super Ted. She makes up clever plans.

—She's having you on, says Kylie.

Super Lily saves rabbits.

—Better not be, says Uncle Paul.

Super Lily creates a 'version, so Grandad can get to the rabbits. Nee nah. Nee nah. It's an emergency. Grandad understood. He read Super Lily's mind. —You see to Lily, Grandad said to Uncle Paul. —And I'll just check on the rabbits.

—Urgggh! I say.

Kylie leans over the wall. She looks at me. Her eyes are black.

—I don't know what you think you're at, she says. —But Michael's waiting for me and if I'm late, if he thinks I've stood him up, then you're for it. Understand?

Grandad coughs. I can hear him close to me. —How's she getting on? he says.

That's code. Secret code.

—Hard to say, says Uncle Paul. —Chris usually deals with this kind of thing. She's the sick expert.

—Perhaps we should just try her back in the car, says Grandad.

That's more secret code.

—Hope for the best.

The rabbits are OK. Super Lily understands.

—Finished, I say, and I wriggle to get off the wall.

—Surprise. Surprise, says Kylie.

I wriggle and Uncle Paul grabs me and spins me round and looks me in the face. He stares at my eyes, my nose, my mouth, and I try not to smile because poorly people don't smile, not when they're being poorly, no way. I didn't smile when I did my yellow sick, and Grandad didn't smile when he couldn't sleep that time and had to stay at Aunty Sheila's, and Mummy doesn't smile when she's bleeding out her bum, and Ben Cley in my class doesn't smile when he's being allergic.

Allergic's like chicken pox and colds. It hides in the things you eat and sometimes it hurts you and sometimes not. Finbar's allergic to cucumber; it gives him spots. Rabbits are allergic to peapods because the pods puff up their bellies and they can't sick them out so they have to sit with the peapods inside them and sometimes it's too much and it pops their rubbish hearts. Ben Cley's allergic to nuts.

Uncle Paul puts me on the ground.

—You'll do, he says.

—Shall we get going then? says Grandad, and he holds out his hand.

Nuts make Ben Cley's tongue grow fat and his face turn red.

I take Grandad's hand.

It happened in assembly once.

—Come on, you, he says.

We were singing 'Light One Thousand Candles' and Jamie Ling sneaked Ben a biscuit. The biscuit was a nut one. Jamie Ling didn't know. Ben's face went red and he grabbed his neck and moaned and groaned. He crashed on the floor and Kelly and Wilma screamed, and Mr Glew, who helps the teachers sometimes, grabbed Ben's emergency bag and pulled out a needle and jabbed it in Ben's leg. Then the ambulance came – nee nah – and took Ben away. It was dead exciting.

Grandad holds my hand a lot. He does it when he takes me down the corridors to school and to the shops and everywhere. He's like my daddy because daddies hold your hand except Grandad's not my daddy because he's old-age and he doesn't look like me and because he's my grandad.

Grandads are grandparents. They're not ordinary parents. Ordinary parents are mummies and daddies and grandparents are ancient wisdom, that's what Finbar says. Ancient is old and wisdom is to do with brains and teeth; falsies, I think. So, I've got an ordinary mummy and one ancient wisdom but I've not got an ordinary daddy, not living with me.

Daddy. Daddy. Daddy.

Sometimes he visits me in my dreams. He sings and claps and whistles to me but I don't see his face. That's because I don't know what he looks like. I know some of him looks like me because that's the rule: mummies and daddies and their children have bits that look the same, like their eyes or noses or skin. But I don't know what we have the same. So I just hear him and I know it's him because he tells me, and I believe him because dreams are dreams and lies are lies, and dreams are inside your head and they belong to you, and lies happen outside your head and they belong to cousins and friends that tell-tale-tit.

I pray to God about my daddy. Dear God, I say, please can I be a rabbit and please can I see my daddy's face? But God's not answered yet, I don't know why. Perhaps he thinks I'm being greedy or I'm not asking right. I do it in secret, under my covers but Finbar says God only hears if you kneel on the floor and make a cross sign on your body and put your hands together like this. I tried it in the bedroom one time but Mummy stopped me. She wasn't very happy.

—Lily, she said. —Pack that in.

—Why? I asked.

—Because . . .

—Because what? I asked.

—Just because, she said, and she pushed her hands through her hair and sighed. —Christ.

—Jesus Christ, I said. —Jesus Christ who died to save us all.

—Stop that, Lily, she said. —It's nonsense.

—Not, I said.

—Get up, she said.

—No, I said.

Mummy leant over, folded her arms on the bed, and got down on her knees.

I smiled. —Dear God . . . I said.

I thought we were going to pray for a daddy together but Mummy put her hand over my mouth.

—Where are you getting it from? she said. She stared at me. —Is it school? Mrs Meadows? I can't believe it's Mrs Meadows.

I wanted to breathe.

—Is it Finbar? she said. She took her hand off my mouth. —Answer me, Lily.

I was gasping.

—Oh never mind, she said. —It doesn't matter. You'll grow out of it.

—Like plimsolls? I said.

—What? said Mummy.

—I've grown out of my plimsolls, I said. —Can I get some new?

Mummy told Mrs Meadows about our God talk the next day and Mrs Meadows laughed when Mummy got to the plimsolls bit, I don't know why, and Mummy laughed too. Then she shook her head and said being a parent was the hardest thing, harder than putting up with Grandad's flat and his smelly rabbits, harder than her college work, dead bloody hard.

—I know, smiled Mrs Meadows and she sort of rubbed Mummy's arm with the side of her finger like Grandad does Lincoln when he's loving her.

Mrs Meadows doesn't do that to any other mummies or daddies. She doesn't do it to Wilma's mum or Jamie Ling's dad; she keeps away from them. Sometimes she pats, not the grown-ups but the children who can read and write and don't do much fidgeting, and sometimes she pats me too. Patting's friendly. It's like what you do to dogs. Mrs Meadows rubs Mummy's arm, then she looks at me and pats me really fast, on my head, like that. It's nice. But normally she's not so great to me. She tells me I should do more concentrating and she makes me copy letters from the board over and over.

She doesn't do any fun things with me like she does with Mummy, like going to the pub and visiting her house and everything. She lives near Uncle Brian and Aunty Sheila, and Mummy says she's got a doorstep and a shed and loads of rooms with loads of books in. She's got a computer and she's got a special machine that can make proper yoghurt, not the purple children's kind, and Mummy wants to live with her, that's what she said. She told me when she came back from the pub.

She tripped over the bedroom bump and she shouted some swear words and woke me up.

—Mummy! I said.

She was on the floor. She sighed. —God, this hole.

—What hole? I said. I couldn't see a hole, just a bump.

—This place is a hole, Lily, she said. —This flat. I shouldn't have to put up with it.

—Oh, I said.

—I should move in with Elaine, she said. —Like she asked me.

—What? I said. —Who?

Mummy smiled and got up off the floor. It took her ages.

—Mrs Meadows wants me to move in with her, she said.

—Oh, I said. —She's my teacher.

Mummy nodded. —But it's a secret, OK? Cross your heart.

And I did, because a secret's a secret and I've not told anybody this one except Grandad because it's dead good news. Mummy will be going to Mrs Meadows' house and Grandad and me will be going to Sweden and that's good, we'll all be going somewhere nice and new. Grandad liked the news. He was interested. He asked me questions about the house and Mrs Meadows and everything.

—Has she got a husband?

I nodded my head.

—Does she still live with him?

I nodded my head, I shook my head. —I don't know.

—So, what do you know?

—She got married, I said. —Up a mountain.

She did too. She didn't get married in a church like Grandad and Granny or in an office like Mummy; she got married up a mountain but it wasn't a Swedes one, it was from Wales and it had snow on and Mrs Meadows wore a woolly white hat and woolly trousers and a big coat made from camels. She had a red nose and so did Mr Meadows. He wore furry boots. Mrs Meadows showed us the photos in class. She called them her wedding photos. She showed them and then said she wanted us to bring in some photos too, not wedding photos from magazines or comics but real ones of grown-ups in our families. She wanted us to talk about them.

How many people live in your house?

One my mother.

I took in Granny and Grandad's wedding photos.

Two my father.

I asked Mummy for her photos too but she said no.

—When you're older, Lily, she said. —We'll go through it all then.

Uncle Paul drives into the rabbit show car park. It's made of blue pebbles. He drives slowly and the pebbles crunch. I can hear them under us. My heart is thumping. I stare out the blue window at the cars and vans and people carrying rabbit boxes and bags of hay. I can feel my heart alive inside me. We're at the rabbit show! It's so exciting.

I stare out of my window, then I stare out of Kylie's except it's not hers any more because she's at Cooller Rollers. Uncle Paul dropped her off. There were lots of teenagers hanging about, doing slouching. Kylie waved and ran to them. Monkey-bag was bouncing on her back. She didn't wave at us. She didn't do any good manners or say goodbye because she was rushing for her boyfriend, that's what Grandad said.

Uncle Paul steers his steering wheel. Steering is like directions. It means left, right, up and down. Uncle Paul's steering left, I think. Left is for witches. It gives you bad luck. I don't want to steer there.

—Go the other way, I say.

—What's this, Lily? Did you see a space? Point it out, he says.

I point. I don't know where the space is but I point over there, to the right way, and he steers his wheel so the car turns from the witches.

186

Space means the sky at night. It's the stars and the dark holes and the cheesy Man-In-The-Moon. Aliens live in it and zoom round it in their saucers. Space is on our planet too but it's a different kind. Mummy wants it but she doesn't get it much because it's hard to find. It's see-through but if you're lucky and if you've got supersonic eyes you can spot it sitting next to things.

—Look! I say, and I point at a van. It's got a bluey-gold cross on the side. It's fantastic-elastic.

—There's the space, Paul, says Grandad. —Next to the barmy-army van.

—Oh! I say.

Grandad has spotted the space. Not me. I spotted a barmy-army van.

—Where's the soldiers? I ask. —Are they inside?

You could get millions of soldiers in there. I don't like soldiers. They have guns.

Grandad turns and smiles at me.

—There's no soldiers, Lily, he says. —Just a few Christians spreading the word.

—Oh, I say. —What word?

Uncle Paul moves his car backwards. He's clever like that. He looks over his shoulder and steers the wheel.

—Put your head down a bit, Lily, he says.

I look at my leggings.

—What's the word? I ask my leggings.

I want to spread the word.

—What's the word, Paul? asks Grandad. —Sausages?

Uncle Paul laughs. —No, not sausages, he says. —Vienna.

—Vienna?

—That's right, Lily. That's the word.

—Well, I never knew that, says Grandad.

Vienna. Vienna. Vienna.

Uncle Paul stops the car.

The cross on the barmy-army van shines through the blue window next to me. It's bluey-gold and Jesus died on it. He died to save us all.

Vienna.

Holy. Holy.

—Out we get, says Uncle Paul. —I'll unload the rabbits.

Uncle Paul opens my door and crunches by. The pebbles aren't blue, I can see. They're grey and dirty like the sky.

Grandad leans in and unclips my strap. —That's you. Out you pop.

I run from the car, over the pebbles, to Uncle Paul.

—Uff! he says.

He lifts the rabbit boxes from the boot and puts them on Grandad's special trolley that he got ages ago from a jumble sale. It's not a supermarket trolley made of wire. It's flat and black with rubbery wheels and a long pole for a handle. I touch the handle. It feels warm.

—These weigh a ton, puffs Uncle Paul.

I nod. I know. I look at the boxes. They're full of rabbits and they're made of wood and they're covered in straps and padlocks.

Grandad leans on the car. He watches Uncle Paul.

—You'll have to ask a steward to help you unload, says Uncle Paul.

Grandad coughs and nods and rubs his hands.

—What's that say? I ask him, and I point at the building where the rabbit show is. There's a big sign hanging on it. It's made of material and it's got huge red letters and numbers. Time numbers, I think.

Grandad wraps his scarf round his neck again. —BRC Three Star Show, Lily, he says. —2.00 p.m. start.

—2.00 p.m. start, I say. —That's proper time, a time number. 2.00 p.m. Two o'clock.

—Very good, he says. —And three star?

He coughs and his breath floats in the air. It looks like fag-puff.

—What does three star mean, Lily?

—Three star's middle-size, I say.

—That's right, he says. —Well done.

I nod. I know. There's one, two, three, four and five star shows, and one stars are the smallest and fives are the largest and Grandad goes to all of them but he only goes to ones to sell off his rabbits. He doesn't show at ones but he does at all the others and he shows the most at fives because they're dead important and give him nerves that make him feel twitchy. Five star shows make him feel very twitchy and three stars don't because he wins these normally. They're OK. They're middle-size and easy-peasy.

Uncle Paul tugs the trolley over the pebbles.

Easy-peasy. Lemon-squeezy. Japanesy. Bumps your kneesy.

Grandad looks up at the cloudy sky, then down at me.

Easy-peasy. Lemon-squeezy. Japan . . .

—Well, come on, he says. —Let's get shifting.

We follow Uncle Paul. He stops the trolley on the little path that leads to the hall. He smiles at us. —Will you be all right from here?

—Should think so, says Grandad.

—Can I pull? I ask.

—No. The rabbits have had enough upset already. You'll bump them.

—Bumps your kneesy, I say.

—What? says Grandad.

—Pardon? says Uncle Paul.

—Easy-peasy. Lemon-squeezy. Japanesy. Bumps your kneesy.

Uncle Paul laughs, and Grandad shakes his head and his falsies clack.

—Must be lovely to be you, he says.

—Lily.

I pull my leggings and Tom's pants out my crack.

—You're wriggling, Lily, says Grandad. —Do you need the loo?

—No, I say.

—Pack it in then. Stand still.

We're in the queue to get inside the show. We've waved bye-bye to Uncle Paul and we've gone through the big wooden doors and we're in the bit near the coat pegs. I'm leaning on a woolly duffel. It smells of muck and old rain. There's a black umbrella that dangles from a top row peg and a spotty plastic mac and a jacket like Grandad's special show one that he's wearing today, that's brown and hairy and has big pockets and knobbly buttons and smells of rabbit wee and hay.

A man knocks off the umbrella as he brushes by. —Bugger, he says.

—That's naughty, I say. —That's a swear word.

Bugger is. Bugger. Bugger. Bugger.

The man stares at me. He picks up the umbrella and puts it on the peg and he turns and shows his back to me. I step sideways and look round him at the queue and the doors that lead into the hall. They're green and there's a lady sitting next to them. She's wearing a flowery dress and she's taking money from the people in the queue and giving them tickets. Grandad says they're raffle tickets for a raffle. We had one of them at school. Mummy got me a ticket but I didn't win anything. Finbar did. His mummy got him seven tickets and he won a packet of Cheese Strings, orange and red flavour. Finbar's lucky.

—Come on, woman, says Grandad. He takes off his woolly hat and unwinds his scarf and puts them in his pockets. He stares at the lady. —We shan't be registered at this rate.

He coughs.

The lady takes some money from a man with no hair and she says something that my supersonic ears can't hear.

—Thank you, dear.

That's what she says. I know because I do the dumb game.

—Take care, dear. Bye.

She gives the man his tickets and he opens the green doors and a whoosh of noise comes out, chattering and rustling, guinea-pigs squeaking, cage doors banging. There's clinking wire sounds and plate and cup sounds too. There must be a food place inside. That means pop and crisps and Penguin biscuits. My heart is beating fast. The man with no hair goes into the hall and the queue shuffles up.

—Stop jiggling, Lily, says Grandad. —Walk normally.

—I'm excited, I say.

—And me, says a lady's voice.

It comes from behind us. I turn and look and Grandad does too.

It's the lady who's got prize guinea-pigs who I've seen before, at the shows. She's got extra special guinea-pigs with dark red sticky-up fur and she brushes their fur with a toothbrush. She's a fussy old lady and she wears flour on her face. She's very floury near her eyes and her mouth. It sticks in her old-age lines.

—Oh, hello there Maud, says Grandad.

That's her name. Maud.

—Hello Jim, she says.

That's Grandad's name. Jim. That's his first name. His second name's Phillips. Jim Phillips. It sounds posh. My first name's Lily, my second is Garner. Lily Garner. That's not so posh.

—Grandad? I say.

—Queue's a long one, Grandad says to Maud.

—Oh yes, she says. —Busy today.

—Did Granny wear flour on her face? I ask. —Grandad? Grandad looks at me.

—What is it, Lily? I'm talking.

—But Grandad, did Granny wear flour on her face?

—Flour? says Grandad.

—Like her, I say, and I point at Maud.

—Oh, says Maud.

—Put that finger away, Lily, says Grandad.

—She's got flour on her face.

—Where? says Maud. —I was doing some baking this morning but I've had a wash.

Maud pats her face.

—Lily, says Grandad.

He stares at my finger and I curl it away. I look at my jellies. I'm in trouble, I don't know why.

Grandad coughs.

—How's your Simon? he says.

—Simon? I say.

I know him.

—Lily, says Grandad. —Please be quiet.

But I do. True-life. He was in Mrs Bagley's class in Year R. He wasn't very nice. He had nits and they were jumping on his head. You could see them jumping up and down.

—Is he on the mend?

The nurse at school gave him a comb.

—I wish, says Maud.

It was black with silver spikes and when he came to school in the mornings he had to comb his nits onto a piece of paper, and there were nit mummies and daddies and babies. I saw. Horrid nit families that suck your blood because that's what nits do.

—He's been for a few more tests but they've no idea. They won't admit it of course.

Mit. Nit.

—It's a shame, says Grandad.

Nit Mit.

—Mmm, says Maud.

Nitwit.

—It's terrible. He's lost so much weight. We had to go to Thorns last week for some new pyjamas. He's wearing ladies.

I look at Maud.

—George thinks we should prepare for the worst, she says.

Grandad shakes his head.

—Aunty Karen's at Thorns, I say. —She sells Hot Pies.

She does.

—Oh, says Maud. —Really? That's interesting.

I nod.

She drives there in her special car that's pink and covered in squiggly writing and pictures of pies puffing wispy smoke so it's like they're hot and ready to eat. She parks her car and goes through the posh doors to zero floor and she stands in a corner near the sweetie counter and she talks about Hot Pies and sells them. She's ever so good. She gives people a plate and a fork and a bit of pie and she smiles at them and never cries. Grandad showed me one time. He took me to see her and she gave me sausage pie, an extra big bit. She said they only do sausage and chicken and mince, no rabbit. So that's good. She smelt of pies and sugary perfume and she was wearing her uniform. It's not like a school uniform, like you have to wear for middle school with black trousers and black shoes and a black boring jumper. It's cool with a hat that looks like a pie and pink trousers and a stripy pink top.

Maud stares at the ceiling, and Grandad fiddles with the stuff in his trouser pockets, he makes a jingly noise. They're not saying anything to each other, not any more. They've gone dead quiet, I don't know why.

Perhaps there's something on the ceiling.

I push my head right back, so it stretches my neck-skin at the front and creases it near my shoulders, creasing it up until it feels squashed and bruised. I look. The ceiling's ordinary. It's normal. It's bright white and there's a crack in it but the crack's not an earthquake crack like Konnie showed us on *Blue Peter*, it's not big enough for houses to fall in and elephants and cars, it's skinny and boring like scribble.

—Karen's your youngest, isn't she? Maud says to the ceiling.

—No. That's Sheila. I've got Donna, Pam, Chris, Karen and then Sheila, says Grandad. —Sheila's getting married.

Maud looks down from the ceiling. I do too.

—She's the one with the dog? she says.

I rub my neck-skin and shake my head.

—No, says Grandad. —None of them have a dog.

—Ah, says Maud, and she pats me on the head like I'm a dog and smell comes out of her and puffs up my nose.

Yuk.

She smells of guinea-pig. She stinks of their torpedo plips. I hate torpedoes. Mr Azad sells them. They're bogging.

The queue shuffles up.

—Here we go again, says Maud.

Grandad pulls his trolley and Maud pulls hers and I follow putting the heel of one jelly right up to the toe of the other. Heel. Toe. Heel. Toe. Heel. We stop on heel.

Maud leans on her trolley. It's not as nice as Grandad's. It's plastic and it's only got two wheels.

—Who had the dog, then? she asks.

—Grace and I had a collie, says Grandad. —But that was when we were first married.

He shakes his head.

—He was a funny old beggar, he says.

Beggar not bugger.

Grandad's dog was a beggar, and he stayed with Grandad and Granny when they lived in the house with the doorstep, I know. Aunty Chris showed me a photo one time when Mummy was doing her college work and Aunty Chris was looking after me. He was brown and black with a white tail and he was called Old Shep and he went round and round, chasing his tail, grunting and growling. He wore a circle in Granny's best carpet.

—Was she angry? I asked Aunty Chris. —Did Granny give Old Shep a smack?

—No, said Aunty Chris. —He couldn't help it. He was a sad case, a bit mental.

Aunty Chris put a finger to her head and screwed it. She gave the nutter sign. We do that at school, at the stupid children, the children who slobber and cry and can't make no friends. We do it at daft-bat Kelly and she gets upset and tells Mrs Chippie the dinner lady but Mrs Chippie's not interested. She bosses Kelly. She tells her to grow up quick and fight her own battles.

—Nothing would've helped Old Shep, said Aunty Chris. —Grandad put him out of his misery in the end. He put him to sleep.

—Can I see? I asked.

—Pardon? said Aunty Chris.

Grandad puts lots of his rabbits to sleep but he won't let me see where, he won't let me visit their special bedroom.

—Can I see Old Shep's bedroom? I asked.

Aunty Chris sighed.

—Can I?

She was peeling a potato and she put it down and looked at it. She seemed quite interested in it.

—Can I?

—His bedroom's far away, she said.

—Far away? Where?

Aunty Chris sighed. —Isle of Skye.

—Isle of Skye? Where's Isle of Skye?

—Far away, said Aunty Chris. She picked up the potato. —It'll be the birds and the bees next, she said.

—Birds and bees what? I asked.

—Lily, she said. She waved the knife. —Your mother's supposed to be the intelligent one, ask her.

Intelligent means brainy and your brain is the purple sponge that's inside your head and helps you to walk and swim and brush your teeth and know facts. Facts are information. Facts are found in information books. Mrs Meadows lets us look at information books on Mondays. There's one about rabbits. It has photos of rabbits and big writing. I can't read the writing but that doesn't matter because I know about rabbits anyway. I know lots of rabbit facts.

Here are some rabbit facts about bums:

If there's poo stuck to the rabbit's bum that means he's poorly.

Rabbits do two kinds of poos, hard round balls and soft shiny stuff. They eat the soft shiny stuff because it's got lots of vitamins in.

Rabbits poo twenty times an hour. An hour's an hour.

Rabbits have a hole in their bums which their poo comes out of and another bum hole for making babies with.

Bucks' holes for making babies with are different to does' holes. Bucks' holes are round. Does' holes aren't.

Put your hand under the rabbit's bum when you lift him because it makes him feel safe.

To learn a rabbit to jump you have to push his bum and shout —JUMP! JUMP! JUMP!

—Right, Jim, says the man in the white coat and hat, not a woolly hat, a material one. —There's your numbers.

He points to some paper stuck on a board on the wall. He's the rabbit show boss. I've seen him before at other shows, in other parts of East and England. He's really tall and he's got a knobbly nose and flappy ears. His hands have got blue lumps on them. They're old-age hands. He's a very important old-age man.

Grandad looks at the board.

—It's a good turnout, he says.

The man in the white coat and hat nods.

—Plenty of English, he says. —Allen and Hamptons have brought theirs in.

—That right? says Grandad. He takes a pencil from behind his ear and writes stuff on his newspaper. —Well, I've nothing to fear there.

He tucks his paper under his arm and he coughs.

—Excuse.

His voice is croaky, and he coughs again.

—Shouldn't you be tucked up in bed, Jim? says the man in the white coat and hat.

Grandad shakes his head. —Better off here, thanks. I'll get more peace.

—That bad? says the man.

I look at Grandad.

—Bad enough, he says.

There's no peace here. Peace is quiet and pigeons flying in the sky and loving Jesus quietly. It's not busy and noisy. It's not full of people and animals, and boxes and bags and coats, and shavings and hay, and tables covered in shiny white cloths. It's not a shiny white cloth.

White's no good, that's what Aunty Chris says; it's a rubbish colour because it gets dirty and shows everything up. She's right, I think, because Grandad has to scrub the white on his rabbits all the time. He does it with a toothbrush like Maud. He scrubs round their bums, near their holes, because the white fur turns yellow there and yellow doesn't win prizes. Black's the best colour, that's what Aunty Chris says. Bethany has a black *Pingu* quilt and black sheets and Aunty Chris doesn't have to do anything with them much, she just puts them in her washing machine with ordinary powder. She doesn't have to use string bags or the magic flowery air in the packet. She's lucky. Her machine's in her kitchen and she never visits the laundry place near Mr Azad's and Mummy wants to be like her, to have a machine in our kitchen too but Grandad won't buy one because Granny managed with soap and a big bucket, and if it was good enough for her, then, that's what Grandad says.

The white cloths on the tables are very white. They're shining bright and they hurt my eyes, and they're going to stay like that for a while, I know, because nobody's putting their sandwiches or pop or Penguin biscuits on them. It's because the tables are for animals only, they're where the animals have to go to get judged, and the cloths are on the tables to make the animals look good, to show up their fur and claws and everything.

Animals get judged and so do people. Animals get judged at shows and people get judged at college and school and everywhere. Mummy's essays get judged and I do too. Mrs Meadows did it to me but I didn't win a prize. I was too rubbish. I got put in the Tortoise group. That's not a prize. Judging's good if you're good and bad if you're rubbish, that's what I think.

Judges do the judging at the shows and there's loads of them here. They wear white coats like the old-age man but they don't wear hats and they have badges on their coats, like the ones Grandad got me for Aunty Sheila's wedding. God. I don't know where those badges are. Mummy's probably got them. I tug Grandad's jacket. I feel sick. Mummy's probably found them and thrown them away.

—Where's my badges? I say.

—Can you hang on? says Grandad. —I'm trying to get my bearings here.

—But my badges! I say.

Mummy's probably thrown them down the shoot for the dustbin men.

—What's this? says the old-age man with the white coat and hat.

She has, I know.

—La la la.

I'm certain sure.

—Something and nothing, says Grandad, and he looks at me.

—La la la, I say.

—Now, stop that, you're being silly, he says.

—La la la. La la la.

—Your mother's got them.

She's got them! She's throwing them!

—NA! I say.

—Lily! Calm down. She's looking after them. She's promised to sew them on your dress.

She's got them. She's sewing them.

—Oh, I say.

A promise is a promise.

—Better?

I nod. Yes.

—Good. Now take a look around. No, don't wander off. Stay with me and look, take your mind off things.

I do as I'm told.

I open my eyes really wide and I take my mind off, like that, and I look.

I look at the tables. There's two of them, for the judging. One's for rabbits and the other's for guinea-pigs, I know, because Grandad says there's only rabbits and cavies at this show, that's what he calls guinea-pigs sometimes, that's their proper posh name. There's no mice or rats or hamsters or gerbils or budgies. There's just rabbits and guinea-pigs and the guinea-pig table is small and has some weighing scales and a wooden box and paper and pencils on it, and the rabbit table has loads of scales and tons of paper and pencils on it and it begins by the green doors and goes down to the stage. I think there's a table on the stage too but I can't see that well because the pens are in the way.

The pens aren't writing pens. They're where the animals have to go when they're not being judged. The pens are made of wire and they're square shaped and they're in rows with spaces between for people to walk down. There's lots of pens in each row and there's pens standing on top of other pens and then more on top of those. Like the hutches in Grandad's bedroom. Like our flats. Rabbit Tower and Guinea-Pig High-Rise. Yes!

—Grandad, I say, and I tug his jacket. —Rabbit Tower. That's where we live!

—Hang on, Lily, says Grandad, and he points at the stage and the big brown piano standing beside it. —So the English are there, at the back?

Oh.

He coughs.

A piano!

—Spot on, says the man in the white coat and hat.

—There's a piano like Miss Baxter plays! I say. —Grandad!

—You're doing it again, Lily.

Grandad coughs and puts his hand over his heart where his ticker is and he looks at me.

—You mustn't interrupt when I'm talking. Be quiet now.

I bow my head.

—That's better.

Miss Baxter gave a show at our school once.

I stare at my jellies.

Not a rabbit show, a music show. She did it to get some money for the extra babies in China. She played China chopsticks on her piano.

China is a country very far away. It's strict with lots of rules like school and the China breed of people have to obey the rules. A rule's a rule. There's a special rule for mummies. They can only have one baby. China is an only-bonely country. But sometimes China mummies forget this rule and have an extra baby and then they have to leave the baby in the forest or at a railway station. They're normally girl babies, I don't know why, and they catch really bad colds and then they die.

Babies aren't supposed to die. Miss Baxter knows this and she knows a man who's trying to keep these babies alive. He's writing letters and moaning and groaning and creeping into China and cuddling the babies and everything. Miss Baxter told us and she showed us a red box with a slot in the top. It was in assembly. —I'm going to play my piano to raise money for this good cause, she said. —Everybody is welcome. Just drop as much as you can afford in this box. The show starts at 7.00.

Mummy wouldn't take me. She said she had no money she could afford, she had an essay to do, and she didn't like Miss Baxter anyway. —She's a frustrated old maid, Mummy said.

Frustrated is like irritated, and maids sit under cows and squeeze their milk. They carry big wooden buckets on poles and wear aprons with lace round and have red circles on their cheeks. There's a maid in 'The House That Jack Built', Mrs Meadows read it to us, and there's a cow with a crumpled horn.

Finbar's big sister took me to the show, and Grandad gave me some money to put in the box, brown money, 2ps and 1ps. Finbar put silver money in. We sat at the front and I could see Miss Baxter's fingers pressing the teeth and her feet pressing the pedals. Her friend Miss Walsh joined in too. She played the trumpet. It was great. Better than assembly.

—Come on then, Lily.

Grandad ruffles my hair with his newspaper.

—Bye, says the man in the white coat and hat.

I give him my secret sign, and I follow Grandad and his trolley, watching the wheels as they roll slowly over the floor through the shavings and hay. They roll over a carrot and some plips and a *Fur & Feather*. There's a picture of Santa on the front of the *Fur & Feather* and I pick it up.

He's sitting on a stool. There's lots of children gathered round him and behind him are rabbits in their wire pens. It's Santa visiting a rabbit show somewhere. Maybe Greenland. Greenland's a bit like Sweden. It's frosty bright with lots of mountains, and it's where Santa lives. I don't know if I believe in him. Finbar does. He says Santa's like Jesus because he's good and kind. He hasn't died to save us all though and Finbar says he'll never do that because he's got his elves to look after and Rudolph with the red nose and he's got tons of presents and stuff to deliver at Christmas. Grandad says he delivered my Bugs Bunny alarm. But there's no chimney in our flat and Santa comes down chimneys, that's what Finbar says, and I didn't hear no sleigh bells. I asked Mummy about Santa.

—Is Santa 'tend? I asked.

—Some people think he is, Lily, she said.

—Do you think that? I asked.

—I don't know what to think, she said.

I drop the *Fur & Feather* on the floor and kick some shavings over Santa's face, then I run to Grandad. A man in a yellow jumper's helping him. He's lifting the rabbit boxes off the trolley and putting them on the floor and then Grandad's moving them with his feet. He pushes the boxes with his feet so they're closer to the rabbit pens and he puffs and pants.

—Are you OK? asks the man in the yellow jumper.

—Can I help? I ask.

Grandad nods. He gives me the padlock keys. His face is sweaty and his mouth is straight, not smiley.

—There's a good girl, he gasps, and he sits on a chair.

There are millions of rabbit shows in the world. They're happening all the time, all over, on Saturdays and Sundays mostly. Finbar says some countries don't have Saturdays and Sundays. He says they have weekends. Weekends happen at the end of weeks. They're like Saturdays and Sundays except they're not because they're joined together. Finbar says there are loads of weekends in Italy. Italy is a hot country and they eat ice-cream and spaghetti hoops there. The people in Italy have black hair and most of them are very beautiful.

Rabbits are very beautiful too. Even the wild ones. They have the kindest faces and they feel warm and soft. Grandad says some people like farmers can't see the beauty in rabbits. He says farmers think rabbits are good for one thing only: the stewpot. That makes me feel shivery and sick.

Run rabbit, run rabbit.

Farmers shoot rabbits.

Run rabbit, run rabbit.

Then they cut their fur off.

Run rabbit, run rabbit.

Then they put the baldy rabbits in a big saucepan of water with carrots and onions and heat it all up.

Run rabbit, run rabbit.

Mummy's eaten rabbit.

Don't you stop.

She went for a meal with this ugly man one time. He wore green boots and a red jacket with fringes on and he had bunches in his hair. He wasn't my daddy, he was Mummy's friend, and I was pleased about that. I want to see my daddy but I didn't want the ugly man to be him, no way. He was ugly and he didn't say anything to me and he smoked and Mummy hates smoking but she let him puff in our bedroom. She was looking for her jumper and he came in and puffed and she chucked her clothes about and then I had to go to sleep with the fag-puff floating round my head. It was horrible. Mummy said he was a friend but I don't think he was a proper one because he wasn't kind, he wasn't like Finbar is with me; he smoked and he made Mummy eat rabbit. True-life. She told me the next day. I was watching *Pet Rescue* and a little rabbit was getting his ear mended on it and he was being ever so good and Mummy sat next to me on the sofa and we cuddled up and it was nice, she was being nice to me, and then she said she didn't mean to but she'd had some pie with this man and it was a lovely flavour and she asked him what was in the pie and he told her it was beer and rabbit.

—MUMMY! I screamed.

I wriggled out her arms. I sat up.

—You ate a rabbit! A real live rabbit!

—No, it was a dead rabbit, said Mummy. —Don't be so sentimental.

—No! I screamed.

Grandad came into the front room.

—What's this? he said. —What's going on?

—Mummy says I'm mental!

—What? said Grandad.

—A dead rabbit! Mummy ate a rabbit!

—Come on now, said Mummy, and she grabbed me and put her arms round me and tried to cuddle me some more.

—No, I said.

I wriggled free.

—It was only a rabbit, she said.

—I hate you! I cried.

I was doing some tears. Mummy hates tears.

—Stop those tears now, she said.

—La la la.

—Just leave her, said Grandad.

—Stop it now.

Mummy put her hands on my shoulders and pressed her fingers in.

—There's no need, Lily.

—Leave her, Donna, said Grandad. —I'll talk to her later.

—There's no need, Lily, she said.

She was pinching me.

—Go away! I cried.

—Stop that now, she said, and she pinched me harder.

—Someone's going to get hurt, said Grandad.

—Not me, she said. Her thumbs were near my mouth. —I'm not being the silly one.

I bit her thumbs.

—FUCK! she said, and she let go of me. —Fuck.

She shook her hands and looked at the floor. I looked at her face. She sniffed. She put her hands between her knees. Sniff. She wasn't very happy, I could tell.

—Soz, I said. —Sorry.

—Come on, Lily, said Grandad. —Best get out of here. Come on now.

He held out his hand.

—I'll put you to bed, he said.

Later, when I was in my 'jamas, Grandad told me a story. It was about when he ate rabbit too. —I was just a boy, Lily, he said. —My Mum and Dad didn't have much money, and rabbits were free. There were so many wild ones running in the fields. Dad caught one most weeks and Mum would skin it and cook it. Those rabbits helped us keep fit and healthy.

—Oh, I said, and I touched my face. My cheeks felt hard and sore. They were covered with dried-up tears. I felt like I was going to cry some more. —Will you eat Lincoln? I asked.

—No, Grandad smiled. —I haven't eaten rabbit in years, and I wouldn't eat Lincoln because she's my special jumping rabbit.

—What about Tamworth? I said. —And Newbiggin-by-the-Sea?

—I wouldn't eat any of my English because they're not for eating. They're for showing.

—Oh, I said.

—For showing, said Grandad. —At shows. Not for the stewpot.

—Oh, I said.

—There's more to rabbits than their meat, said Grandad.

—That's what showing's about. There's their coat to consider and their size and their shape and their breed. You know about breed, don't you, Lily?

I nodded. Grandad had told me about it before, lots of times. He'd told me that there are Eng*lish* people from Eng*land* and African people from Africa and Indian people from India and Swedish people from Sweden, and English and Swedish have white skin and African have black skin and Indian have browny skin, and Indian people are smaller than English, and African have black scratchy hair and Swedish, Indian and English people don't. So there's an English breed of people and an Indian one, an African one and a Swedish one. And it's the same with rabbits. Except they're not all called after countries. Some are called . . .

—What's the breed with the floppy ears? asked Grandad.

Some are called after . . .

—F . . . lop, said Grandad.

What?

—F . . . lop f . . . lop f . . . lop, said Grandad.

Sounds?

—Lop, I said.

—Clever girl, said Grandad. —And . . . ? Do you know any more? Different kinds of Lop? The . . .

Grandad hunched up, made himself small.

—Hi ho, hi ho, he said.

—Dwarves! I said. —Snow White and the Seven Dwarves! Dwarf Lop! Dwarf Lop!

—And . . . ? Grandad hunched himself even smaller. —Teeny weeny . . .

—Yes! I said. I knew this one. —Mini Lop!

—Good. Grandad nodded. —What other breeds besides Lop? What do I breed?

—Easy-peasy: English.

—Yes, and . . . what other breeds do you see at the shows?

—Mmm . . .

—Think of sunshine, said Grandad. —And putting that cream on, sun something cream.

I shook my head.

—Tan, said Grandad.

—Oh, I said. Then it came to me. Just like that. —Silver Wolf?

—Close, said Grandad. —But it's fox not wolf. Silver Fox. And there's a Swiss Fox. That's a rare one. Other rares are the Tri Colour Dutch, Sallander T, and Blue Vienna. Mind you the Mini Lop was rare once.

—They're Fancy, I then said, because I was remembering, like in a dream, stuff about the shows.

—Well! said Grandad.

I smiled and did my secret rabbit sign. I was even smelling the shows in my head, the poo and wee and hay, the hot chocolate drinking chocolate, the fag and pipe puff. I coughed. —Fancy, Fur and . . .

—Rex. Grandad smiled. —We'll make a fancier out of you yet, Lily Garner, he said.

—OK, park yourself, says Grandad.

He points at the stairs that go to the stage, and I do as I'm told. I pretend I'm driving Uncle Paul's bluey car and I look in my mirror and steer my steering wheel and I move backwards because I'm good at that. Brmm. Brmm. I don't trip or anything. See. I'm a natural. My leg-wheels bump into the stairs and I stop. Eeek! I pull on my brakes and sit down. I park myself. But it's a long way for my bum to go and it's like I'm whooshing through the air until my bum hits a step.

Uff!

—Ow!

I'm parked, on step number one. I stretch my leg-wheels out.

—Here, says Grandad, and he hands me my plate. It's full of stuff: a crispy cake, a Penguin biscuit and a packet of Monster Munch. I rest it carefully on my leg-wheels.
—I'm going to have to go. Won't be long.

I nod. I know.

He won't be long but he has to go and see to his rabbits. He's got to leave me and settle them into their pens with hay and water and carrots. He's got to talk to them and tell them to be good and to lie still when the judges look at them and ruffle their fur and pull their ears and count their spots.

—I'll be over there. See? I won't be far.

I nod my head and Grandad bends his creaky knees and puts my raspberry Panda on the floor.

—Mind you don't knock it over, he says, and then he goes, not very far, to the pens, and it's OK.

He's leaving me but it's OK because he's not leaving me true-life. He's still about. I can see his spiky hair and his rabbit-show jacket and I can hear his croaky voice with my supersonic ears.

—In you go, Hull, he says. —Hup.

I take a bite of my crispy cake. It's sticky. It's made of honey and sugar and Rice Krispies. Grandad got me it from one of the ladies behind the counter. It cost 15p.

The old-age man in the white coat and hat walks up to me and smiles.

—Hello, missy, he says.

I chew my crispy cake. —Mmm, I say.

—You're going to have to mind out the way, he says. —I need up.

—Mmm, I say.

—Shift then, he says.

He's got a silver cup in his hand and a wooden shield covered in little metal circles.

—Your Grandad's name's on here. Did you know that? he says, and he waves the shield.

—Mmm, I say, and I shift my bum along the step. I do it carefully because I don't want to spill my stuff.

—Three times.

The old-age man stares at the shield.

—Mmm, I say, and I swallow a lump of my crispy cake.

—Nice to see you're taking an interest, he says.

I take another bite.

—Got to get on, he says, and he clomps past me.

I can hear his shoes banging on the stage and the stage boards going CREEEK, and I reach for my Panda and take a sip. It's raspberry flavour but it's blue like Uncle Paul's bluey windows. It turns your tongue blue. It's cool.

—Dearie me, says a lady. —That can't be good for you. Look at the colour of that.

She parks her trolley and nudges a fat lady and this lady parks her trolley too.

—What flavour's that then? she says. She pulls a face. —Paint stripper?

She laughs and dribble comes out her mouth and she wipes it up with the back of her hand. She's not very pretty. She's got chubby cheeks and a blobby mole on her chin and she's got scruffy grey hair pushed under a hairband. The hairband's got writing on in puffy paint. Probably her name. Bethany's got one with her name on. She got it at the seaside. She went under the sea to Disneyland and she went to the seaside too and she bought the hairband with her seaside money. She didn't buy me one.

—She's not talking to us, says the fat lady's friend.

I blow bubbles in my drink.

—You belong to Jim Phillips, don't you, love? says the fat lady.

I blow some more bubbles. I'm not supposed to talk to strangers.

—Jim's your grandad, isn't he?

I take a sip of drink.

—Not as friendly as Jim, she says, and she winks at her friend, I don't know why.

She crouches down to undo the travel box that's on her trolley, and the other lady crouches too, and they put their heads close together and they whisper. I can't work out their whispers. They sound rude like someone going to the loo. Psst. Psst. Psst. I shuffle my bum. Perhaps I can see their lips. No. I shuffle my bum again. I still can't see and Tom's pants are up my crack and I can't pull them out because of the plate on my knees.

I sip my drink.

The ladies click open the locks on their travel boxes and undo the straps. The boxes aren't normal size. They're wide and ever so long.

I blow more bubbles.

The fat lady puts her hands into her box. —Typical, she says.

I don't know why.

Her friend nods and the fat lady lifts a rabbit out of her box. He's a giant, grey, with huge floppy ears, and he makes her wobble. Wibble wobble. She drops him in one of the big wire pens pushed against the stage. There's only four of them and they stand on the floor, side by side, and there's nothing on top or under them. They're made of extra thick wire.

—Phew! she says.

Her friend smiles. Then she pulls a rabbit from her box

and he's a giant too and she drops him into the next-door pen, and the sawdust flies up around him and he blinks his eyes.

—Well.

She locks the pen and claps her hands.

—Time for a snack.

—Some of Marjorie's coffee cake, says the fat lady, and they waddle off down the hall.

I watch the giant rabbits. They don't do anything. They sit very still and they blink their eyes and they breathe. That's important. Breathing. It's important for their hearts.

One time, Mrs Meadows did a Pets Day. She said we could bring our pets into class and show them off and talk about them.

—As long as nobody brings a crocodile or a mountain lion, she said, and then she laughed – Ha! Ha! – like that and we laughed too because it's nice making noise because we're not allowed normally, especially when we're doing our reading and writing, no way.

We laughed and laughed and my throat was getting sore like Grandad's does when he's feeling poorly.

—CHILDREN!

Mrs Meadows banged the register on her knees and scared us.

—QUIET!

We did as we were told.

—Right, she said. —Any questions?

Finbar asked if he could bring Zippy Snake.

—How long is he? she asked. —Is he big?

Finbar picked up his ruler.

—Same as this, he said.

—Just a little one, then, she said. —That's fine but I don't want you bringing him in your pocket, he must be in a tank or a margarine carton or something like that. OK?

Finbar's mummy drove Finbar and Zippy to school in her big white car. She helped Finbar carry Zippy into the classroom. Zippy was in his tank, on his twig. He was wound round his twig and he looked ever so happy. Finbar's mummy patted Finbar on the head and told him to have a lovely day. Sometimes his mummy's kind like that.

I looked at Zippy. It wasn't fair. Kelly had her worm, Wilma had her woodlice, Ben had his rat, and Jamie Ling had his thing that changed colours, and Finbar had Zippy the snake, and I didn't have nothing. I had some *Fur & Feather*s and a photo of Chesterfield winning a prize and some certificates and one rosette and my diary with the plip in but I didn't have a real live pet.

I'd asked Grandad if I could take in some rabbits, some nice baby does, but he'd said no, rabbits have supersonic ears and it wouldn't be good for them, children squashing round, squealing and screaming at them.

—But it's noisy at shows, I'd said.

—I'm not going to argue, Lily, he'd said. —What if someone feeds them chewing gum, what if someone takes in a dog? Dogs hate rabbits. They'll snarl and bark and you know how that'll upset them. It could kill them. Rabbits have very fragile hearts. Do you know what fragile means?

I'd shrugged my shoulders.

—Breakable. Eggshells are fragile, Lily, and so are rabbits' hearts.

But Mrs Meadows invited a pet man from a pet shop and he brought a rabbit and a dog. The rabbit was a giant one with long floppy ears and the dog was small like a Furby. The pet man put the rabbit and the dog on the mat together, side by side, and I was scared. I thought the dog was going to fragile the giant rabbit's heart.

—Don't, I said.

—It's all right, said the pet man. —The rabbit won't eat him.

I shook my head. It didn't make sense to me. Rabbits eat carrots and greens and mix and hay, not dogs.

The pet man stroked the rabbit and patted the dog.

—Which one do you like best? he said. —Rabbit or dog?

I stuck up my hand, and he nodded at me.

—Rabbit, I said.

—Why's that? smiled the man. —Because he's the biggest?

—No, I said.

He was stupid, that man.

—My grandad's got English, I said, and I held up the rosette. —He wins prizes.

—Aah, said the pet man. —The English Spot.

—Yes, I said.

—So why do you like rabbits better than dogs, Lily? said Mrs Meadows. She was sitting on her teacher's chair near the Knex.

—They've got supersonic ears, I said.

—You mean they can hear a pin drop? said the pet man.

I looked at Mrs Meadows. She was being nice. She was smiling and nodding and encouraging me. —Go on, Lily. Can they hear something as quiet as a pin dropping on the floor?

—Yes, I said. —True-life.

The pet man fiddled with his coat. He was wearing a white coat like a judge but he didn't have rabbit badges on it, just writing on the pocket near his boobies and a picture of a fish blowing bubbles.

—Well, he said, and he looked at me. —You're right, Lily. Rabbits can hear incredibly well but so can dogs, and dogs can answer back, dogs will hear a noise and bark in response.

—Oh, I said.

—Yes, and if a dog hears a frightening noise, Lily, then it'll bark fiercely in response to scare the maker of that noise away, whereas rabbits would be too timid to answer back even if they could.

—Oh, I said.

I didn't like the pet man. He was muddling me.

—Do you understand, Lily? said Mrs Meadows.

—No, I said.

—OK, said the pet man. —Let me put it simply. Rabbits are beautiful creatures but they're no match for dogs. They have excellent hearing but they can't do anything about what they hear, except run away.

—Well, I don't think that's a bad thing, do you, children? said Mrs Meadows. —Sometimes it's better to run than stay and fight and get hurt, don't you think?

I finish my Panda and blow into the empty bottle.
It makes a nice whistling noise. I whistle 'Spice Up
Your Life' and then I shove the bottle between my legs,
between my food plate and my crack so it looks like I've
got a willy. I stare at my willy and put my finger in it.
Willies are so stupid. They're like worms. I wiggle my
finger. Yuk. Fancy having an ugly worm in your pants.

—Stop it! I say to the giant rabbits.

They're staring at me with their sad eyes. Giant rabbits
always have sad eyes. Perhaps because of their fragile
hearts. Perhaps because they're too giant to run around
and play or do anything.

Fee Fi Fo Fum.

Rabbit can't budge because of his tum, his bloody
big bum.

Ho hum.

Yum yum.

That's a poem. I made it up. Just now. In my head.
All by myself. I'm good at poems. Because I can be
very imaginative, Mrs Meadows says, when I'm not
fidgeting. Imaginative means using your imagination
and imagination is something to do with your brain,
but it's not to do with the facts and information bit of
your brain, it's to do with the colourful bit where dreams
and pictures and make-believe happen. Mrs Meadows
says you can get famous from being imaginative at
poems; you can be on telly and make lots of money
and meet the Queen and get to wear glittery clothes and
things. I might get famous one day too, Mrs Meadows
says, if I learn how to write my poems down. That'd
be cool.

—Wouldn't it? I say to the rabbits, and they blink at me.

Sad eyes.

What a surprise.

I open my Monster Munch.

Flies.

A lovely smell puffs from the bag. If I was a boy I'd swap my willy for a packet of Monster Munch, any day.

—Chesterfield, whispers Grandad.

I nod.

We're standing by the piano. It's in the corner by the stage. It's not on the stage because that would take up too much space, that's what Grandad says. It's big and brown and its lid is up so you can see its teeth. They're white and black. The white teeth are long and the black are short because black teeth are mouldy and rotten and they can't grow. Kelly's got black teeth. She's in my class but she's not a piano. She's a Tortoise and she's got black teeth because she eats too many sugary sweeties and Tortoises shouldn't do that because they're only supposed to eat green healthy stuff, the same as rabbits.

—Are you watching, Lily? whispers Grandad.

I nod. I'm watching a man with hairy whiskers carry Chesterfield to the long table covered in the white cloth, the one near the piano. The man wears a coat like the old-age man but no hat.

—He's a judge, I say.

—That's right, whispers Grandad.

—He's going to look at Chesterfield, I say. —To see if he can get him a BOB.

—That's right. But keep your voice down. We mustn't put them off.

The judge puts Chesterfield on the table. Then another judge comes with another English rabbit and puts him on the table too.

—Is that Hull? I ask.

—Quieter, please, Lily, says Grandad. He fiddles with his shirt, around the collar. —Hull and the others will be brought out later. There's a lot of English to get through.

—Oh, I say.

Grandad nods.

—I'm going to have to sit down, he says, and he puts one hand on the piano and some of its teeth go plink, really loud.

—Grandad! I say.

—Sorry, he says, and he bends his creaky knees and pulls a stool out from under the piano. It's long and green with a spongy seat. Grandad brushes the seat with a hand, then sits. He undoes his jacket. —That's better.

He pats the spongy seat.

—There's room for a little one, he says. —Come on, Lily.

I do as I'm told. I sit beside him and I hold his hand. It feels wet and cold.

We watch another judge come to the table and another and another but the last one doesn't bring a rabbit with him, he brings some paper clipped to a board instead. He's like the man who came to Grandad's door, who wanted to take the rabbits away. Except he's not that man because he tucks the board under his arm to feel in his pocket and I can see there's certificates clipped to the board. He's a judge and he loves rabbits and he doesn't want to take them away; he wants to give them certificates like the ones Grandad's pinned on Granny's wardrobe. Certificates are prizes like rosettes and rosettes are rose-shaped and certificates are white with crinkly edges, like crinkly crisps. The crinkly edges are pinky-red.

The man with the certificates gets a pen out of his pocket and clicks it. He nods at the judges who hold the rabbits still on the shiny white cloth.

—In the round, says the man with the certificates. —Let's begin.

The judges stroke the rabbits. The rabbits are all English Spots with black pointy ears and noses and black stripes running down their backs and black spots on their sides. The judges brush their hands along the rabbits' sides. They're show rabbits, the ones Mummy doesn't like, the creepy-perfect ones. Except they're not. Because most of them are playing tricks. Grandad's explained it to me. It's to do with the rules. A rule's a rule. The judges are like teachers and God and they're like what Mummy wants to be; they're like solicitors who make up rules and they look at the rabbits to check they're doing the rules properly. Normally loads of rabbits do the rules wrong and there's just one excellent rabbit that's doing them right, that's not playing tricks or anything. This excellent rabbit is the winner. She gets the BOB. BOB doesn't mean poo or squits. It's a prize, a certificate and sometimes a rosette, and it means Best Of Breed. Grandad's rabbits are mostly BOBs and sometimes they're Best Fancy too and sometimes they're BISs. A BIS is better than a BOB and a Fancy. A BIS means Best in Show. The rabbit that wins the BIS is the most perfect rabbit in the whole wide show and it's not doing anything wrong at all.

—Beautiful, whispers Grandad. —Are you watching, Lily?

I nod. I'm watching.

The man with whiskers strokes and pats Chesterfield. He's wearing white gloves on his hands. The other judges wear white gloves too and they stroke and pat their rabbits and number five with the board asks them questions and writes down loads of words.

—Moulting, anybody? he asks.

—Mmm, mumbles judge number two. He ruffles his rabbit's fur.

—Stray spots?

—Mmm, mumbles judge number three, and he points to a spot on his rabbit's side.

—Missing cheek spots, anybody?

—Mmm, mumbles number four, and he points to his rabbit's head.

—Balanced work? Head and saddle? Haunches?

—This buck here, mumbles number one with the whiskers. He places his hands over Chesterfield's bum.

—Good, whispers Grandad. —Well done.

Number five scribbles with his pen. He fills one page with scribble and starts on the next. He's getting sweaty. He's got sweats under his arms, big round circles, and the other judges have got some too and number three's baldy head is shining wet. They're wearing themselves out, doing too much like Mummy. They fluff up the rabbits' fur with their gloves. They look in the rabbits' ears. They pat and stroke the rabbits, patting and stroking, patting and stroking; their arms and hands doing movements like old-age steam trains chugging along. Then the man with whiskers suddenly throws Chesterfield on his back. Then hup! on his bum. Then hup! on his back.

—There he goes, whispers Grandad.

I nod.

Chesterfield goes hup! and so do all the other bunnies, hup! in the air.

—Beautiful, whispers Grandad. —Poetry in motion.

—Oh Grandad, I say. —I know about that. I'm imaginative at poetry . . .

—Later, please, Lily. I'm trying to concentrate.

—Bunny bunny. It isn't funny . . .

—Shush, keep your voice down! whispers Grandad. —You mustn't disturb the judges.

I do as I'm told. I close my mouth and swallow my voice right down and I hear a water noise in my head. It's not fair. I don't know why I have to shush. The ladies behind the counter are clinking cups and plates, the guinea-pigs are squeaking, doors are banging, and the English judges are mumbling.

I swing my legs. I wriggle.

Something's tickling my crack. It's tickling under my skin. It's hot. A sign. I need to tell Grandad. I need to bring my voice back up and tell him I'm having a sign.

—Grandad.

Not a metal sign with a picture on, or writing.

—Grandad.

Not my secret rabbit sign. But a body sign.

Body signs tell us things, Mrs Meadows says. They

give us information. They tell us if we're hungry (the sign for this is tummy rumbles) or tired (yawns) or busting for a wee (hot tickles). I'm always getting hot tickles. I get them in literacy hour especially and when I ask Mrs Meadows if I can go to the loo she tells me to pretend I'm a puppy because puppies can forget their hot tickles and hold in their wee until their owners let them out to do it. Then it whooshes from their willies and cracks, down the sides of lampposts normally. But I'm no good at pretending I'm a puppy because I'm a Tortoise and they wee when they like and I want to be a Rabbit and they wee when they like too, they get their hot tickles and jump in their wee corners and just piddle, like that.

—Grandad, I say. —I'm busting. My body's doing me a sign.

—Quiet, says Grandad, and he squeezes my hand.

—But I'll pee Tom's pants! I say. —I'll pee my leggings! I did it at Aunty Chris's, Grandad! I'll do it again!

Judge number five makes a tutting noise and taps his pen on his board. He stares at Grandad and me.

—You'll get me disqualified, whispers Grandad.

I hold my crack. I wriggle. I keep wriggling, I can't help it, and Grandad sighs. He lets go of my hand.

—Stand up, he says.

I hold my crack and I stand slowly so the wee doesn't rush out. Grandad copies me. He doesn't hold his crack because men don't have them, but he stands slowly and carefully.

—Right, he sighs. —The loos.

He looks round the hall and I do too because I know about loos, I know how to spot them. They have pink doors for ladies and blue doors for men and the doors have pictures on. They're not very good pictures normally. There's a man that goes on the door to the men's toilets and a lady that goes on the door to the ladies' and they don't have ears or eyes or mouths or fingers and their arms and legs are fat. The man has a square, that's his jacket, and the lady has a triangle and sometimes there's a wheelchair too. They're toilet signs, not body ones, and they're instead of words because words are difficult for children like me.

—I can't see them, whispers Grandad. —Can you?

I hold his hand and shake my head. I can see some judges, that's all. They're carrying more English rabbits to the table. They pass my eyes and then there's zero, nought, nothing in my way, and I can see right to the back of the hall. I can see the green doors and the feed man and his sacks of mix and hay and I can see the loos, pink and blue. Top marks! Top marks! Yes!

—Grandad! I say.

He squeezes my hand.

—There's the loos!

Sometimes Grandad lets me go to the loos on my own at the shows. It's safe, he says, because nobody robs little girls at the shows, they only steal rabbits away. One time somebody tried to steal Lincoln. They fiddled with the padlock on her pen. Grandad showed me. There was a bit of metal stuck in the keyhole. Poor Lincoln. The robbers would've made her have babies, that's what Grandad said.

—Ow! I say.

Grandad's holding my hand ever so tight and he's squashing my fingers.

—Grandad, I say.

I look up at him but he doesn't look at me. His mouth is straight, not smiley, and his eyes are staring at the 'pig pens like he's seen a scary thing, Dracula or Mickey or a ghost. Brr. I shiver. Perhaps he's seen a ghost.

—Grandad? I say. —Is it a ghost?

A scary ghost floating round the 'pig pens.

Grandad shakes his head but doesn't say no.

—Something like that, Lily, he says.

God.

He's seen something like a ghost. That's what he says. Down by the 'pig pens. I look. I have to look. There's Maud. She's not a ghost. She's a floury-faced lady and she's fussing with a guinea-pig. She's holding it in the air and she's kissing it yuk! on the nose. There's loads of chairs piled up and there's a man in a long black coat with curly hair. He's got curly hair and he's all eyes and I'm all eyes and he's looking at me.

Jesus. Mary.

—Grandad, I say. My mouth is wobbly.

It's the smelly man.

Grandad lets go of my hand. —There they are! he says.

He's a stranger. He's danger. He does tricks and he's looking at me.

—The loos are near the feed stall. Can you see?

He's a ghost.

—Is he the ghost?

My heart is thumping.

—Ghost? says Grandad, and he glances at me and I point at the smelly man and Grandad doesn't look but his mouth stays straight, not smiley, and I know it's true, true-life.

The smelly man is watching me. He's a smelly ghost.

Grandad puts his hands on my shoulders and turns me. —The loos are there, at the far end, he says. —See?

There's the blue door and the pink door, and they're not near the smelly man, the ghost man.

—Now, scoot!

They're far far away.

Grandad pushes me.

—Come on, Lily! Hurry, please. Scoot!

I feel whizzy. I'm running and jumping. It's like I'm Lincoln. Hup! Hup! Hup! I do the triple. Down the hall. Hup! I go. Hup! Past the judging table and the rabbit pens and the sacks of mix and hay. Hup! To the pink door. I'm puffing and panting. I gob on the floor. I hold my belly and feel my wee. It's tickling me. I turn to wave at Grandad. But he's not looking. His arms are folded across his chest and he's staring at the 'pig pens and the ghost man, I know.

He's waiting for something to happen. He's doing what Mrs Meadows does. She folds her arms like that when she's annoyed with Finbar and me, and she's waiting for us to settle down and behave.

—I'm waiting, she says. —Lily Garner. Finbar Rex Smedley. Yes, you!

Her voice is strict and she waits and waits and we try to behave, honest to God, but it's hard because we're just being cheerful and bright because we're dead good friends.

Finbar believes in ghosts. Not cartoon ones like on *Scooby Doo*, like Casper the friendly ghost. But real-on-this-planet ones. Finbar believes in them more than he believes in Santa and Jesus Christ who died to save us all. He believes because he's seen one. He was visited.

Real-on-this-planet ghosts are people who've been put in the churchyard but didn't want to be. They're in the middle between dead and alive. They make woo noises and they're floaty and see-through and go poof! from one place to another like magic.

Granny's in the churchyard but she's not a ghost. She was ready to be there, that's what Aunty Sheila says. She was ready for Grandad to put her in a box under the ground. She wanted to turn into bones. She didn't want to stay alive on this planet Earth and see me and Tom and Bethany and Baby Pod and Grandad's rabbits and Lincoln jumping. Hup! Hup! She didn't want to see the sunshine any more or get up with the birds. Get up! Get up! Get out of bed! Cheer up! Cheer up! She didn't want any more of that because she was fed up.

Finbar's not allowed in the churchyard. His mummy won't let him, that's what he says. She won't let him go to Azad's either because she thinks it stinks. But that's where he saw the ghost. He needed some scratchings for

Zippy the snake. He begged and begged but his mummy wouldn't budge.

—Wait for the pub to open, she said.

—But Zippy's starving, he said.

—Zippy'll live, she said.

Finbar's mummy is heart-yes sometimes. Zippy was hanging off his twig. He looked flat. His tongue wouldn't come out. He looked sad. Finbar told me. He had to do something. So he pinched 10p from his mummy's purse and went to Azad's, all by himself. He was ever so brave. He creeped from his flat. He ran through hell-hole warren. A crazy-on-drugs man jumped out of a dark corner and grabbed his Superman bag. Finbar grabbed it back. He kicked the man in the willy and ran to the lift. Kelly was in there, sitting on the floor. She was singing nobody likes me. She put her arms round Finbar's legs. She tried to kiss him. But he punched her in the nose and ran from the lift. He ran from Rabbit Tower and through the play-park. He ran past the garages and he saw Mickey with some of Grandad's rabbits and he judoed Mickey to let the rabbits go. It was like on *Free Willy*. Mickey let them go. They were ever so grateful. They jumped and hid under a car. It was getting dark. A drunk daddy came singing down the street. Finbar hid behind a dustbin. He was puffing and panting. He checked his 10p was still in his pocket and then he felt the cold hands on his shoulders. Ghost hands! He gulped and turned around.

—It was my brother, Finbar said. —Cross my heart.

—Your brother? I said.

—Kieran, he said.

—Kieran? I said.

—Kieran who went away on the motorbike, he said.

—Your big brother? I said.

—It was horrible, Finbar said.

He was shivering and his eyes were wet. Sometimes Finbar's a liar. I think he was lying about Mickey and the rabbits and the crazy-on-drugs man, but I don't think he was lying about Kelly and Kieran. He wasn't 'tending about Kieran.

—He was bleeding, he said.

—True-life? I said.

—Not wet blood, he said. —Dry ghost blood. He had a hole in his head, just there. He was floating.

—This is scary, I said.

—He was floating in the air and he came up to my ear. He whispered in my ear.

—I don't like scary.

—He told me a secret.

—A secret's a secret, I said. —You have to keep a secret.

—Oh, said Finbar.

I didn't want no ghost secret.

—You mustn't tell anybody . . .

—Oh, said Finbar.

—Or he'll find out and he'll be cross, he'll come back, I said. —You mustn't tell me.

—Oh, said Finbar.

—Soz, I said.

There's somebody in the loo. They've been in there ages.
Parp. Parp. It's disgusting. They won't shut up.

—Shut up, I whisper, and I pinch my crack to keep
in my wee.

Parp. Parp.

I'm busting.

I jump up and down.

—Hurry up. Hurry up.

The pink door opens. The door from the hall. It's a
girl. I look at her. A guinea-pig squeaks. The door closes.
She looks at me. Parp! Parp! We giggle.

—She's been ages, I say, and I nod at the loo. —I'm
busting.

—And me.

The girl crosses her legs and leans on the sink.

—I'm going to wet myself, I say.

—And me, she says.

She's wearing a furry hairband with rabbit ears on.

—That's good, I say, and I want to give her my
secret sign but I can't let go of my crack. —Your
hairband's good.

She smiles. —Woolies, she says.

I don't know what she means.

Parp!

The girl nods at the sink and her rabbit ears jiggle.

—I'm going to do it in there, she says. —I'm going to widdle in there.

—True-life? I say.

Paarp!

—I do it at home, she says. —When Daddy's taking too long.

—I don't have a daddy, I say.

—Wicked! she says, and she fetches the chair that's under the machine, not the towel machine but the machine full of sticks with a picture of a lady on the front. The lady's wearing a swimsuit and she's skipping. She's got a stupid smile on her face.

—They're for ladies who can have babies, I say, and I point at the sticks.

—My mummy's having a baby, the girl says, and she puts the chair near the sink and stands on it. —She's always having them.

—I'm an only-bonely, I say.

—Wicked! she says, and she fiddles with her leggings.

Paarp!

She giggles.

—I hate leggings, I say.

She pulls hers down.

—And me, she says.

She's wearing flowery knickers and she pulls these down too and sticks her bum in the sink and wees. Whoosh!

—Cool, I say.

—I'm going to be your friend, she says. —I've decided.

—Honest? I say.

She nods and pulls up her things.

—Your turn, she says, and she gets off the chair.

I climb up. —Don't look at my boy pants, friend, I say. —Promise.

—Cross my heart and hope to fry, she says.

Paarp!

That's not me.

—Ah. Oooh.

That's me.

—Finished, I say, and I jump from the chair. —Hold hands?

My friend nods and we hold hands and open the pink door together.

—We've got to be careful, I say.

—Why? she says.

—There's a smelly man. He's like a ghost. He's outside, I say. —I think he's after me.

We peek through the door into the hall.

—Can you see him? she whispers.

—Hello there, says a man with a long black beard.

—Aargh! we say.

He's not the ghost but he's sitting in a deckchair by the door and he stinks of pipe and he's got a bunch of carrots in his lap and he waves the carrots at us.

—Would you like one?

—No way! I say, and I look at my friend.

—Hate carrots, she says, and we giggle.

—With ears like that? says the man.

My friend touches her rabbit ears.

—Are they real? asks the man. —Can I stroke them?

—Don't let him, I whisper to my friend.

—Is he the smelly man? she says.

I shake my head. —He's different, I say.

—What's this? The man smiles. He shows his yellow teeth.

—But he's probably a child-catcher, I whisper. He's got black dots all over his nose.

—He'll probably steal us.

—What's this? says the child-catcher.

—He will! I whisper. —Run!

I pull my friend. She knocks into the child-catcher. She knocks his deckchair and all his carrots. She squeals.

—GIRLS! shouts the child-catcher.

His carrots fall crash! to the ground.

—RUN NOW! I shout.

—GIRLS!

—RUN!

Run rabbit. Run rabbit.

Don't you stop.

We run and run.

We run down the hall. We run through the shavings and hay. We run past the men's loos, the feed stall, a man in an apron.

—CHILDREN! he shouts.

We run past the pop counter, the chinking mugs, the hot chocolate drinking chocolate, Penguin biscuits, Panda pop and crispy cake.

Run rabbit. Run rabbit.

We run round the rabbit pens.

We run past some judges carrying rabbits.

We run to the stage.

Wham!

Our bellies bash into the stage.

—Phew! I say. —Phewyerr!

I waft my arms. I hold my belly. There's spit in my mouth and I gob it out.

—We're safe. Home.

I turn round. We're close to the giant bunnies with their giant sad eyes.

—We're home, I say.

Home sweet home. That's what Grandad and Granny called their house with the doorstep, Grandad told me. Home, home where the buffalo roam. Except there weren't any buffaloes. There was just Granny and Grandad and Old Shep and Mummy and her sisters.

—Can you see the child-catcher? pants my friend.

I look round the hall.

—I can see my grandad, I say.

He's at the end of the rabbit judging table and he's sitting on a chair that's wood like the ones we have at school. It's next to a heater. Grandad holds his hands in front of the heater and warms their fronts and backs. He does this in our flat too. He sits in his easy chair and warms his hands on the front-room fire. The fire's made of electric. It's not a proper fire like the one him and Granny had in their home sweet home. That was made of sticks and coal. Coal is hard black stuff and it comes from the ground like rock. Men have to dig to find it. They dig tunnels and it's like they're rabbits digging warrens except they don't use their bodies to dig with, they use spades and big machines.

—My grandad's over there, I say, and I point at him and then I see the smelly man, the ghost. He's holding two plastic cups and they're puffy with steam. He smiles and gives one to Grandad. Then he leans against the wall. —God.

The ghost knows Grandad. Grandad saw the ghost and now they're talking.

—He's almighty and religion, says my friend.

They're drinking cups of tea together.

—He goes to church, says my friend.

—What? I say.

The ghost's drinking tea with Grandad.

—Him?

I point at the smelly-man ghost.

—No, says my friend. —God. He's religion. He wears a white dress.

Grandad scrunches himself so I can't see his face properly, just his blobby nose, a bit of his mouth. He sips his tea in front of the heater, the fiery flames.

—It's not a nancy dress, says my friend. —God's not a nancy.

—Shush, I say, and I flap my hand because the ghost's saying something and I can't hear what.

His lips move. I watch his lips. He's not moving them wide like Mummy does in the dumb game. He's not even doing them like Grandad did when he was on the telephone to Peter. I can't work out any words.

—You know that man? I say, and I point at him again. —Can you see?

My friend nods. Her rabbit ears shiver.

—He's the ghost, I say.

—Wicked! she says.

She stares.

—Nah. He's not see-through, she says. —Ghosts are see-through.

—Oh, I say.

I look at him.

—Oh yes.

He's wearing his black coat and it's undone and he's got a woolly jumper underneath and trousers with zips and things like Kylie's. He's not see-through and he's not floating, his trainers are stuck to the ground.

—He's an alien, says my friend.

—They're green, I say.

—They don't have to be, she says. —They're talented at disguises. They've got the power. They have these rings and they rub them and then they change, just like that. There's lots of aliens about. They come from Jupiter in their ships.

Grandad puts his plastic cup on the heater. He glances round the hall. He sees my friend and he sees me but he doesn't nod or smile. I wave and do my secret sign. He doesn't wave back. He's being rude, I don't know why. He coughs and looks at the man, then he shakes his head.

—Girls go to school to get more cool, says my friend. —Boys go to Jupiter to get more stupider. The moon's made of cheese. Can you believe that?

The man walks up and down. He does small steps. Heel. Toe. Heel. Toe. Forwards and back. He says loads to Grandad. He goes on and on and I can't work out any words. He could be an alien. He stops by the heater and he puts his cup next to Grandad's and he notices me.

Jesus. Mary.

He's all eyes.

He fiddles in his coat pocket.

Alien eyes.

His coat is black.

He takes his hand out of his pocket and clicks his fingers and then there's a coin. Just like that. Shining silver in his fingers. He flicks the magic coin and it spins and he catches it before Grandad can see. He smiles.

—Wallace and Gromit went to the moon, says my friend.

He fiddles in his pocket again and tugs something out. It's more money, not silver but paper. It's brown. He shows it to Grandad.

—The penguin one was rubbish, says my friend. —Did you see the penguin one?

Grandad looks at the money, and the alien man smiles at me.

—I don't like penguins, I say. My mouth's wobbly.

Mary. Joseph.

The man's winking his alien eye at me.

—What about Pingu?

—Pingu stinks.

I grab my friend and pull her from the stage.

—Come on!

—OI! she says.

—Come on! I say. —Run!

We run past the rabbit pens. We run back down the hall. There's a gap between the rabbit pens. We run through the gap. We whiz and drop on the floor.

—Phew, I say.

—Wicked! says my friend.

Her furry ears are flopping over her face. She pushes them straight. I look around.

—It was the alien man, I say.

Brilliant. He's not followed me.

—He needs to die, says my friend. —We can shoot him. Bang bang bang!

—We've not got guns, I say. I don't like guns.

—We'll track him then, she says. —This way.

My friend crawls through the shavings and hay. I copy her. She lies on her belly and does froggy legs like she's swimming at Splash World. I do the same. She wriggles over the warm floor. I follow her. We're tracking the alien man. We're like the Red Indian people. We put our ears to the floor and we listen hard.

—This way, says my friend.

We wriggle to the rabbit judging table. There are loads of rabbits on it, lots of different breeds, and there are judges round it, mumbling and murmuring. One judge is cuddling a Lop. I know it's a Lop because of its ears. The judge takes the Lop away from the table and leaves a space.

—Through there, says my friend.

We wriggle through the space and then we're at the white cloth. It's long and dangles down over the side of the table. It nearly touches the floor. My friend wriggles and pushes it with her head. It brushes over her hair. I follow her. This is so exciting. We're under the table and it's dark like nighttime. I can hear blurry shuffles. I can hear my heart. Thump. Thump. Thumping. It's so exciting. I blink and the dark turns to dusty bits and my friend points to the judges' boots and shoes moving below the cloth. There's some brown shoes poking right beside us and I can see plips stuck to the toes and the laces tied into bows. My friend tugs one bow and it comes undone, true-life! We put our hands over our mouths so our giggles won't escape and our shoulders go up and down. Tee hee hee. Like that. Then the brown shoes move but the judge in the shoes doesn't trip over his lace which is good, I think it's good, because he's holding a rabbit and could drop it and hurt it. —I'll just put this one away, he says; that's how I know he's holding a rabbit.

My friend taps me on the shoulder. She makes a signal like one potato two potato, then she crawls along, under the table. I follow her. My nose is close to her bum. Her bum smells of soap and piddle. She stops. My nose jabs her bum.

—Listen for alien language, she whispers.

—Gobbly gobbly? I whisper. —Like that?

—Yes, she whispers.

We put our hands behind our ears. We do concentrating. We hear with our ears and listen with the rest of our bodies. We hear the aliens gobbling. We don't know how many there are. We listen to their squeaky gobbly noises. It goes into our ears and hurts our brains.

—There's zillions of them, my friend says.

—From Jupiter, I say.

—Yes, she says. —Out in the hall.

—Investigating the rabbits, I say.

She nods. —Aliens enjoy animals, she says.

She crawls a bit further. We're near the end of the table where Grandad's sitting. I can see Grandad's chair, its legs. Chairs have legs. It's true. My friend stops. I do too. God. I can hear gobbly gobbly. It's the alien man, his voice, I know. He sounds like he did in the play-park. Growly. Deep. I can see his trainers. They're walking about. I gulp. I listen. His gobbly gobbly turns into human language.

—Ancient history, he says.

Ancient's wisdom. But I don't know history.

—What's history? I whisper.

—The olden days, says my friend. —Dead people. They're history.

—Oh, I say.

My granny's dead.

—Why can't she forget? he says. —Put it behind her, move on.

She's history.

—She has moved on, says Grandad.

She's bones under the ground.

Grandad coughs.

—La la la, I say.

—She's still mouthing off, says the alien man.

—I want to be a rabbit, I say.

—Well, what do you expect? says Grandad.

—La la la, I say.

—Well, sorry I couldn't stay away, says the alien man.

—I want to be a rabbit.

—I'm not made of stone.

Granny's doorstep-stone.

—Come on then, says my friend. She crawls backwards. —This is boring. Let's go.

We're under the table. We crawl backwards, far from the alien man. His voice gets quieter. It turns into whispers. Then zero, nought, nothing, just the sounds of the judges moving the rabbits on the table above us. We're safe. I can breathe. I sit and my friend sits too. She looks at me.

—This is our cage, she says.

—What? I say.

I can breathe. I can do it properly.

—We're playing rabbits, says my friend. —This is our cage. This is the top.

She touches the table above our heads.

—This is the door.

She pats the white cloth.

—And we're the rabbits.

She smiles at me.

—Cages are cruel, I say.

That's right, that's true. Zoos have cages for elephants and tigers and lions and they're made of cold metal and they're cruel, that's what Mummy told me; they stop the animals from running about and eating humans and being happy. Rabbits don't eat humans. They eat mix and greens and hay and they're happy because they live in warrens and hutches.

—Rabbits live in hutches, I say. —Not cages.

—Hutches, says my friend.

—Yes, I say.

—OK, she says.

—We're baby rabbits, I say. —They share hutches.

—Wicked! she says. —I'm biggest with the important ears, and you're little, you're sleeping.

—OK, I say.

—Sleep then, she says.

I do as I'm told. I curl up like I'm in my mummy's nest box. I close my eyes and lick my skin. I've not got much fur. I taste salty. —I'm Totnes, I say. —That's my name.

I enjoy my mummy's boobies.

—Sniff, says my friend. —Sniff. Sniff. I'm exploring. Dig. Dig.

—Snore, I say. —Snore. Snore.

Then the important old-age man shouts really loud and wakes me.

—THIS IS AN ANNOUNCEMENT, he shouts. —WE APPEAR TO HAVE LOST A LITTLE GIRL. HER NAME IS JESSICA AND SHE'S WEARING A VERY DISTINCTIVE HAIRBAND WITH RABBIT EARS ATTACHED. JESSICA RABBIT, CAN YOU COME TO THE STAGE NOW PLEASE? YOUR GRANNY'S WORRIED ABOUT YOU.

—I'm Jessica, says my friend, and she looks at me.

—Oh, I say. I blink my eyes.

—Do you think they mean me? she says. —I think they mean me.

—You've got a very instinctive hairband, I say.

—Bye, she says, and she pushes her head at the white cloth, the door to our hutch, and she hops out.

—My name's Lily, I say, and I watch her jump away.

It's not fair. I lick my salty rabbit skin. This happens to me all the time. I make friends. Then I lose them, dead quick. I don't know why. Once I even thought I was going to lose Finbar. Finbar's my best friend. I never want to lose him but his mummy and daddy were going to take him and his brothers away to Manchester. Finbar's daddy was going to play football with Manchester United. That's what Finbar said. But then Finbar's daddy fell off a ladder and hurt his head and couldn't do headers any more, so Manchester United didn't want him. I was ever so pleased when Finbar told me. True-life.

It's quiet under the table. It's lonely without Jessica. I lick my rabbit skin and wait for the old-age man to do an announcement about me. I taste the salt and close my eyes and it goes dark in my head. The dark is black. It's boring. I open my eyes. I don't know what to do.

I look at the gap at the bottom of the white cloth where the judges' boots and shoes move about. The boots and shoes are black and brown with black or brown laces. They're boring. There's no jellies or teenager shoes with sparkly bits and flashing lights. There's no wellies or glittery sandals. I push my head under the cloth and that's better, I can see lots more. There's interesting stuff like men's legs and ladies' legs, and travel boxes pushed under pens, and a see-through bag stuffed with greens. I can see a woolly glove that's on its own lying in some shavings and some shiny gold paper, a Crunchie wrapper, I think.

Crunchies are wrapped in gold and they're chocolate with gold in the middle that fizzes in your mouth. I had one of them in my selection box at Christmas and I gave a bite to Mummy. She was ever so pleased. She said it was nearly as nice as Aero and she cuddled me. Grandad got me my Bugs Bunny alarm at Christmas and Aunty Pam gave me the selection box and Mummy got me a stocking. It was full of bits: penny chews that cost one penny and a bag of marbles and a mermaid Barbie. Mermaids swim in the sea. They're like people and they're like fish too. They've got a face and a body but they've not got legs because they've got a fish tail instead and that's how they swim. Finbar doesn't believe about mermaids. He believes about Jesus Christ who died to save us all but not about mermaids because you can't get mixed-up fish and people, that's what he says, and that's what Aunty Sheila says too. She says some things don't go together because they're too different like Grandad and Mummy. It's the same as the pairs game we do at school where gerbils can't go with chipmunks and rabbits can't go with pussy cats. Rabbits go with rabbits, that's right, I know, but that confuses me because I'm a girl and I'm a tortoise and sometimes I pretend to be a rabbit, I want to be a rabbit, so I'm mixing me up, I am.

I crawl backwards and the cloth falls and my hutch door closes on me. I'm a mixed up Lily rabbit and I sit and lick my paws. My hutch is empty, there's no water bowl or carrots or hay. It's long and dark like a tunnel, a burrow, a warren under the ground.

Wild rabbits dig warrens in fields. They have big strong legs and they dig up the grass and potatoes, cabbages and mud. They dig right down into the middle of planet Earth. First they make long entrance tunnels, then lots of other tunnels to join them up. Entrance means come in. It's like a door. You can come in and you can go out too as long as you don't get in anybody's way. The tunnel-warrens are for all the rabbits, for mummies and daddies and babies, for old-age rabbits and teenagers and children. They're like homes. They don't have windows or lights or cookers or fridges or beds but they're comfy and cosy and dry, and they're ruled by the King and Queen.

The King and Queen are the top buck and top doe. The King's OK but the Queen's bossy and heart-yes. She keeps a bit of the warren for herself. She sits in it and plips in it and she won't make space in it for any of the other bunnies. Sometimes she'll let them visit but mostly she nips them to make them go away.

I hop along my warren. I'm on my own. I'm a mixed up Lily rabbit and I want to find my family.

One's my father.

Two's my mother.

Three's my brother.

My family's left me because I fell asleep and they got hungry and needed to chomp some vegetables, I know. They're outside in the farmer's field, that's where they go. I hop along the entrance tunnel. I want to join them. I sniff the air. It smells fresh and clean like tablecloth. It's making me excited. My nose twitches and sniffs. I love fresh air. I want to feel it on my fur. I want to hop and jump in it with all my family but I'm scared. Sometimes the farmer's guarding his field with his gun.

Run rabbit, run rabbit.

He shoots at us. Bang! He shot my granny. Bang! Bang!

Run rabbit, run rabbit.

He put her in a pie. I'm missing her.

Don't you stop.

I stop.

I listen with my supersonic ears. I hear whispering like grass blowing. I hear trees creaking. I hear shuffling like my family moving about, nipping and pulling the vegetables. The sky is cloudy and white. I push it with my head and then it's gone, it's turned to cloth and it's tickling the back of my neck, and I don't know where I am. There's no field. A bright light's hurting my eyes. God. I do know where I am.

Sometimes rabbits get so frightened their eyes grow big in their heads and their bodies won't move and they want to run but can't.

Run rabbit, run rabbit.

I can't.

I do know where I am.

Grandad's in his creaky chair. I see his knobbly shoulders and his silvery hair. I see one of his old-age hands resting on his knee. I see the fiery heater flames and they're flicking and whispering like grass. I see the alien man. He's wearing trainers and he's looking at his feet. He's sort of shuffling his feet, scuffing them on the floor.

—I can't let this go, Jim, he says. —We're talking about my flesh and blood.

Flesh. I don't know what that means but I do know blood. Blood's red and it makes your body work because it goes round your body like nerves. It pumps your heart and turns you happy and alive. It helps ladies to make babies. It's good but it's bad too. It messes Grandad's hankies and it pours from rabbits' bums and Mummy's bum and it dripped out my nose. Miss Musters' hands shake when she sees blood and it floods from Aunty Pam, and you have to keep lots inside your body or else you feel sad and ill, and sometimes, this is horrible, you shrivel up and die. Dracula sucks blood out of you and makes you shrivel up and die.

Grandad coughs. —This isn't getting us anywhere, he says.

—Tell me about it, says the flesh-and-blood man, and he puts his hands in his pockets and looks away from Grandad. —Oh hello.

He looks at me.

My eyes are popping out my head and I want to move but I can't. I'm a scaredy-cat rabbit and the blood man's smiling at me. I feel sick but rabbits can't be sick. I want to poo.

—La la la, I say.

—Lily? says Grandad. —Is that you?

Grandad's voice sounds shivery. I think he's looking at me but I don't know, I can't see. My eyes are stuck. They're popping.

The flesh-and-blood man moves closer. He lifts up his coat and crouches down low and he smiles.

—Been listening in? he says.

He lets go of his coat and puts his hands on the floor. His coat is black.

—Lily, says Grandad. —Run along now.

It spreads out around him and it looks like a bat, like rubbery bat skin. Bats are sexywexy, that's what Finbar says; and some bats are OK, like Batman, and some are not, like Dracula.

Nobody likes me.

Dracula's stranger-danger. He sucked my granny, that's what Mickey says.

Everybody hates me.

My heart is going to pop.

—Lily, says Grandad. —Scoot!

—Calm down, Jim, says the flesh-and-blood man.

I think I'll go and eat worms.

—Just leave her be, says Grandad, and he creaks in his chair and gets up.

I can see him in my eye corner. He coughs. I can see his rabbit show jacket, the sleeve, his wrinkly hand. He's reaching out. He grabs the flesh-and-blood man's shoulder.

—Got me, says the flesh-and-blood man. He shudders, then winks.

—Just leave her alone, Jed, says Grandad.

Jed?

The blood man smiles at me.

It's Jed.

I say his name inside my head.

Jed. Jed. Jed.

It doesn't make sense to me.

He's the flesh-and-blood man, the smelly man, the alien man.

His coat is black.

It's Jed, not Peter.

He sighs.

Jed.

His breath blows out and touches my face and it's like fag-puff, it smells dirty. I crinkle up my nose.

—You give my love to your mum, he says, Jed says.

He knows Grandad and Grandad knows him and he knows my mummy.

—La la la, I say.

—Ah, he says, and then he tickles me with his finger, tickling me like Grandad tickles his rabbits, and I can feel his dried-up skin and his nail. They're scratchy and they hurt me. I want to get away.

—Jed, says Grandad.

—I'm hearing you, he says. —Give us a break.

—La la la, I say.

I want to move. I move.

Run rabbit, run rabbit.

I crawl backwards.

Don't you stop.

I'm under the table. I'm in my warren, my hutch. The cloth falls. My hutch door closes on me.

—La la la.

My heart is thumping.

—There, says Jed, the alien man, the flesh-and-blood man. —No harm done. Happy now?

Grandad coughs. He coughs and coughs, and the blood man sighs. I see his hands and knees through the gap at the bottom of my hutch door. He presses on his hands and pushes himself up and his coat sways and swoops. It sounds like bird. I can see his trainers. They're white with blue stripes and they're moving away from me. I close my eyes. It's dark in my head.

Baby rabbits are born blind and deaf.

I hear whispering and coughing. I stuff my paws in my ears.

They only open their eyes and ears when they're ready.

It's dark. It's quiet. I can't hear anything. Just my heart.

Baby rabbits are called the same as baby cats.

They're kittens and they grow up to be bucks and does.

Bucks and does stay awake in the day and sleep at night.

Wild bucks and does listen out for foxes and badgers and buzzards when they sleep.

Buzzards are birds and they eat rabbits. They don't buzz.

Bees buzz and they sting you with their bums.

Rabbits sit on their bums when they're awake and they lie on their sides when they're asleep.

Wild rabbits sleep on their sides and they listen out and sometimes, if they've got babies, they open their eyes and keep watch too.

Wild rabbits watch their babies to keep them safe but rabbits in hutches don't because they've got walls and holey wire and nest boxes and human beings to do it for them.

Rabbits in hutches are lazy. They don't use their ears or eyes or brains.

Wild rabbits have big brains. Rabbits in hutches don't.

Rabbits in hutches have stopped using their brains and so they've made them shrink.

One time Grandad couldn't sleep. His arms ached and his chest felt sore and he was uncomfortable on his camp bed. He was tossing and turning night after night and he didn't know what to do. Mummy said he ought to start college and write some essays because that would soon tire him out. —Don't wind me up, Donna, he said.

You can wind up clocks and watches with knobs and keys and you can wind up people by being naughty or cheeky or rude. Mummy winds Grandad, and I wind Mummy and Mrs Meadows, and Mrs Meadows winds Wilma and all the Tortoises. Mummy and Mrs Meadows are winding most of the time and I am too, I don't know why. I do it by accident. I try to be nice and good but something goes wrong with me, and I get excited and silly and all over the place, and then I'm winding.

—Soz, Grandad, I said.

I get shouted at or smacked if I wind or made to do extra work in class. It's not nice and I try to stop it happening to me.

—It's your mother who should be saying sorry, said Grandad.

—Oh, I said.

—Well, is that the time? she said. —I'm off to the library.

Mummy got two manuals about lady solicitors and a picture book about rabbits and a tape from the library. She gave me the picture book and Grandad the tape.

—There, she said. —I'm not all bad.

I said thank you but Grandad didn't. He was rude. He just took the tape and put it in his machine. Soft pretty music came out of the machine and a lady's voice that was whispery even when Grandad turned her up. She talked about sleeping. She said loads of stuff that didn't make sense to me but Grandad understood. He had to try a few things out, that's what he told me; he had to do some experiments. I'm good at experiments and I wanted to help but Grandad wouldn't let me. He said he had to do them all on his own.

Experiment Number One: stay up really late for one week. A week's a week. Grandad did as he was told. He waited until the big hand and the little hand pointed to 12, not 12 dinner-time but 12 at night when it's black and cold and teenagers do sexywexy in the park. But he still couldn't sleep.

Experiment Number Two: go to bed really early for one week. Grandad went just after *Pet Rescue*, the same time as me, but he snored for a minute, that's all. A minute's a minute. —I'm fed up, Lily, he moaned. —I've really had enough.

Grandad threw the tape away, and Mummy saw.

—That belongs to the library! she said. —I'll get charged for that!

—It belongs in the bin. It's bloody rubbish, he said.

Poor Grandad. He was fed up. He was turning just like Granny. She got fed up too. Aunty Sheila told me when we were in the churchyard looking for Granny's doorstep-stone. God. Granny had gone under the stone, under the ground because she was fed up. She'd turned into bones. Dracula had sucked her. This was frightening me.

Experiment Number Three: eat all your medicines and drink lots of beer. This was a stupid experiment. It made Grandad groan and wobble round the kitchen and it made Mummy shake him and shout in his face and it frightened me even more.

—Clear off, said Grandad to Mummy.

—La la la, I said.

—OFF! said Grandad, and he lifted his hand like he was going to whack Mummy but then he didn't, he fell and crashed on the cooker. He hurt his head.

—YOU STUPID OLD FOOL! shouted Mummy.

It was bleeding, I could see.

—La la la, I said. —La la la.

Mummy ran into the hall. She phoned Doctor Whitworth and he came straight away. Nee nah. Nee nah. It's an emergency. He had his doctor's bag that's brown and full of medicines, that I tried to pick up once, but couldn't because it's too heavy.

—What have you been doing to yourself, Jim? he said, and he put his bag down, and crouched and stared at Grandad's face.

Grandad was sitting at the table. He was holding a hanky to his head and he was drinking another bottle of beer.

—You don't need that, Jim, said Doctor Whitworth, and he moved the beer away. Then he pulled the skin round Grandad's eyes and they popped like Wigan's did when she was checked by the man with the board, the one who rang Granny's doorbell that time. —Hmm, let's see your tongue.

Grandad stuck it out. It was purple and slimy. Yuk.

—I can't sleep, he mumbled. —I've had enough.

—I'm sure you have, Jim, said Doctor Whitworth. —Can you take off your shirt?

Doctor Whitworth helped Grandad with the buttons and pushed the shirt off his shoulders. Then he tapped Grandad's skin with his cold fingers. He tapped his chest and bony back.

—One thing's for sure, Jim, he said. —A man in your condition shouldn't be sleeping on a camp bed.

—What? I said.

I didn't understand. Condition's what you put in your washing machine, it's like the flowery packet. You can put it on your hair as well to make it nice and soft. But Grandad wasn't soft. He was bony and stiff and sore. He was fed up. He'd had enough. He coughed. His shoulders scrunched up and his knobbly spine stuck out. I could see it poking through his holey vest.

—It's never been a problem before, he said.

Mummy sighed and looked at me. —Lily, she said. —Go and play in the bedroom.

I looked at her. —I don't want to, I said.

I wanted to stay and watch Doctor Whitworth make Grandad better. I wanted to see Grandad get better.

—Do it, Lily, said Mummy. —Now!

—Here.

Doctor Whitworth was fiddling around inside his

special bag. He pulled out a pen and smiled and gave it to me.

—See if you can draw me a picture.

The pen was white with a heart and some writing on. I couldn't read the writing and the heart was black and really small.

—Thank you, said Mummy.

I looked at the pen.

—It's nothing, said Doctor Whitworth. —I get them from reps all the time.

—Well, go and draw something, Lily, said Mummy. —Go on.

I took the pen and went into the hall. I opened the bedroom door. I could see the bin by Mummy's desk. It was full of crumpled pieces of paper, the rubbish bits from her essays. I stepped over the bump and I threw the pen like that and it landed on the paper. I jumped on the bed and lay down. The heart wasn't normal and red and alive. I stared at the ceiling. I didn't want to think about the heart. I stared at the big white swirls on the ceiling and I did some concentrating. I was on Mummy and Daddy's marriage bed. I could feel the lacy pillows and the fluffy blanket under me. I could feel thoughts and imagination growing in my head.

I coughed a pretend cough. I was getting old. I wasn't a little girl any more. I was growing old and poorly and sad. My body was wrinkly and my skin was itchy and dry. I had scabs on my bum and my cough was sharper than daggers. It made me squeal and bend my creaky knees. I curled up. My legs were covered in grey hairs and knobbly bumps. I coughed and clacked my falsies.

I was ancient wisdom and my body was being cruel and heart-yes to me but the bed was being kind. It was looking after my tired bones. It was warming me like a mummy-doe warms her babies. Then ping! I had a thought. Grandad could sleep in this bed with me and Mummy could sleep on the camp bed. Top marks to me. Top marks. Yes!

I jumped off the bed and ran into the hall. The front door was open. Doctor Whitworth was saying goodbye.

—NA! I shouted, because I wanted him to wait and hear my plan.

I was puffing and panting and he bent his head and looked down at me and told me to take my time. I swallowed big breaths. Mummy tutted and folded her arms.

—What is it now, Lily? she said.

I described my plan and Doctor Whitworth smiled and nodded but he wasn't listening to me, not really, I could tell. He was hearing but not listening and it was the same with Mummy because they'd already thought of a plan and they were going to do that. They'd decided. They were sending Grandad to Aunty Sheila's for a rest, they said. He would stay in Joe's room, in Joe's spare bed, until he felt better. Spare means extra. It's like plus. Joe's got his own bed plus another one. He's got an extra bed and now he was going to get my grandad too.

The flat felt funny without Grandad. Not funny ha-ha but funny sad. There were sad empty spaces in the front room and kitchen and everywhere. Grandad's things were about, his books and his chair and his rabbits but I couldn't see him or touch him or feel his skin. I couldn't sit on his knee. I couldn't hear him. There were no noises coming from his room. There were no coughs or groans or mumbles or Hup, Lincoln! That's it girl. Hup! Hup! Hup! He phoned me one time and that was nice but it was horrid too. His voice sounded quiet and far away. He said he hoped I was being good. The phone was heavy. It smelt of Grandad's runny medicine and it made me feel shivery and when Grandad wanted me to say something about school and the rabbits and Finbar I couldn't. My tongue wouldn't work. I thought I was going to be sick. I gulped and wanted to cry.

I was missing him much more than I've ever missed Granny. I wanted him back. I prayed for him to hurry up and get better and come home to the flat. I wanted him normal and around and Mummy did too because she had her college work and me to look after and the rabbits and she was feeling worn out. She told me, she told her sisters and she even told Mrs Ahmed but Mrs Ahmed was rude and didn't say one word. She just bashed her mat on the corridor wall to make the dust fly out. Mummy got annoyed then and said hello, are you there? But Mrs Ahmed had zipped her lips. She wouldn't speak or smile or anything. She stepped through the dusty clouds and disappeared – poof! – into her flat.

Mummy had promised to look after the rabbits, a promise is a promise, and I had promised to help. But I couldn't reach all the hutches to put in the mix and hay and I couldn't clean any of them because I'm rubbish at that and get too much mess on the floor. Grandad said we had to clean six hutches every day, that's his rule. You have to clean six one day, and six the next, and on and on, because it stops the rabbits getting sick and the room turning smelly. Mummy said it was the most revolting job. She screwed up her face and put a hanky over her nose and she cleaned dead fast and she thumped the rabbits if they got in her way. It upset me and Newbiggin-by-the-Sea. Newbiggin nipped Mummy and Mummy screamed and threw the dustpan at Newbiggin's head. Poor Newbiggin-by-the-Sea. I stood on tiptoes and kissed my fingers and pressed them through the holey wire and she kissed them back, she gave them a lick, but Mummy saw and shouted and screamed some more. —YOU'LL CATCH GERMS! she said.

Aunty Karen sent us Uncle Ben in the end. She wanted him out of her flat because he was just watching telly and driving her mad. She said he could take care of the rabbits and Mummy said good, he could wash up too. Uncle Ben didn't say anything. He didn't even sing she'll be coming round the mountain when she comes. He just followed Mummy and listened and nodded. He nodded when she showed him the rabbits and Granny's wardrobe where Grandad keeps the shavings and hay, and he nodded when she showed him the cloths and the Fairy Liquid and the sink with all the dirty plates and mugs piled up. She was being dead bossy. She told him he had to wear two hats, one with Rabbit-Keeper on, the other with Washer-Up on, but then she forgot to give Uncle Ben the hats and I couldn't find them for him anywhere.

It's Jed. He touched me. I felt his nail on me and his hard skin, and Grandad called him Jed. —Leave her alone, Jed, he said.

I shake my head. It's puddling me.

It's Jed, not Peter, not Peter Potter. It's Jed and he knows my grandad and he knows my mummy and my mummy knows him, I think.

She was fizzing and sparking. Jed's a rabbit fancier, that's what she told me.

God.

She was fizzing and sparking, and he's horrid, that's what she told me.

I shake my head. My eyes are closed and my ears are blocked.

He's horrid.

He touched me.

He's blood.

I don't know what to do.

I can't see anything or hear anything except my thoughts, and they're going on and on like Mrs Meadows does in class, like Mummy does when she's cross with me. I want them to shut up and go away. I want to hear my heart, that's all. My cousin Pod had to go into hospital about his heart. The doctors said there

was a hole in it because when they listened it didn't
sound right. I can hear mine now. It's thumping and
thumping. It doesn't sound right either. It might have
a hole. Holes are dangerous. They make jumpers fall to
bits. Jesus. Mary.

Someone pulls my jellies.

—NA! I say, and I kick my legs and my eyes flick open
and my ears go pop. It's Jed reaching under the table and
tugging me!

—Don't be silly. It's me.

—What? I say.

Grandad?

—The man's gone now, he says. —So you can come
out, sweetheart. Please.

It sounds like Grandad, but it could still be Jed. He
could be tricking me. I swallow a breath and feel with
my hands. I do it carefully. I feel a bit of sleeve and it's
hairy like Grandad's show jacket, not rubbery like bat.

—Grandad! I say.

It's him. Praise be.

—Come here, Lily, he says, and he gives my jellies
another tug and then he lets go.

I turn on my knees. There's dusty bits in front of my
eyes but I can see Grandad's blobby nose and his pointy
white face staring in at me. He's crouched on the floor
with his head poking under the tablecloth. He's playing
the rabbit game but he's too old-aged and wobbly. He
puts his hand up to his mouth and he coughs, then
coughs again and nearly topples over.

—Ah, I say, and I crawl to him and give him a kiss.
His skin tastes sticky.

—Thank you, he mumbles. —Now, let's get you out of here. Come on.

He huffs and puffs and shuffles backwards on his creaky knees and I do as I'm told and I follow him. The white cloth strokes our heads, then the light is bright like it's a summery day. We're out from under the table. I blink and sit. I can see the orangey hall floor and Grandad's chair and the heater flames. I can't see Jed or his trainers or his long black coat. Good. That's good. I cuddle Grandad. He's on his knees next to me.

—I think you're going to have to help me up, Lily, he says.

—Oh, I say, and I look at him.

—Mmm, he says, and he screws his face and flattens his hands on the floor and straightens his arms and pushes. His face turns red, then purple like he's choking.

—Grandad! I say.

He lets out a big breath of air.

—My legs have locked, he pants.

I look at his legs. They're locked but they can't be because they're not houses or cupboards or doors.

—How are we going to do this?

He shuffles a bit and lifts his arm and slides it round my shoulders.

—Ow! I say.

His arm is heavy on my shoulders and it presses and squashes me.

—Hang on, he says, and he flaps his hand and coughs and coughs. He sounds like Baby Pod's shaker with the beads inside, rattly and rainy. —This probably isn't . . .

I can't get him off me.

He coughs. —The best way, he says.

I'm getting closer and closer to the floor. I can see little blobs of green paint on the floor and a mark like a cross.

—Grandad, I whisper.

Jesus died on a cross. He died to save us all.

My breath is going from me.

—Grandad.

I'm scrunching into a ball.

—Are you all right, you two? asks another voice.

I squint my eyes.

—Do you need some help?

It's a lady. She's wearing brown shoes and yellow trousers.

I stretch my hand out.

—My knees, croaks Grandad. —They've locked.

I'm like the girl on *Blue Peter* when the earthquake happened. The earthquake cracked up the girl's street and the buildings came tumbling down and she got trapped, true-life!

—Oh dear, that's nasty, says the lady.

It was horrid. Bits of brick flew in the girl's mouth and jabbed her eyes. They hit her on the head. She was five, nearly six, and that's the same age as me. She was scared and couldn't move. She was trapped under the ground but she was lucky. She had pretty fingers and they were sticking in the air. She could feel the air blowing round them and she wiggled and waved them and a man saw and he dug under the building with a machine. He rescued her. I want to be rescued. I tap the lady's shoes.

—Here, she says, and she crouches and I smell Polo mints and then I see her big round face smiling at me. It's a miracle. Holy. Holy. She puts her hands on Grandad's shoulders and she pushes him and he moves and it's better, lighter; my body's coming undone.

—I'm sorry, croaks Grandad.

—I don't know, she says, and she holds Grandad under his arms and she grunts like an old pig and pulls him up.

—Hurrah! I say.

Grandad's off me and I try to stand. Woah! I wobble. My leggings are up my crack and I tug them out and the lady tugs Grandad. She's wearing a T-shirt with a rabbit on the front and the rabbit's holding his paws up like this, feeling her boobies. Grandad's face falls on her boobies. He mumbles a word, —Sorry.

—Not to worry, Jim, she says. She knows Grandad's name. —That's what they're there for.

Perhaps she knows me. I give her my secret sign but she's too busy. She walks Grandad to his chair. His feet shuffle and drag on the floor.

—Well, she says, and she helps him to sit. He flumps like a shopping bag. —You should take it easy, Jim.

She rubs her hands and wipes them on her trousers.

—I'd like to, he says.

—You need to, she says, then she smiles and pats his knee and looks at me. —You'll help him, won't you, dear? Come on.

She grabs another chair and puts it next to Grandad.

—You keep him company, she says.

I know what that means. It's like a gang, like Finbar

has at Megadeath. His gang's
of boys. My gang's called Englis.
just Grandad and me. I'm his compan... it's full
the chair.

—Hello, I say.

—Hello, he says, and he fiddles in his trouser pocket and pulls out his hanky with the blood spots on.

The lady looks at her fingernails. They're pale pink and her cheeks are a bit pink too.

—I'm sorry if I hurt you back there, Lily, says Grandad.

—S'all right, I say.

He blows his nose.

—Would you like some water, Jim? asks the lady.

—Please, he says. —Thank you.

—Keep up the good fight, she says, and she picks up the two plastic cups that are on top of the heater and hurries off down the hall.

—Who's she? I ask.

—She shows Harlequins, says Grandad. —I can't remember her name.

—They're Fancy, I say.

—Rex, says Grandad, and he wipes his face and neck with his hanky.

His hands shake. They're cold, I know. They're bluey-white, and blue means cold because it's on taps, and white means cold too because that's ice and snow. Grandad tucks his hanky back in his pocket, then leans forward to warm his hands. He stares into the heater flames. They jiggle and fidget like me, like they've got ants in their pants and can't keep still. Ants are tiny and snakes like Zippy, or animals like ʌ nsh like fish. They're insects and they crawl ʌp walls and they're ever so busy. There are hundreds in the concrete tube in the play-park. They crawl in lines, one behind the other, all over the naughty drawings, but they've not crawled in my pants, no way! That's something Mrs Meadows made up. She says I've got them in my pants but it's like a story, I think, a story about my fidgeting.

—Lily.

Grandad watches the flames and he makes a noise like he's got a biscuit stuck in his throat and he's trying to get it out.

—Lily, he says again. —About Jed. You know?

I know. God.

—I think we ought to keep him a secret. Just between you and me.

Grandad licks his lips. There's white stuff on them, like dried-up spit.

—I don't think we should tell anybody that he was here. Understand?

I nod, I shake my head.

He's a horrid man.

Grandad looks at me. —You don't understand?

He's flesh-and-blood.

Grandad sighs. —I'm not sure I can explain.

Jed's flesh-and-blood and he's horrid and Grandad can't explain about him even though he's good at explaining normally. He explains to me about rabbits and show-jumping and being perfect and Sweden and breeds and everything. He's patient; Mummy's not. Poor

Grandad. Jed's worn him out because he's horrid and a secret.

—It's very complicated, says Grandad. —I . . . he . . .

—Here we are, says the lady with the rabbit T-shirt. She walks in front of me. —Your water, Jim.

—Ah, says Grandad.

The lady gives Grandad a plastic cup. She's got him some water. She didn't get any for me.

—You look a little perkier.

—Thank you, says Grandad, and his shaky hands wobble the cup and water splashes on the floor.

—Oh, dear.

The lady quickly kicks shavings over the puddle.

Doctor Foster went to Gloucester.

Grandad sips some water.

In a shower of rain.

Then he holds out the cup. Shaky. Shaky.

The lady stomps the shavings down.

He stepped in a puddle.

—Thank you, says Grandad. —If you would.

Right up to his middle.

—Of course.

The lady takes the cup and puts it on the heater.

And never went there again.

—LADIES AND GENTLEMEN, says the old-age man in the white coat and hat. His voice booms round the hall.

—Oh! I say.

He's on the stage and he's speaking into a micro-phone like he's famous at poems, like he's on *Top of the Pops*.

—CAN I HAVE YOUR ATTENTION PLEASE.

—I'll move out of your way, says the lady, and she leans on the wall.

—ONE TWO. ONE TWO.

The old-age man taps his microphone and blows into it. Whuff! Like that.

—NOW, TO THE SERIOUS PART OF THE PRO-CEEDINGS. THE CAVY RESULTS ARE STILL BEING TALLIED SO WE'LL START WITH THE RABBITS, THE PRIZES . . .

He points his microphone at the stuff on the table, the wooden shield and three silver cups.

—AND THE JUDGES.

He swings his arm and points at the judges behind him, a lady and two men.

—I know him, I say. —That judge.

He's the one who had the board and the certificates.

—I know him, Grandad, I say.

The lady with the T-shirt looks at me. She puts a finger to her lips. She's telling me to zip. She's being bossy.

Grandad puts his hands on his chair and tries to push himself straight. —Fancy, Fur and Rex, he says.

—MR KEITH FISHER, OUR JUDGE FOR THE FANCY CLASS, the old-age man says into his micro-phone, and the man who had the board stands and he bows and everybody claps, all the people standing near the stage and the people leaning against the 'pig pens and rabbit pens and the people sitting on the seats near the food counter.

—FUR CLASS: MISS CHRISTINE SWIDELLS.

The lady judge gives the same wave as the human

276

Queen does. A little wave with her hand like that. Then there's more clapping and some whistling too, the sort that Aunty Sheila gets when she walks down the street. Phew-phew.

—REX CLASS: MR ROBERT GURGERSKI.

The other man nods. He's wearing a tie like clowns wear that spins round and shoots water. It's glittery and blue.

—AND THE RESULTS ARE . . .

Results are marks. I wriggle. The rabbits are getting their marks and I'm getting excited. I'm getting ants.

—Lily, says Grandad. —Here.

The old-age man takes a piece of paper from his white coat pocket and Grandad takes my hand and puts it inside his jacket on his chest. My hand's on his chest where his ticker is and his chest feels warm and his ticks are ticking faster than my Bugs Bunny alarm. I can feel them pressing through his shirt.

—I'm excited inside but look at me . . .

I look.

—I'm calm outside and that's how you should be. Try. Please.

—GET ON WITH IT! someone shouts.

—Patience, ladies and gentlemen.

The old-age man unfolds the piece of paper and flaps it, and I try to stop my ants.

Tick tick tick.

I cross my legs.

—Now, as you know the judges' reports will be published in the next issue of the *Fur & Feather* and the Best Of Breed certificates have already been awarded.

It's been an extremely good turnout for all classes and the judges have had a difficult job deciding on their winners.

—Oh yes? says Grandad.

Tick tick tick.

—Fancy first, the old-age man says, and he blows into his microphone again. —AND THE BEST FANCY GOES TO JIM PHILLIPS FOR HIS BLACK ENGLISH SPOT, LINCOLN, A BEAUTIFUL DOE! WELL DONE JIM!

Everyone claps.

—Grandad! Grandad!

I kiss Grandad, I hug him round his neck, and he sort of kisses me, then he coughs.

—JIM, IF YOU CAN COME UP HERE AND COLLECT YOUR PRIZE.

He coughs and I smell a smell like the dirty washing box at home. Yuk. It's coming from his mouth.

—Lily, he says.

It's his breathing and it smells of washing box and fish, the fish like Mummy gives me sometimes, that's good for my bones, that she mashes and puts on my toast.

—Please, you're choking me.

I let go of Grandad.

—WHERE IS HE? JIM?

I move from his fishy mouth.

—HAVE WE GOT JIM PHILLIPS?

—HE'S HERE! the lady shouts. She bends and pats Grandad's arm. —Shall I be your walking stick?

—Please, says Grandad, and he looks at me. —Are you coming, Lily?

—Come on, says the lady, and she helps him up.
—You won't be a minute.

A minute's a minute.

—IS THAT JIM? says the old-age man. —COME
ON, JIM.

The claps get louder and Grandad looks at me and
the lady tugs on his arm. —Don't be a fusspot, she says.
—You'll be all right won't you, dear?

She stares at me. The rabbit is feeling her boobies.
She's got big wobbly ones like Aunty Chris has. Grandad
coughs. The lady smiles and leads him away.

Aunty Chris is my pretend mummy.

Grandad and the lady walk to the stage.

I wish Aunty Chris was here.

They walk ever so slowly like they're being married.

Daisy, Daisy, give me an answer do.

They're holding each other and they're walking slowly
and people are watching and clapping and saying well
done.

I'm half crazy all for the love of you.

I look around me. Give my love to your mum, that's
what Jed said.

It won't be a stylish marriage.

I can't afford a carriage.

He was talking about my proper mummy, I know.

But you'll look sweet.

Upon the seat.

Not Aunty Chris.

Of a bicycle made for two.

Grandad married Granny hundreds of years ago. It was after the Second World War. The Second World War was when the English fought battles with the Nazis. Nazi is like nasty and the Nazi leader was a man with a moustache, not Aladdin but somebody else. He had shiny black hair and he stuck his hand out like this, like he was measuring tall things all the time. That was his sign. My sign's better. It's more expressive. Expressive means showing-off. Not rude showing-off but clever showing-off with brains. This is a song from the war.

My Brother Sylvest.

Forty medals cross his chest.

Big chest.

Grandad sings this song. His daddy taught him it because he was a soldier in the war. He blasted a gun. He didn't want to but the policemen made him. It was their rule. A rule's a rule. Grandad's daddy had to fight in the war or else the policemen said they'd lock him in prison. Prison's icy cold and full of men and spiders. Grandad's daddy didn't want to go there.

It's a sad story. He didn't enjoy the war, that's what Aunty Sheila says; it was hard for him. Coal's hard: it's black. Black's like bats and nighttime and Batman

Dracula. It doesn't show any dirt. Tables are hard too, and bricks and cheese, and reading and writing. Hard is hard. It's not soft. The war wasn't soft for Grandad's daddy and that's a shame, Aunty Sheila says, because he was a kind and gentle man. Grandad's kind and gentle too. Kind means giving people presents and cuddling them, and gentle means loving everything soft like rabbits and the love of your life.

Granny was the love of Grandad's life. She had curly hair and she made his sandwiches for work and she painted their doorstep white and she got up with the birds. She loved Grandad and he loved her and they made babies together but that was after they got married, I think.

They got married in a church. Not the church with the churchyard where Granny's under the ground but a different church that's in a different part of East and England. Granny wore her sister's dress. She wasn't an only-bonely. She had a sister called Elizabeth who worked in a button factory and Granny worked there too until she married Grandad.

Grandad's got a photo of their wedding. I took it to school when we were doing our project about how many people live in your house. It's not colourful. Grandad's in posh black trousers and a white shirt and black tie and a black jacket and Granny's wearing her sister's white dress. They're standing very close together on the church steps. Granny's holding a bunch of flowers in her hands. There's nobody with them, just the church behind them and the steps under them and the grass at the bottom of the steps. You can tell it's grass. It's not green in the photo, it's grey, but it's jaggy and sticky-up like grass, so you know that it's grass.

Grandad keeps his marriage photo on the shelf above the fire in the front room. It's in the middle of the shelf and then on one side there's a picture of Aunty Sheila and Aunty Karen, and on the other side there's a picture of Aunty Pam and Aunty Chris and Mummy. Mummy's wearing a shirt with zigzags on and she's got very long hair and she's sort of got her hands in her hair and she's fluffing it out. She looks like Mummy but she doesn't as well because she's not so fat and her hair's pretty and she's doing a kiss shape with her lips.

Mummy hates this photo. She wants Grandad to throw it away but he won't because he's keeping it for his memories, that's what he says. Memories are important things that happen to you, that you keep in your mind or on shelves, and you think about a lot. I've not got many memories because I'm at first school. Memories happen more to humans when they get older. They don't happen to rabbits at all. True-life! Rabbits don't have memories because their brains won't let them. They know about eating and drinking and sexywexy and they know how to sniff and dig and jump and that's it, so thank you Jesus, Mary, Joseph. They can't take photos and they don't have memories about their babies or running around outside in the rabbit run or being at shows and winning BOBs. Bristol doesn't have any memories about being ticklish with Wigston, and Kettering doesn't have memories about being perishing, and Lincoln won't have any memories about Sweden and doing the triple. Hup! Hup! Hup! She'll have zero, nothing, nought memories about that.

I hold the silver cup. The lady with the rabbit T-shirt gave it to me when she helped Grandad sit down. She's leaning on the wall now and Grandad's huddled by the heater and I'm next to him and I'm in charge of the cup. That means I have to take care of it and make sure it doesn't crash on the floor. It's a very important job because the cup's silver with a lid on. It's shiny and it's Lincoln's prize.

Grandad's won loads of cups. Some are the same as this one, some are smaller and haven't got lids, and some have got pictures of rabbits on. I like the rabbit ones best but I don't get to see them or any of the others much. Grandad's allowed to keep them and the certificates and rosettes and sometimes he can take the BIS home for a while too. He can't keep the BIS. His name's put on it if he wins and he can borrow it for a bit but he can't keep it for ever and ever amen. He doesn't mind. There's not much room in our flat for prizes, there's not enough shelves, that's what he says. The certificates and rosettes can stick on the side of Granny's wardrobe but the cups and the BIS need shelves to stand on. We've got shelves in the kitchen but they're for jars and tins and mugs. So the cups and the BIS go to Aunty Sheila to look after. She puts them in her room with all her memories. The room's at the top of her stairs. It's not a bedroom, it's a box, that's what it's called, and it's got hundreds of shelves and a cupboard. Grandad's cups are on the shelves with photos of Granny and Grandad, my cousins and aunties, and Mummy and me. Then in the cupboard Aunty Sheila's got her dresses and her school books and her toys and her diary from when she was a little girl. Kylie's not allowed in the box because she's rude and laughs and upsets Aunty Sheila. But I went in there at Christmas when Aunty Sheila invited us round for turkey sandwiches. Aunty Sheila and Mummy fell out and so Aunty Sheila took me away to see the box. It was fantastic-elastic. I could look at everything but I couldn't touch.

I take the lid off the silver cup and put it on my knees. The cup looks yellow inside and not so shiny. Soldiers and kings used to drink beer from these cups in the olden days, I know. They didn't have shelves. They kept their cups in bags and carried them everywhere. Their cups were precious. Precious means special and stones. Special stones were stuck on the cups, red and green and diamonds. Mrs Meadows showed us a picture of a king's cup. She got it from the computer. We're lucky. We've got a computer in our class. It doesn't do the internet or essays or grown-up stuff like that. It's not a proper computer, that's what Finbar says. It's too old, and I don't like to think about it much because I can't go on it. I'm a Tortoise and I can't work the knobs.

I blow into the cup. The yellow turns steamy. I put the lid back on so the steam doesn't escape, then I wipe the outside with my sleeve and stare into it. I can see my face in the silver and everything else in the hall. It's a bit like my Barbie mirror except it's not because my Barbie mirror makes me look normal and the cup makes me look bulgy and big. My doe eyes look bulgy and my nose and my mouth, and my hair's sort of stretchy and my chin's a pointy triangle. It's funny.

—Grandad, I say.

I show him the cup. I hold it near his ear and it makes his ear look flappy like an elephant's. But he's not interested, I can tell. He's staring at the stage and the fat lady with the hairband.

—I know her, I say.

She's waving one of the other cups and she's stomping from the stage, stomping down the stairs.

—WELL DONE, EILEEN, says the old-age man into his microphone. —THAT WAS THE WINNER OF THE BEST FUR. EILEEN PURDY FOR ENGLEBERT, A MAGNIFICENT BRITISH GIANT!

—She talked to me, Grandad, I say, and I hold the cup by his mouth but not too close because he might get cross with me. I watch the silver and I wait for his mouth to open, for him to answer me. But he's zipped his lips. There's dribble on them. Yuk. That's all.

I put the cup on my knees. Grandad's concentrating, I'm sure. He's waiting to see if Lincoln gets the BIS. He's staring at the stage and he's waiting and wishing. I wish. I wish I had a baby sister and I wish I had a daddy and I wish I was a rabbit and Lincoln wins the BIS.

Grandad mumbles.

—What? I ask.

I can't hear what he says. He's mumbling and his legs are shaking.

—Are you excited? I ask.

He is, true-life. He's excited outside and that's not fair. He should be calm outside. Calm outside, excited inside, that's what he told me.

—Be calm, Grandad, I say. —Stop it.

He mumbles and fiddles with his collar. His face is thin and pointy and sad.

—Cheer up, I say.

He's sad and he's excited. He should be happy and excited. That's right, that's best. His shoulder's pressing into me.

—Grandad, I say.

He's being silly. The lady with the rabbit T-shirt is in front of us, leaning on the wall, and Grandad's pressing into me and staring at her bum. He's stopped staring at the stage and he's staring at her bum. Her yellow trousers are tight and they make her bum look big and round and yellow like the Man-In-The-Moon.

—Grandad! I say. —That's rude.

It is. You shouldn't stare at people's bums or any of their other bits, like their teeth or cracks because it's rude, Aunty Sheila told me. It's rude to stare, or to make trump noises, or to stick your tongue out like this. Nah nah. I wiggle my tongue at the lady's big bum.

Grandad shakes and mumbles. His breath sounds like gurgly water. His body presses and rubs on mine. He's giving me burns like the China ones that Finbar does with his fingers. He's hurting and squashing me like he did before.

—Grandad! I say.

His hands flap.

—Grandad!

His falsies clack, and his arm flops and knocks the silver cup. Crash! The lid smashes on the floor!

—GRANDAD! GRANDAD!

The lady with the rabbit T-shirt turns.

—JIM! she says. —MY GOD!

Maud's flour face stares at me and her bony fingers fiddle with my hair. We're in the kitchen, behind the counter where they sell the pop and crisps and Penguin biscuits, and we're sitting on a bench. It's hard and brown like the ones we use for PE, that we run along and jump over, that aren't very comfy. It's by the table where the sandwiches are made and it's hurting my bum. I wriggle. Maud's sitting close to me.

—There, there, she says.

She smells of floury powder and guinea-pig plips.

I look down at my knees.

—Dear, dear, she says.

She's so annoying me. She stinks of guinea-pigs and they're silly creatures, that's what Grandad says; they just hurry about like rats with no tails. They can't hop or jump or send body messages like rabbits can. They don't have proper language.

I stare at my knees. My leggings are red but my knees are black and dirty because I've been crawling on them pretending to be a rabbit. I want to be a rabbit. I do. I want to send a message to my grandad.

Get up! Get up! Get out of bed!

That's what I want to say.

Cheer up! Cheer up! The sun is red!

That's my message.

Get up, Grandad. I'm sleepy and hungry and this bench is hard and it's hurting my bum and I want to go home. Don't keep snoring in the hall. Doctor Whitworth will be cross. You need a proper bed, not the floor. Stop jiggling your legs and get up off the floor.

Rock a bye baby.

The lady with the rabbit T-shirt put Grandad on the floor. A man helped her. They said Grandad needed a sleep, and Maud cuddled me and took me away.

—La la la.

His falsies were loose in his mouth.

—Hush, dear, says Maud. She fiddles with my hair.

—La la la. La la la.

I've not got much hair and she's pulling and picking at it with her fingers. I think she's looking for scabs but I've not got them. Kelly has. She's got them all over her head and sometimes she picks them in class and puts them on the table so we can see. They're horrid and crusty with dried-up blood.

—Stop it, I say.

I stare at Maud and pull my head away.

—Oh, she says, and she drops her arm, her hand, her bony fingers. Her fingers are like witch's fingers twitching in her lap.

Oh God. Dear God.

Brr. I'm perishing cold.

—I think she's tired, says the lady who does the pop and crisps and Penguin biscuits. —Are you tired, lovey?

She's standing by the sink. She's in a pink dress

and she's wearing pink gloves, the washing-up kind. One pink hand's in the sink, stirring the plates round in the water and the plates clink like Grandad's at breakfast-time.

—What do you think? she says. —Tired?

I nod, I shake my head.

This is my treat. Not many children get to see behind the counter, that's what Maud says. But I don't care. I don't care about the pop lady and the fridge and the oven and the big brown bins. I want to be with Grandad. I'm tired but I only want to sleep with him, next to him like Granny did in their marriage bed. I want to be with him. But they won't let me. Maud took me away.

—Grandad, I say.

His silver cup's on top of the fridge. He's got the BOB and the Fancy and he wants to know if he's got the BIS. But he's sleeping.

Rock you, rock you.

I look at the door.

Get up! Get up! Get out of bed!

It's closed. It's like Grandad's front door, closed so you can't see the dirty grey corridors and the crazy-on-drugs men and everything bad that happens outside.

Grandad's outside.

—Where's Grandad? I say.

I look at the counter. It's shut with metal and padlocks like Mr Azad's shop at nighttime.

—She's a bit agitated, says the lady.

I can't see through to the hall.

—La la la, I say.

Grandad's outside in the hall. He's on the floor by the heater.

—Don't fret, dumpling, says Maud, and she strokes me with her bony fingers.

She called me dumpling. Dumplings are furry and squidgy and you eat them with meat. Granny made them for Grandad's tea. I know. He told me.

—La la la, I say.

There was dark on his trousers near his willy. His legs were shaking. He was weeing his pants.

—La la la, I say.

—We should get her to sleep, says the pop lady.

—La la la. La la la.

—Are you tired, dumpling? say Maud. —Would you like a little nap? You look all washed out.

—Yes, have a little sleep, princess, says the pop lady. —You can rest your head on Maud.

The pop lady pulls off her pink gloves and they make a snapping sound. She throws them in the sink. Then she crouches in front of me and smiles without showing her teeth, like Finbar's mummy does when she kisses Finbar bye-bye in class and sees me in her eye corners. A grown-up smile, I think.

My teeth chatter.

I'm jealous of Finbar. He's got a mummy and a daddy, brothers and sisters, three grandads and four grannies, and they're all alive and that hurts me because that's what jealous means. You hurt inside and sometimes you can turn green too. Mummy gets jealous of Aunty Sheila but she's not turned green, not yet, and I get jealous of Finbar and of my cousin Joe because he's got an extra bed. Grandad slept in Joe's extra bed one time and left me feeling lonely. He was with Joe when Joe got frightened by all the nighttime noises and he snored with him and that's not happened to me, never ever, but it might in Sweden, true-life. I asked Grandad if we could share a bed there and he said maybe, it was all in the future but maybe, who knows?

—Is that a promise? I asked.

—It's a maybe, Lily, he said.

—We're going to Sweden, I tell the pop lady. —Grandad promised me. We're going on a plane, to a hotel and everything. We're going with Lincoln. She's a jumping rabbit.

The pop lady looks at me. —Well, she says, she smiles. —Well, you'll need a rest before you go there. It's a long journey, isn't it, Maud?

—I can't place Sweden, says Maud.

—It's next to Poland, says the pop lady. —She'll have to fly or take a boat. It's over the sea. Here . . .

The pop lady pushes her hands between her knees.

—What about a story? You put your head on Maud's lap and I'll tell you about the time I went to Sweden and met a Swedish prince.

—A Swedish prince! says Maud. —Was he handsome?

—Oh very, says the pop lady, and she winks at me. —Once upon a time. Put your head down now, here on Maud's lap.

—I don't want my hair fussing, I say.

—That's fine, says the pop lady. —Head down now. I do as I'm told. I lay on my side and she helps me curl up, and I put my head on Maud. Her trousers are warm. They smell of coffee.

—There, says Maud.

—That's it, says the pop lady.

I curl my knees to my belly. Dr Whitworth says sleep mends your body. It makes you happy. I hope Grandad's happy.

—That's it. Off we go, off to Sweden.

It's dark in my head and I can't see anything. I don't know where I am. I can smell lots of stuff but it's all mixed up and I can hear tapping and voices and squeaking, not guinea-pig squeaking, another kind. I feel cold and shivery. My eyes are sticky like the poorly rabbits on *Pet Rescue*.

—Sticky, I mumble.

I sound strange. My voice is blurry and my mouth rubs on something warm and woolly, a jumper I think. I'm bouncing along. Somebody's holding and carrying me. There are fingers prodding the tops of my legs, hands pressing into my bum.

—She's stirring, a man says.

Stirring's what you do with spoons.

—Lily? Are you awake?

The man's close to me. It's Uncle Paul, I'm certain sure.

—Lily?

—Mmm, I say.

I blink and yawn and I see fuzzy white light and it's all around me and Uncle Paul. It shines over his brown hair. My eyes shut. I'm sleepy and safe. Uncle Paul's carrying me and Grandad's pulling his trolley. I can hear it squeaking behind me. I shiver and blink some more and I see blue and a 7 and a 7 and a 7. We're at Grandad's door. We're home sweet home. I can hear keys and the door opening. I bounce along. The door slams. Bang! It hurts my ears. Then everything sounds different, quieter. I hear footsteps going pad pad pad and another voice.

—Thanks, put her there, Paul.

It's Mummy.

Then woah! I'm getting lower. Uncle Paul's hands are dropping me and I land on something soft.

—I'll just see to the rabbits, he says.

I curl my arms and legs.

—OK, says Mummy.

I'm on something soft.

—Don't worry, says Uncle Paul.

I blink and roll up my tongue like Grandad's carpet that went in the lift and I taste fur and wet. I feel around with my achy fingers. I feel my Teletubby jumper, my leggings and a fringy bit of cushion.

—Sofa, I mumble.

I'm in the front room.

—Hello, says Mummy.

I open my eyes.

—How are you?

Everything's bright. I rub my eyes and Mummy is sitting beside me.

—You've had a sleep, she says.

She's wearing her black tracksuit with the white lines on and her big green cardigan. She pushes my legs ever so gently.

—Sit up.

I do as I'm told but I'm wobbly and whizzy and my eyes are stinging. I blink. The curtains are closed and the light's on.

—Is it nighttime? I ask. My voice is mumbly.

—Teatime, she says, and she looks at me. —Are you OK?

I nod, I shake my head.

She's sitting next to me and her face is puffy, I don't know why. It shines puffy and big under the light and it's like Kelly's face when she gets upset. It's not normal. Nobody likes her. Everybody hates her. Daft-bat Kelly. She's a cry-baby. Not like Mummy. Mummy hates tears. Her eyes are red.

—Here, she says, and her arms wrap round me for a cuddle.

She's being dead nice. Perhaps she's finished her essay. That's why her face is puffy and her eyes are red. She's all worn out but that's not bad, it's good, because now she's got time and space to give to me.

—Excellent, Mummy, I say. —You've done your essay.

—Not quite, she says, and she lets go of me and strokes my arm with the side of her finger.

—Mummy! I say.

She's doing what Mrs Meadows does to her in class in the mornings. It's a surprise to me. She rubs my arm in that special way. Aunty Sheila surprised me with my girl-girl dress and Grandad surprised me with my badges and now Mummy's surprising me too.

—It's surprise surprise day!

Mummy sighs and stops her stroking. She looks down

at her hands. She opens and closes them like she's squeezing stuff but she's not because her hands are empty. Empty isn't full. It's when something's not there, it's missing.

—Where's Uncle Paul? I ask.

He's missing.

—Seeing to the rabbits, says Mummy.

—Is he helping Grandad? I ask. —Where's Grandad?

He's missing too.

—Is he in his room?

He's not with us because he doesn't like being close to Mummy and she doesn't like being close to him, I know.

—Is he having a lie-down? I ask. —He was sleeping at the show, Mummy. He was excited because Lincoln got the BOB and the Fancy but he needed a sleep. He was shaky.

I wiggle and jiggle my legs like Grandad, like that.

—OK, Lily, says Mummy.

—A lady and a man put him on the floor.

There was dark on his trousers near his willy and he smelt of human wee.

—OK, Lily.

His falsies were loose in his mouth.

—La la la, I say.

Mummy puts a hand on my knee.

—Quiet, Lily, she says.

Her eyes are watery and her mouth is scrunching up.

—What? I ask. —Where's Grandad?

—Please, she says.

She squeezes my knee and she sniffs.

—Is he in his bedroom? I ask. —Is he sleeping?

All things bright and beautiful have to go to sleep, that's what Grandad says.

Sometimes they wake up.

—He's only sleeping, I say. —Isn't he, Mummy?

Sometimes they never do.

—The man closed his eyes, I say.

He put Grandad on the floor and he closed Grandad's eyes with his fingers because he needed a sleep.

—Grandad was sleeping, I say.

—I know.

Mummy lets out a long sad sound.

—He still is, she says. —In a way.

She pats my knee. —I'll be going to see him soon.

She stares at the fire.

It's cold. The bars aren't red.

—Uncle Paul will take me, and Mrs Meadows will be babysitting you, how about that?

—Mrs Meadows? I say.

—I think you'll have a nice time.

Mrs Meadows is my teacher and Mummy's friend. She's not my babysitter; Grandad is.

—I want Grandad, I say.

I want to sit on the sofa and eat crisps and talk about Sweden and rabbits and things.

—You can't have him, Mummy sighs. —I've told you. He's not here. I'm going to see him with Aunty Chris and Sheila and Karen and Pam. And Mrs Meadows will be looking after you.

That's not fair. I kick my jellies against the sofa.

—Lily, please! says Mummy. —Look, you can show Mrs Meadows your new dress.

Mummy turns and fiddles under the cushion behind her back and pulls out a blue carrier, like the ones you get from Mr Azad's. She holds it upside down and my pink girl-girl dress falls out on my knees. She's done my dress. It's covered in badges, I can see.

—Oh, Mummy! I say.

—You can put it on if you want. Take off your jumper, she says.

I pull at my jumper but it gets stuck on my head, so Mummy has to help me. She tugs and then I'm in the light again.

—OK, she says, and she rolls up my new dress and slips it over me. —Arms in.

She smooths and pats and buttons the dress and she pinches out the sleeves with her fingers. She fusses them until they look just right.

—It'll feel a bit tight because you're still wearing your T-shirt and leggings, she says.

It feels lovely. It's velteen. It's got rabbit badges stitched all over and my favourite is on the pocket. I touch the little black rabbit in the middle of the red circle. I tickle his ears.

—Thank you, Mummy, I say.

—Well, it's not really my taste but . . .

—You didn't throw them away, I say.

—No, of course I didn't, Lily.

Mummy makes a funny noise in her throat like a gulp.

—Of course not. You've got me all wrong.

She gulps some more, then tears come out of her eyes.

I can see.

They're real.

—Mummy! I say.

They're making wet lines on her face.

I don't know what to do.

—La la la, I say.

Mummy gulps and gulps and she puts her hands over her eyes.

—Don't, I say, and I try to cuddle her. —La la la.

I pretend I'm Aunty Chris cuddling and calming and loving me.

—There, there. Don't cry. La la la.

I'm Aunty Chris and Mummy is me and I'm caring for her.

—La la la.

I stroke her black hair with the grey bits in.

—La la la.

I can feel her head under her hair. It's big and full of brain. She's not a Tortoise. My hands are shaky. She's the intelligent one and my teacher is her friend. She gulps and shudders. Her hair is black. She feels hot. His coat was black. It was made of bat. Give my love to your mum, that's what he said. I am. I'm loving her. Flesh-and-blood. My heart is beating fast. I've got to keep him secret, that's what Grandad said. A secret's a secret. But sometimes if you cross your fingers when you tell a secret it doesn't matter. I let go of Mummy. She sniffles and wipes her eyes with her cardigan sleeve. Then the room is quiet like at school in class, when everything goes quiet all of a sudden. I cross my fingers.

—Mummy, I say.

—I had to keep these on, says a voice.

—Oh, I say.

It's Uncle Paul. He's in the doorway. He's wearing his gloves and he claps them together.

—They were kicking like anything, he sighs. —I think they sensed it wasn't Jim.

I uncross my fingers.

The rabbits were kicking.

They do that when they're frightened.

Run rabbit, run rabbit.

They thump their feet, and nip and kick, and stare with popping eyes.

They sensed it wasn't Jim.

That's Grandad's name. Jim. Jim Phillips.

It wasn't Jim.

—It wasn't me, I said one time when I knocked the mix all over Grandad's floor.

—Well, it certainly wasn't me, said Grandad.

Uncle Paul takes off his gloves and sits in Grandad's easy chair. He's been putting the rabbits away and now he's sitting in Grandad's chair but he's Uncle Paul, not Grandad, and he belongs to Aunty Chris and Tom and Bethany, not to Mummy or me.

—Hello, Lily, he says. —Wide awake I see, and wearing a dress. Is that your special dress for Aunty Sheila's wedding?

Uncle Paul speaks to me but he's not looking at me, not properly. He's looking at Mummy.

—What a lot of lovely badges.

She's hunched up and staring at the photos on the shelf above the fire, the photos of her and her sisters and the one of Grandad and Granny getting married. There's snot bubbling out of her nose.

—Where's Grandad, Uncle Paul? I say. —Is he with Old Shep?

I think that's where he is, sleeping with Old Shep on the Isle of Skye.

—If you like, says Uncle Paul, and he pushes himself out of Grandad's chair.

—Yeehah! I say. —He's with Old Shep!

Grandad's with Beamish and Old Shep and the mummy bunnies who can't get off their bums. It's true, I know. He's sleeping in the special bedroom.

—I want to go there, Uncle Paul, I say.

—Really, princess? he says, and he bends and lifts me off the sofa. —Maybe you should go and see to the rabbits first. They probably need a feed. Can you do that?

He cuddles me and smiles. His nose is big and his lips are too and one of his teeth is shiny silver like Grandad's cup.

—Grandad got the Fancy, I say.

—I know, he says. —He did well.

—Where's his cup? I ask.

—With the rabbits, he says, and he carries me into the hall and puts me down and turns me to face Grandad's door. —Go and see to them, Lily. They're waiting for you.

—Mummy was crying, I say. —She doesn't like tears.

—I know, says Uncle Paul, and he strokes my back like Grandad strokes his rabbits to get them going. —I'll just have a word with her.

Uncle Paul goes into the front room and closes the door. He's in the front room and I'm here on my own and it feels cold behind me and cold in front. I'm an only-bonely-lonely. Uncle Paul's left me to be with Mummy, and Grandad's left me too because he's not in the flat with his perfect rabbits, and he's not even in Joe's room with the extra bed. He's sleeping with Old Shep on the Isle of Skye instead. Old Shep's been sleeping for a hundred years. I'm five, nearly six, and a hundred is more than that. It's an even number, a big one.

—Grandad, I say.

I can't feel his skin or sit on his knee or anything. I'm missing him. I'll be missing him for a hundred years.

He's not my dad.

—La la la.

He's too old-age and he doesn't look like me. He's ancient wisdom and he's kind and patient and he's interested in rabbits.

I want to see his rabbits.

—La la la.

I want to see Lincoln and Chesterfield and Newbiggin-by-the-Sea. I want to be a rabbit. I know lots of rabbit facts. I'm a fancier. I am.

God.

A thought pings in my head. It's in my head and I shake my head and grab the handle on Grandad's bedroom door. The handle's thin and shiny and I can see my face in it, my eyes staring back at me. My big doe eyes.

Jed.

I feel sick.

He's a fancier.

There's a sick taste in my mouth.

I gulp.

My thought is growing.

I'm all eyes and he's all eyes.

My sick tastes yellow and sweet.

Blood is sweet. He's blood.

—NA! I say, and I close my eyes and pull the handle.

Mummies and daddies and children have bits that look the same.

I shake my head.

I want the thought out of me.

I want to be a rabbit.

I push the door.

Rabbit sounds fill my supersonic ears. Nighttime sounds.

He's not my daddy.

The rabbits are making nighttime sounds.

No way.

I breathe. I listen to the sounds. Mummy says it's teatime but these belong to the nighttime. Shuffling and sniffing and munching and snoring. I open my eyes. I breathe. They're happening in the dark.

The room is dead dark. The curtains are shut, and I can see shapes, that's all. The shape of the hutches lined up by the wall, the humps of the rabbits moving about in the hutches, Granny's wardrobe with Grandad's camp bed leaning against it, the piles of *Fur & Feather*s that Grandad uses for jumps.

—HUP, LINCOLN! he shouts in the mornings. —HUP! HUP!

He always wakes me and he always wakes Mummy too.

—THOSE BLOODY RABBITS! she shouts.

—HUP, LINCOLN! he shouts. —THAT'S IT GIRL!

Grandad jumps Lincoln and then he cooks my breakfast and takes me to school or gives me a bath. He's nice like that. But sometimes on Sundays he puts Lincoln back and has an extra lie-down. Then I wake him. I sneak into his room and it's dark like this and he moves in his camp bed and it groans and squeaks and he says, —Is that you, Lily? Put the light on would you?

—OK, Sergeant, I say, and I do my secret sign.

—No messing about, he says.

—No messing, I say, and I feel on the wall by the door. I stand on my toes and feel up high because that's where the switch is. I can reach the switch. Bethany can't. She's four and she's too babyish.

I click the switch, I do it now, and I rub my eyes and blink. There's purple blobs floating round the hutches. I blink again. That's better. No blobs, just proper yellow bulb colour. I know all about bulbs. Mr Azad sells tons from his shop, even teeny-weeny ones for sewing machines. Mummy got a teeny one for her machine. She was ever so grateful.

—Excellent, she said to Mr Azad. —That's saved a trip into town.

—Our aim is to please, Mrs Garner.

—Not Mrs, she said. —Not now.

I close the door.

Mummy daggered my daddy, that's what Finbar told me.

Grandad's shirts and trousers flap against the door, the coat hangers jangling.

I haven't got a daddy.

We will rock you, rock you, rock you.

I get free school dinners because I haven't got a daddy, that's right.

The rabbits are going barmy-bonkers.

That's true.

The rabbits thump their back paws in the shavings and hay.

I breathe.

They put their front paws on the holey wire and scrabble. They're excited outside.

I breathe.

They always are when the light goes on.

—Hello rabbits, I say.

I love Grandad's rabbits.

—Here rabby rabby rabbits, I say.

They're English breed, Black English Spot. They all look the same but they're not the same, not really. They've got different personalities. Some of them are happy and some are silly and some are horrid and some are grumpy and some get too stressed out. Lincoln's a spirit, and Tamworth and Chesterfield are always at it, and Totnes loved Bristol's boobies. They're like Mummy and Finbar and Mrs Meadows and Kelly and Aunty Sheila and Aunty Chris and Grandad and me and everybody in the whole wide world on this planet Earth. Some of them win prizes and some don't and some eat their babies but only if they're hungry and not getting enough mix and greens.

Oh dear.

—Here rabby rabby rabbits, I say, and I make a squashy sound with my lips. —Would you like some mix? Rabby rabby rabbits?

I open Granny's wardrobe and the big sack of mix that's next to the hay bag. I spoon some mix into the jug and I take the jug to the hutches. The rabbits are interested in me. They paw the wire and they turn their heads so they can see. Rabbits' eyes are on the sides of their heads. They're rubbish really. They can't see in front or behind and they can't work out colours. It's a shame.

I put the jug on the floor and I point at my dress.

—This is pink, I say, and I turn around. —Barbie pink. Girls wear pink not boys. It's for Aunty Sheila's wedding.

Weddings are for men and ladies that love each other. I spin round and round.

Give my love to your mum, that's what he said.

I spin round and round and round. I feel the air on my legs and my dress goes whoosh! and it spreads out and the pink velteen and the red badges and the black badges and the white and blue and yellow mix and whirl. They make me feel dizzy. Woah! I crumple on the floor.

—Bugger, I say.

There's plips and mix all around me. I kicked the jug. No, I didn't. It wasn't me. There's hay stuck in my jellies.

—Bloody bum.

I'm in my new dress on the dirty floor. Mummy will be cross, double-cross, I know. I stand up quick.

—WHEN THE RED RED ROBIN COMES BOB BOB BOBBING ALONG ALONG.

—Oh, I say.

That's Granny's doorbell. She got it from QD.

—THERE'LL BE NO MORE SOBBING WHEN HE STARTS SINGING HIS OLD SWEET SONG.

Poor Granny. She's in the churchyard.

—GET UP! GET UP! GET OUT OF BED!

But she wanted to be there, that's what Aunty Sheila said.

—CHEER UP! CHEER UP! THE SUN IS RED!

It doesn't make sense to me.

—LIVE . . .

Probably because I'm a Tortoise and I'm dead slow.

—LOVE . . .

I'm in the Tortoise group at school. There's six of us and one's my best friend Finbar. I'm going to marry him because he's the same size as me.

—LAUGH . . .

That means funny ha-ha.

—AND BE HAPPY!

Grandad was happy when he married Granny and he was sad when she died. She left him and broke his heart and made him cry. Hearts can break and they can go pop and they can stop ticking, true-life. I know all about hearts. Rabbits have rubbish hearts and sometimes humans do too.

With thanks to my agent Jane Bradish-Ellames and my editor Carole Welch for their support and good advice; to the Eastern Arts Board for the grant; to Rose Cowan for introducing me to the world of rabbits; and especially to Andrew Cowan for pushing me to get it right.

LYNNE BRYAN

Gorgeous

She's sexy, brassy, forty-eight and in her prime. Mrs Rita Swales, owner of a successful housesitting agency in the Midland town of Cranley, has come a long way from an impoverished youth and the drudgery of mothering four sons. With an ardent suitor wrapped around her plump little finger, the only fly in her ointment is her husband Collis, still malingering after his industrial accident. Thus the day of Rita's party for her agency's fifth anniversary becomes the day of reckoning for her life – will she stay true to her past, or grasp all that the future offers? In this bittersweet, sensual and beautifully crafted novel, Lynne Bryan traces the path of a strong and vital woman from teenage to maturity.

SCEPTRE